He'd never felt l

As Joshua thought of his father's death, anger seethed inside him. He'd never felt rage like this before, and he wasn't sure how to handle those feelings now. He'd seen his two older brothers punch a wall in anger or frustration, but he'd never understood what drove them to do crazy things like that. He'd always derived so much satisfaction from staying in control, from finding the pattern and walking in beauty. Without harmony there was only chaos.

He glanced at the woman, Nydia, who had allied herself with him. Try as he might, his feelings toward her were anything but moderate. And a healer needed moderation. Love, judging from what he'd seen of it, seldom led to that. He'd always believed it was the last thing he needed.

Until now.

Dear Reader,

Welcome to Four Winds, New Mexico! It's one of those magical towns where no one is who they seem to be...and everyone has a secret. And the sexy Blackhorse brothers are just the perfect tour guides we need.

Harlequin Intrigue is proud to present the FOUR WINDS miniseries by bestselling author Aimée Thurlo. She's been called a "master of the desert country as well as adventure" by Tony Hillerman, and a favorite author by you, our readers.

Join Aimée for all the stories of the Blackhorse brothers and the town in which they live. Don't miss *Her Shadow* in March.

For a free newsletter, or signed bookmarks, you can write Aimée at P.O. Box 2747, Corrales, NM 87048.

Happy reading!

Sincerely,

Debra Matteucci
Senior Editor & Editorial Coordinator
Harlequin Books
300 East 42nd Street
New York, NY 10017

Aimée Thurlo
HER HERO

Harlequin Books

TORONTO • NEW YORK • LONDON
AMSTERDAM • PARIS • SYDNEY • HAMBURG
STOCKHOLM • ATHENS • TOKYO • MILAN
MADRID • WARSAW • BUDAPEST • AUCKLAND

To Debra M. Huntley F. and the staff at
Harlequin Intrigue. You are the most supportive and
terrific bunch of people in the industry.
It's a pleasure to work with you all.

ISBN 0-373-22441-9

HER HERO

Copyright © 1997 by Aimée Thurlo

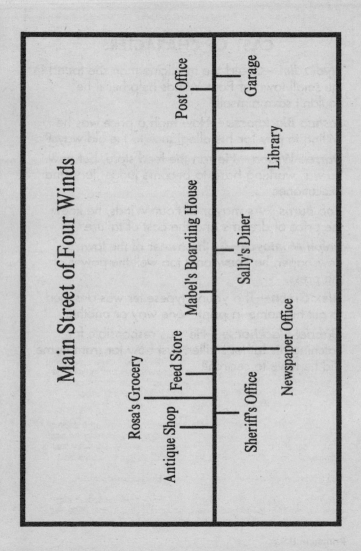

Main Street of Four Winds

Rosa's Grocery
Feed Store
Antique Shop
Mabel's Boarding House
Post Office

Sheriff's Office
Newspaper Office
Sally's Diner
Library
Garage

CAST OF CHARACTERS

Nydia Jim—Could the medicine man she found in the small town of Four Winds help her if he couldn't save himself?

Joshua Blackhorse—How high a price was he willing to pay for his allegiance to the old ways?

Darren Wilson—He ran the feed store, but now he was working hard to become judge, jury and executioner.

Bob Burns—As mayor of Four Winds, he knew the price of dreams and the cost of failure.

Ralph Montoya—As the owner of the town's newspaper, he knew only too well the power of the press.

Alex Green—The young typesetter was destined to get his name in print—one way or another.

Gabriel Blackhorse—He was responsible for catching his father's killer. Just how far from home did he have to search?

Chapter One

As she waited for the gas tank to fill up, Nydia Jim unfolded a small hand-drawn map and placed it on top of the hood of her truck. It had been several months since she'd last visited Four Winds, New Mexico, and although she remembered sketching the route to the medicine man's hogan, she'd never actually been there. The reasons for her visit had been far different then.

She thought back to her brief meeting with Joshua Blackhorse. As she pictured him in her mind, a twinge of awareness swept through her. Tall, like all of the Blackhorse brothers, with a broad, muscular build, piercing black eyes and an air of unshakable confidence, he was certainly a man any woman with a pulse would find hard to forget.

Not that she'd let him know it when they'd met. She'd acted cool enough, hiding her attraction under layers of professionalism. As an anthropologist, she'd learned how to remain analytical and objective in all kinds of situations. It was a skill she'd had to teach herself over the years, rather than something that came naturally, however. She'd always been more comfortable going by gut feeling than anything else.

Nydia folded up her map and stuck it in the back pocket of her jeans. It was hopeless. She'd been driving around for hours and still hadn't seen the *hataalii*'s hogan. So much for the myth about Navajos never getting lost. It was late afternoon, and she had no intention of wasting the entire day searching just to prove she could find it on her own. Before getting under way again, she'd get better directions to Joshua's place.

As she approached the counter, ready to settle her bill, the attendant, Charley according to his name tag, was busy speaking to two men. From the conversation, she gathered that the burly military type was, surprisingly, the town's librarian. The other man, who seemed irritable and annoyed that he wasn't getting Charley's complete attention, was the mayor of Four Winds.

She gave him a long, speculative look, aware that his attention was elsewhere as he arranged for the sale of his son's bicycle and some kind of all-terrain vehicle to Charley.

The man seemed stressed, with the gaunt face of a businessman burning the candle at both ends. In Nydia's experience, administrative types often became that way. Always pushing to get things done took a toll on a person's serenity.

Nydia waited for her turn, then, when the mayor was busy writing down a description of the rest of the items he wanted to sell, she managed to catch Charley's attention. The attendant took one look at her map and laughed.

"The map you have is for his old place. He's been building a new hogan on some land he and his father own west of town."

"Can you tell me exactly how to get there?" He started to tell her, but when she realized how complicated the directions were, she held up a hand and pulled out a small tape recorder she kept in her purse. It was as much a tool for her work as the notebooks stacked on the rear bench of her truck. "Here," she said, holding it out. "Speak into this. That way, I won't have to keep coming back and bothering you."

He smiled. "No problem. Head back out the way you came in, and drive until the road crosses a little creek. Just past there, as you go up the hill, there's a dirt road, and beside it is a big boulder with a red *X* on it. Turn there, then keep going north until you see a water tower. Then turn left and drive farther up into the forest about three miles. You can't miss it."

"Thanks." The directions were the kind she found familiar, since she'd been born and raised on the Navajo reservation. There, most homes were found through landmarks rather than street signs. She wouldn't get lost again.

Nydia returned to her old Ford pickup, slipped behind the wheel and pulled out into the street, relieved she'd finally be able to find Joshua and conduct her business. She had family back on the rez who needed his healing services, and she'd promised to bring him back with her. Unfortunately, time was working against her. Her father-in-law's belief in the old ways was so strong that without the ceremony he felt he needed, he continued to grow worse, though the doctors she'd brought in had been at a loss to explain it.

Spotting an elderly man standing by the front of a decrepit-looking Volkswagen van parked on the side of the road, Nydia slowed down. The vehicle had a flat, and the Navajo man trying to change the tire looked almost as ancient as his vehicle.

She pulled off the road behind him and stopped, ready to help. A half hour wasn't going to be critical to her father-in-law, but it might be to this old man. "Good afternoon, Uncle," she said, using the term to denote respect, not actual kinship.

As she approached, she realized the man wasn't nearly as old as she'd thought at first. In fact, now that she could see him more clearly, he appeared curiously ageless. His copper skin shone in the sun, accentuating his weathered face. But it was his eyes that held her attention. They were a dark gray instead of black, and they were bright and eagle sharp.

"I have a flat," he said, his breathing labored as he rolled the spare in front of him. "At least it's only on the bottom of the tire."

"I'll handle it, Uncle." She smiled at his little joke. "I'm used to this. In my work, I drive on bad roads a lot, and I have to deal with flat tires all the time."

Fortunately, the man had one of those ancient but very useful cross-type lug wrenches, and with the extra leverage it provided it didn't take long for her to change the tire. She hadn't been speaking idly when she'd told him she was used to that type of work. After two years as a widow, she prided herself on being able to take care of almost anything.

Nydia pulled the little scissors jack out from under the van, stood up and wiped her hands. "It's all done."

"You must let me give you something in payment," the man said. "I don't have much money, but perhaps I have some item in my inventory that interests you."

Nydia read the sign on the side of the van. Curious Goods—Prices To Fit Every Customer. A shiver of recognition ran through her. When she'd visited Four Winds several months back, she'd come to research a story about a skinwalker bowl. She remembered the story Lanie Blackhorse had told her, of acquiring the bowl from a peddler who'd been traveling through town. She wondered if this was the same man.

Curiosity drove her. As he slid open the side door of the worn vehicle and pulled down a little folding table, she peered inside. Everything on the various built-in shelves looked like inexpensive fifties-era collectibles or ordinary dime-store merchandise like plastic sunglasses and ceramic roadrunners.

"Are you the gentleman who sold a woman at Four Winds a skinwalker bowl last year?"

He shrugged. "I'm getting old. It's hard to remember things I sold last week, let alone last year. I buy, sell and trade merchandise everywhere." The peddler reached toward the front of the van and pulled something out of one corner. "You are one of the *dineh*, our people. Maybe this will catch your eye." The man unfolded the most beautiful Yei Navajo rug she'd ever seen, one that depicted the Holy People. It was about six feet long, and was divided into three sections, each showcasing a water-sprinkler deity in blue, black or gold. Rainbow-guardian figures protected the borders.

"Uncle, I can't accept that. It's not a fair trade. This rug will bring you a good price."

"From some, perhaps." He folded it into fourths, then held it out in his arms. "Take it, please. A gift to please an old man. This rug deserves an owner who will appreciate its beauty and value it as a precious thing."

"I couldn't possibly…" The rug was simply exquisite, and obviously genuine. She recognized the weaving pattern of her people, and the natural dyes the People used to create distinctive colors. Imitators of the Navajo designs had yet to successfully duplicate the deep Ganado red, a blend of crimson and brown, much like the vibrant colors that covered the ground during a fiery sunset.

She rubbed her hand lightly over the weave, feeling its softness. According to Navajo customs, the lanolin present in wool had been preserved in the yarn, making this rug as soft and supple as a blanket. As she studied the beautiful patterns, she found herself wishing it really could be hers.

"It is a gift. Take it. The rug calls to you," he said softly.

She *did* want it, and there seemed no danger in accepting something like this. It wasn't like the skinwalker bowl she'd heard so much about, an abomination from the time it was created.

"Let me pay you something for it, at least."

He shook his head. "It is freely given, and has now been freely accepted."

Nydia gathered the rug up carefully, and held it, still feeling guilty for having accepted the valuable gift. "Is there something else I can do for you?"

He held her gaze for a long time. "Hear me now, Navajo woman. Be careful with this rug. The weaver who created it was proud of her design, and, unable to mar the perfection of her work, constructed it without a flaw."

"A flaw?" The notion sounded vaguely familiar, like a story she'd heard long ago but couldn't quite remember. She tried to clear her thoughts, but she couldn't look away from the peddler's penetrating gaze, or push back the cobwebs that encircled her mind.

"Spider Woman first taught our weavers to create beautiful blankets, then later, rugs, as today. At first, as a tribute to her, a small hole was left in the center of each blanket or rug, resembling the spider hole in the center of Spider Woman's web. Later, a thin line from the center to the edge became a traditional part of such work. It is said that Spider Woman became angry that the weaver of this rug denied her the tribute, so she spun webs in the weaver's mind, clouding her reason. It is also said the rug's owners will share a similar fate until the time when the curse ends or the blanket is destroyed."

Nydia came to her senses slowly, blinking several times. She had no idea how long she'd stood there. She vaguely remembered the peddler saying goodbye. But all she could see now was his van disappearing over the horizon.

Suppressing a shudder, she went back to her pickup and stored the rug carefully behind the seat. "Good trick," she muttered. The peddler had wanted to add a touch of mysticism to the gift, and he'd done an admirable job of it. If the story was true, it had probably come about because the weaver and subsequently the elders who'd owned it had succumbed to dementia at some point in their lives. As an anthropologist, she knew stories often grew into legends that way.

Chiding herself for having lost almost another hour, she hurried on toward the singer's, or medicine man's, hogan. Nydia had hoped to complete her mission and be on her way home before dark, but the sun had nearly set now. So much depended on her. The life of her father-in-law and the trust of her own child hung in the balance. She had to find Joshua Blackhorse and bring him back with her as quickly as possible.

Nydia passed the water tower but, after fifteen minutes of driving through the pines, she pulled to a stop. Somehow, she must have taken a wrong turn. There was certainly no sign of a hogan anywhere. She'd have to backtrack. The question was how far.

Everything was quiet except for the rustle of the wind through the pine trees. As she put the truck in reverse, she heard a whisper-soft voice coming from within her. It was like her own thoughts, yet not. Her heart began to pound.

A Navajo man is about to become involved in murder.

She heard it as clearly as if it had been spoken, though there had been no audible sound. She shook her head. The peddler had probably put some hypnotic suggestion in her mind, which also explained her earlier distortion of time. She shouldn't have lowered her guard and allowed him to give her a gift. She'd suspected him of being the one who'd given Lanie Blackhorse the bowl. But accepting the rug had seemed so inconsequential, she hadn't counted on him playing mind games with her.

Once again the whisper-soft voice in her head warned her, *There's going to be a murder.*

Nydia shook her head, trying to free herself from the annoying, persistent thought. This was ridiculous. She'd been reading too many mysteries lately—that was all.

As Nydia turned around and drove back up the hill toward the water tower, two closely spaced rifle shots cracked through the air. Nydia hit the brakes, slid to a stop and glanced around quickly. About a hundred yards ahead beside a pine, she could see the outline of a man aiming a rifle. The man fired again, and the blast reverberated in the confines of her truck.

Nydia pushed down hard on the truck's horn. It wasn't deer season. Maybe the man was a poacher. As the horn blast echoed through the forest, the shooter ran off into the woods. The man was clumsy in his haste to escape, stumbling and almost falling down twice.

Nydia drove over the ridge, wondering what he'd been shooting at. In a small clearing below, she could see a blue pickup and a nearly completed log hogan partially hidden by a cluster of pines. Another vehicle was in the trees farther away.

Nydia drove down the hill, her heart pounding, dreading what she might find. As she entered the clearing, she saw a man lying on his back beside the blue pickup, his shirt soaked with blood.

She wasn't squeamish. She'd been raised in the country, where people hunted or butchered livestock, but she'd never seen anything like this before in her life. She stopped the truck, reached under the seat for her first-aid kit, knowing instinctively that it was woefully inadequate to meet the wounded man's needs.

Nydia went to his side. The dime-sized wound in the

center of his chest made her breath catch in her throat. This man needed an emergency medical team right now. Nydia noticed his face as she crouched down. His strong good looks reminded her of Joshua, but his age suggested he was Joshua's father or some other relative of that generation. She knew it wasn't either of the singer's brothers; she'd met them when she'd been in Four Winds a few months ago.

Through the open door of the blue pickup, only a dozen feet away, she saw a portable phone on the seat and a rifle in a rack below the rear window. Glancing around to be certain she was alone, Nydia ran toward the vehicle. The elder Blackhorse must have been shot as he'd tried to reach the truck to arm himself and call for help.

Nydia was almost to the telephone when a hand clamped onto her wrist. The manaclelike hold effectively immobilized her entire arm. Unable to see directly behind her, she reached back desperately with her free hand, aiming for his face. Her arm was forced away firmly, and brought down beside the other. Quickly, her captor shifted both her hands into one of his. Terrified, she struggled wildly.

"Stop fighting," he commanded, then as if to make his point, jerked her back toward him.

Nydia slammed into a man's bare chest. It was solid and hard, and felt a bit like running into a brick wall. As his breath touched her cheek, her skin prickled, her heart thumping loudly in her chest. "What...what do you want?"

"I want you away from the truck," came the reply.

His voice was low, and held a velvety smoothness that affected her more than it had a right to. Without further word, he moved her aside as if she weighed nothing more than a feather. His strength amazed her.

At last his grip eased, and taking advantage of the moment, Nydia jumped away. As she turned to face him, she inhaled sharply. The man who had held her was Joshua Blackhorse. Without taking his eyes off her, he reached down and retrieved a rifle on the ground at his feet.

As she remembered from their first encounter, Joshua possessed a mesmerizing quality that made him totally unforgettable. His shirt was open and hung down over a pair of faded jeans. His chest gleamed with perspiration, and small scratches crisscrossed his bronzed skin. An intense virility defined him.

As his eyes gleamed down on her, a shiver raced up her spine. Yet on a level she wasn't sure she could explain, even to herself, she sensed something dark and deadly within him.

"You have nothing to fear from me, now that I know who you are," he said, and went directly to the man on the ground.

Nydia rushed back to the truck and lifted the other rifle out of the rack. She'd heard of Navajo singers turning bad before. It was said that by taking the life of a close relative, they could gain the powers of a skinwalker. "Stop where you are."

Joshua glanced back at her, but ignored her order. "My father needs me, woman."

"Set down your weapon or I *will* shoot you," she said, her voice shaky but determined.

"The rifle you're holding is my father's. It's not loaded."

Nydia's stomach fell, fear spiraling through her. She opened the bolt action, and the chamber and clip below were empty. She took a step back, wondering if Joshua would come after her now that she'd angered him. But his attention was focused solely on his father.

Nydia forced herself to calm down. Had he wanted her dead, he could have killed her by now. She'd never heard him approach. And if Joshua had wanted his father dead to gain skinwalker powers, why was he helping him now? She recognized the herbs that Joshua had taken from a pouch on his belt and was applying to his father's wound. They were ones commonly used on the reservation to stop bleeding. Then she heard him start a powerful sing. His voice was like a raging fire that robbed the oxygen from her lungs. She understood now why he was so sought-after as a singer and why so many of the People placed their trust in him. It was more than charisma. His prayer was vibrant, as if he possessed the magic that could summon the Earth Mother herself.

As he glanced up, she saw that his eyes now blazed with pain. Unable to bear the raw emotions there, Nydia looked away. As her gaze fell on the rifle by his side, she felt a cold chill envelop her, and common sense returned.

She had no way of knowing what had happened here. What she did know was that she needed help, and so did the gravely wounded man. She used the phone in her hand and dialed the operator, uncertain if 911 would work here. Joshua didn't try to stop her. As soon as help was on the way, she announced that the police and medical help would be there soon.

Joshua nodded and went on with his sing. Finally, he paused to replace the herb and met her gaze. "Regardless of how it seems, I didn't do this," he said. "But I *will* punish whoever did."

"If you didn't shoot your father, who did?"

"There was a man up on the ridge. He's responsible for this. When my father can talk, he'll confirm what I'm saying."

Nydia didn't respond. As Joshua renewed the sing, she once more sensed the raw power that came from him. She watched him apply pressure to certain points around his father's chest, trying in vain to stem the flow of blood that continued despite the herbs.

She was no doctor, but it didn't take a degree in medicine to see that the man on the ground was dying. As the blood drained away the elder Blackhorse's life, Joshua's song became distorted by loss and dark despair. It seemed to lose its vitality, as if the healer's faith was slowly being shattered.

Nydia felt his anguish with each mournful phrase. She felt the moisture gathering in her lashes and tried to push the emotions back. If there was ever a situation that called for staying cool and analytical, this was it. She couldn't afford to forget the look in Joshua's eyes when he'd first appeared. There had been something dark and frightening there. It might have been directed at the attacker, if Joshua's story was true, but she had no way of knowing for sure.

As the dying man's breathing became shallower, Nydia heard Joshua redouble his efforts, singing and applying herbs with a desperation that she couldn't believe would ever come from a murderer.

A ragged gasp came from the wounded man. The next instant, there was only silence.

Joshua's hands curled into fists as he leaned over his father's body. The strangled, desperate cry that he uttered came from his soul.

Nydia mourned his loss, but with a burst of will, forced herself to think clearly. Moving quickly, she picked up Joshua's rifle from the ground.

When Joshua rose back to his knees, he saw her holding his weapon. He stood slowly. "Woman, my father is dead, and his murderer is out there, running free. Give me that rifle. I have a killer to hunt down."

"No," she said calmly. "You're not going anywhere until the sheriff arrives."

"As we talk, the killer gets farther away. It'll be completely dark soon."

Nydia hesitated. She wanted to believe him. There was

something about Joshua that made it nearly impossible to think him capable of such a crime. But the facts were less plain. She finally shook her head. "You're staying. I'm honestly not sure what's going on here, but that's not up to me to decide. You'll have to settle this with the sheriff."

"I'm a healer. I don't take lives, especially my father's."

She sensed the truth in his words, but she just couldn't be sure. He was charismatic, and his voice had an oddly compelling timbre that would make anything he said sound plausible. "What happened, then? How could someone sneak up on you? It's so quiet."

"My father and I did hear a vehicle approach, but neither of us was concerned. A lot of fishermen come out this way. Then, fifteen minutes or so later, someone fired two shots at us from up on that ridge. I was closest to the trees, so my father told me to go into the forest and outflank the sniper. I almost had him, too. But then you drove up. The sniper fired once more, hitting my father, then ran when you honked the horn. I couldn't catch him, but I picked up the weapon he discarded. It's my own rifle."

"Are you're telling me that the murder weapon belongs to you?"

"I reported it stolen last week. I've never even fired it. Now, you have to give me the rifle and let me go. You're playing right into the murderer's hands by keeping me here while he escapes. Don't help him get away twice."

The words stung. If his story was true, then in her effort to help, she'd given a killer the opportunity to escape. But that was no answer. She couldn't fix what had already happened. It was the present she had to worry about. "I can't let you go. It may have happened the way you said, or it may not. In either case, you have to talk to the sheriff first."

The gathering darkness around them seemed to concentrate into the obsidian eyes that held hers. The impact of his strength of will and determination almost overwhelmed her. She felt the battle going on within him and his struggle to control his emotions. For one wild moment, she felt a primal desire to touch him and soothe his anguish. Though he didn't realize it, she desperately wanted his story to be true, if only to help those who were counting on her. Everything she had ever heard about Joshua Blackhorse supported her belief in his innocence now. Unfortunately, the facts were less clear.

"Look, if nothing else, you are the last person who should be tracking the killer," she said.

Joshua said nothing and remained rock still, but that stillness was too pronounced to pass as natural. It was more in line with a man who was conserving his energy.

"Tell me this," he said. "Did you see anyone when you came over the hill?"

"There *was* someone." Nydia searched her mind for a clearer image of the person she'd seen standing in the shadows. If memory served her right, it had been a much smaller man than Joshua. But she couldn't be one hundred percent certain.

Hearing a vehicle, Nydia turned her head for a second and saw flashing red-and-blue lights approaching. By the time she glanced back at Joshua, he'd moved toward the road and was standing there waiting. She lowered the rifle. Had he wanted to, he could have easily made his escape then, not just moved. More to the point, once again he'd never made a sound. She remembered the clumsiness of the gunman she'd seen by the tree, the man who'd fired the shots. Comparing the two men in her mind, she became certain they couldn't have been the same person.

A minute later, the sheriff pulled up and stepped out of his Jeep. She recognized Gabriel Blackhorse from her last visit to Four Winds.

Grim faced, Gabriel went directly to his father's side and

knelt by the body. Finally, he looked up at his brother. "What happened?"

Joshua gave his brother the same story he'd told her, pointing to the spot where the gunman had hidden. "Whoever it was is long gone now, probably. But I may still be able to track him."

Gabriel looked at Nydia curiously, as if wondering what she was doing here, but focused on the more vital question. "Can you confirm my brother's story?"

"I came here to look for the *hataalii*, because my father-in-law is sick. When I drove up, I saw the gunman briefly, but not clearly enough to identify him. Your brother was not with your father when I reached him, but arrived shortly after I did." She recapped what she'd found upon her arrival, and what had happened subsequently.

Joshua's voice was taut as he glared at his brother. "I *am* the best tracker, but time is slipping by. I have to get going before the man covers his trail."

"I can't let you do that." Gabriel said. "This is my job, and you have to trust me to do it the right way." Turning to Nydia, he said, "Mrs. Jim, I want you to take me to where you saw the sniper." When she nodded, he turned his attention back to his brother. The sheriff met his younger brother's fierce gaze. "We'll catch whoever did this, but not by going off half-cocked. You, of all people, should know the value of patience, Tree."

Nydia looked at Joshua, wondering now if her errand of mercy to Four Winds would become nothing more than a waste of time, a dream that, like so many others, faded into nothing when one got too close. The emotions flickering in Joshua's eyes now had nothing to do with harmony and balance. There were some very un*hataalii*like emotions there, and she sensed that until he restored his inner balance, Joshua could not act as a healer. Despairingly, she thought of the errand that had brought her here. Joshua was the only known keeper of the ancient song needed to restore her father-in-law's health.

She thought of her son, John, and the faith he'd placed in her when he'd asked her to bring Joshua back to his grandfather. She couldn't fail him. But before she could fulfill her promise to John, this matter facing the *hataalii* would have to be resolved.

As the flashing lights of another vehicle appeared at the top of the hill, Gabriel motioned to his brother. "Ride back with them. I need to have gunpowder-residue tests run on your hands to prove that you didn't fire the rifle. That will clear you in the eyes of the court."

"I'm not guilty and you know it. What we need now is to work together to catch our father's killer. Let's get going while the trail is still there."

"No, Tree. Clearing you is the first order of business. Do as I say."

She heard the whisper in her mind once again. *Stay on your guard,* the inner voice warned. As she saw Joshua stick his hand absently into his pocket, a cold chill ran up her spine and she stepped back. In a heartbeat, the air was filled with a red powder that made her eyes sting. She began to cough, unable to stop. By the time the spasm passed and her eyes cleared, Joshua was gone.

Chapter Two

Joshua ran as silently as his father had taught him many years ago. Neither of his brothers would be able to follow his trail. Fuzz and Shadow were the fighters in the family—quick to anger, loyal to a fault, but they were lacking in the old skills.

Admittedly, Gabriel was persistent and would eventually find him. After all, he'd just injured his brother's pride on two counts: by showing little faith in Gabriel's methods of catching the killer, and by deliberately flouting his judgment.

Joshua returned to the north side of the ridge where his father's killer had run after Nydia Jim had appeared. The forest extended for miles in almost every direction, but the killer had left a trail Joshua could follow even in the twilight. He reached the dirt track he knew led to the road and followed the tire imprints he found there. They led toward the highway. The killer had driven into the trees, hiding his vehicle before he stalked them.

Joshua moved cross-country, making a straight line for the highway, yet knowing that unless he could get a vehicle, he wouldn't be able to go any farther than that in pursuit. He was moving through a thicket of scrub oak when the wind suddenly rose. Wind carried messages. He listened carefully. The sound of a vehicle rose in the distance. It wasn't his brother's Jeep; he could tell.

He hurried toward the sound instead of away. He was no thief, but desperate times called for desperate measures. Hiding in the shadow of some pines, he waited until the vehicle's headlights appeared, then jumped out into the track, waving his hands in the air.

The pickup stopped abruptly, and he saw the driver was Nydia. Not giving her time to react, he jumped up onto the driver's-side running board, threw open the door and grabbed both of her arms before she could move.

"What do you think you're doing?" she yelled, struggling to loosen his grip.

To his surprise, as he pulled her out of the truck, she managed to snag the car keys, holding them tightly in her fist. "I need your truck, woman." He noted her expression. Nydia Jim was afraid, but not too afraid to stand up to him.

"You said you're not guilty, but by your actions you're going to make it tough for your brother to prove otherwise. You're not helping by running away, you're just muddying the waters."

He lowered her arms to her sides, and glowered at her. His size alone had intimidated men twice her weight, and he'd learned how to make people back down with one look. It was the best way he'd found to avoid violence. "The keys," he snapped.

Nydia swallowed hard, and her voice nearly cracked as she answered. "No. You can have the truck with me as driver, or nothing at all."

"I *can* take the keys from you, but I have no desire to hurt you in the process."

Nydia studied his expression, then smiled hesitantly. "You aren't a violent man, *hataalii*. Stop trying to make me believe you're something you're not."

Frustration ate at him, but he had to admire her courage.

She was right, too. He would not risk harming her or anyone else to get what he wanted. "All right. You're my driver. Head back to the highway slowly while I study the ground and look for signs of a trail."

Nydia did as he asked, keeping her eyes on the road. He might have believed she wasn't in the least bit afraid if she hadn't kept a death grip on the wheel.

"You worked very hard to become a *hataalii*," she said. "Your brothers follow modern ways, and so did your father, so I suspect you had to overcome their doubts to follow a traditional path. You apprenticed for years, and put your heart into learning. Now you finally have the knowledge of a singer, and our people look to you, even though you're still very young. Don't throw all that away. Your brother is the sheriff, a trained police officer. Let him prove your innocence, then you'll be free to use your own skills, your knowledge of people and the Way, to track down the killer. You'll have a better chance of catching him if you work with the law instead of running from it."

"You should be concerned with your own problems, not the ones I face. Why are you getting involved in this? Haven't you even stopped to wonder if I'm trying to become a skinwalker by killing my father?"

"It crossed my mind, but logic works against that theory. If you'd wanted to follow the path of a skinwalker, you had the perfect opportunity last year when your brothers discovered the bowl that held a Navajo witch's power. I heard the stories—that's why I came to Four Winds before, remember? You knew about the bowl, too, yet you chose to stay on the rez with the singer who was your teacher to learn a new healing song. You didn't come to Four Winds to claim the bowl and its power."

"I'm of no use to you as a healer until the killer is punished," he said, hating to admit that. "You're wasting your time."

"My father-in-law is ill now. My son, who is following the old ways, heard about you, and it was he who convinced my father-in-law that you could help. I came here today to find you. Since the *hataalii* who taught you passed away, you are the only one who knows the ancient life-giving song my father-in-law needs. As a *hataalii* you have a debt you owe the People. You can't turn your back on someone who needs you, who will pay for your services and asks nothing of you except the knowledge that you alone have."

The lengths to which Nydia was willing to go to fulfill the promise she'd made to those back on the reservation spoke of loyalty and love. Under any other circumstances, he would have done whatever was necessary to help her. A woman like Nydia, whose courage matched her capacity to love, deserved better than she would get from him. "If I could go with you now, I would," he said softly.

Joshua kept his eyes on the road, focused on the task that had brought him out here. The fresh mud that lay in small clumps along the road made him suspect they were on the right track. It was the same color as the patches of mud found back by the water tower. "I'm sorry that your father-in-law is ill, but believe me when I tell you that I can't help you, not now anyway."

"Can't or won't?"

"Both. There's no harmony inside me right now. You know about our ways, so you know I'm telling the truth when I say that the Holy People I would call upon in my sing would not help the patient. They'd only see the anger and pain I'm feeling. Those emotions destroy my abilities as a singer."

He saw the sadness that crossed her eyes and felt his gut wrench. Nydia was no stranger to sorrow; he'd sensed that in her the first time they'd met. It was as if a shadow covered her heart. Maybe she still mourned her husband. He knew she was a widow.

But their moment in time had come and gone months ago. Neither of them had been ready to pursue the attraction, both too focused on the responsibilities they each had in their own lives. There had been no chance to get to know her then, and there was no chance now, though he'd harbored some wild dreams about his next meeting with this lovely, enticing widow.

The rumbling sound of a powerful engine filled the air, and brought his thoughts back into focus. He gestured by pursing his lips Navajo-style toward the closest rise. "A big truck or Jeep is coming from that direction. If it's my brother, he'll catch us unless you speed up."

She pressed down on the accelerator, and her pickup reluctantly cooperated.

"Does Gabriel know you came after me?"

"Yes," she said, and explained that she'd driven off before he could stop her.

"He'll have the state police out helping him by now. Stay alert for roadblocks." He watched her out of the corner of his eye, intrigued by Nydia. She was beautiful, with thick black hair that cascaded over her shoulders. Though small, her body's generous curves called out for a man's touch. But there was a hard edge of determination just beyond that lovely exterior, too. If instinct served him right, she was a woman used to getting what she wanted through persistence. It was what she was doing now, as she fought to do whatever she had to in order to bring him back to the reservation with her.

"Do you have any idea who might have wanted your father dead?" she asked.

Her question brought his thoughts back to the present with a jolt. "No. My dad was the sheriff of Four Winds for many years before Gabriel took the office. He made enemies, of course, but it makes no sense that they'd wait this long to strike out at him.''

"Is it possible that *you* were the target, not your father?"

"No. I was standing several feet away from him when the first shot came. The bullet struck a tree right beside my dad. The sniper wasn't aiming at me, and the shot was too close to be a warning of any kind.'' He gave her a long sideways glance. She was using her intelligence and logic to help him now, though softer feelings were at the core of what was driving her. He couldn't help but wonder what it would be like to be the sole object of all her gentle emotions.

"Let's track this from another angle," she said, interrupting his thoughts. "Who in town knew where your father would be this afternoon?''

He paused, his restless gaze moving slowly over the area, gliding off objects like the fallen branches that littered the road. "Almost anyone at Four Winds," he answered at last. Clearly, she was trying to fulfill her own goals, but he was surprisingly glad she was with him now. She made a good ally.

"That doesn't narrow the field much.''

"Yes, it does, somewhat. It's not a big community, unless you count livestock and pets.''

Nydia chuckled and glanced at him, surprised by the joke. But then she saw his somber expression and realized he hadn't been joking. "Narrow it down some more. Whoever murdered your father must not care much for you, either, since he was trying to frame you.''

"True, and circumstances really worked in his favor, too, like you appearing on the scene. Your testimony might have helped him reinforce the frame.''

"But his luck wasn't perfect. Obviously, that part of his plan didn't work. For now, though, let's stick to the facts. Someone is out to destroy you. Who hates you that much?''

Joshua considered the question for a long time before answering. "I have no idea. I've never lost a patient, and I've never knowingly wronged anyone." He shook his head slowly. "I have no idea who the killer could be."

Nydia slowed down as they reached a section of the road where water and sediment from the recent rains had collected. Mud splattered all over the front of the truck as she hit a pothole.

"This road continues on into Four Winds, nowhere else. The killer came this way. I've been watching the sides of the road carefully for any signs that he left the road and went cross-country, but I found none. This is our first break. The killer's vehicle will probably have mud splattered all over it."

"But you can't assume that anyone with a mud-splattered vehicle is a suspect," she countered.

"If you're worried that I'm going to turn vigilante and go after the innocent, don't. I want my father's killer, not a convenient scapegoat."

As he thought of his father, anger once again seethed inside him, and he tried to repress it. He'd never felt rage like this before, and he wasn't sure how to handle those feelings now. He'd seen his two older brothers punch a wall in anger or frustration more than once, bloodying their knuckles in the process, but he'd never understood what drove them to do crazy things like that. He'd always derived more satisfaction from staying in control, from finding the pattern and walking in beauty. Without harmony, there was only chaos.

He glanced at the woman who had allied herself with him. He'd forced himself to think of her as an attractive distraction when he'd first met her months before. A singer needed moderation. Love, judging from what he'd seen of it through Gabriel, seldom led to that. Though it obviously offered other rewards, he'd always believed that love was the last thing he'd need if he wanted to stay centered.

Of course, that hadn't meant he couldn't enjoy a woman's company, and that special magic they had that brought out the gentler side of a man. But he didn't think he could afford the confusion a woman created when she got into a man's heart.

"So what's the plan? I drive you around town and you check out the cars?" she asked.

"Can you think of something better? Your truck isn't known there, so we shouldn't alert anyone unless they see me."

As they entered Four Winds, the familiar buildings of Main Street made his gut clench. His father had dedicated his life to protecting Four Winds, and this was how he'd been repaid. This time, he surrendered to the anger raging inside him, allowing the heat to rise to his face.

The blast of a siren jolted him out of his thoughts. "Turn here," he said quickly. "Now!"

Nydia sped around the corner he indicated, but the state-police vehicle stayed with her. "I'm going to pull over."

"No. Head down the alley just ahead." He knew he could jump out of the truck and hide in a dozen places there. As a kid, he'd played with his brothers in this spot near the old well.

"It's okay. He's not after us after all." She slowed down and pulled off the road, the tension washing out of her.

"No! Don't stop!" When she ignored him, he glanced at her and saw the curious expression on her face. It was as if she was listening to something.

"Don't worry."

A moment later, the police vehicle sped past them, much to Joshua's surprise. "How in the blazes did you know he'd do that?"

Nydia shrugged. "I just felt we'd be okay, I guess," she said.

"What do you mean?" Joshua knew she was holding something back. He generally could tell when people did that. As a *hataalii*, he'd learned the signs, the hesitancy, the subtle changes in tone.

"Look, what does it matter now? I was right, so don't worry about it."

He could tell that something was bothering her, but this was not the time to press for answers. As she pulled back onto Main Street, Joshua ducked down. "You'll have to do all the searching for me until we're on a side street. It will be easier if people in town don't see me at all. And we'll have to be quick. It won't be long until it's completely dark. There are no streetlights in Four Winds, just a few business signs and everyone's porch lights."

"There's a pickup by the library that looks real shiny under the outside light, like it has been washed very recently," she said.

Joshua glanced up slightly, then ducked back down. Jake Field's truck was perfectly clean; even the tires on the librarian's truck had been washed. "Good observation. Nobody's truck is that free of dust out here."

She continued past Sally's Diner, where a family was just getting into a dusty but not mud-splattered station wagon.

"We should be near the feed store now. What about the truck there?"

"There are no vehicles there."

"There should be a green truck in the alley."

"Sorry. The alley is empty, but it's late, you know. It's close to nine."

He looked up. Darren Wilson's pickup was normally parked in the alley next to his feed store, but it sure wasn't there now. As speculations rose in his mind, a feeling of oppressiveness settled over him. The people here were all longtime friends, yet now a killer hid among them.

"You really care about this town, don't you?" she observed, watching his face.

"This is my home, and the residents of Four Winds are at the center of everything I love about this place. It's hard for me to believe one of them is a killer."

"There's a coin-operated car wash ahead. Two carloads of kids are waiting for their turn with the sprayers. Recognize any of them?" she asked.

He took a quick look. "The boy in the right stall is the son of the woman who owns Sally's Diner. He saved my sister-in-law's life once. It couldn't have been him."

"If you say so. What about the others? And don't discount the women, either. Women are usually better shots than men."

He raised one eyebrow. "Sweeping statement, wouldn't you say?"

"No, actually it's based on studies done gauging the skills of each sex at different tasks. For the record, females are usually more effective predators in nature, too."

"Speed up a bit. The woman leaning against the beat-up sedan is my sister-in-law, Lanie. If anyone can spot me, it'll be her. She's a teacher now, and they notice everything. The other woman is Marlee. She owns the boardinghouse. We're lucky with her. She doesn't notice much of anything except my brother Lucas."

When she reached the end of Main Street, Nydia turned onto a side street that led to a residential area. "That's it for the ride. You can't question anyone if you're wanted by the law. Word could already be out about your father. People won't talk to you. And you can't do any more tracking—there's almost no traffic here. Someone's likely to call in a report of a suspicious vehicle casing the homes, and we'd have either the state police or your brother here in a flash. It's time to go talk to the sheriff."

Joshua gestured up the road. "Keep going a little farther. There's an area of high ground ahead. When you get there, drive up behind the stand of pines. It's possible the killer managed to find a hiding place for his vehicle near the highway, avoiding the drive through town to his home until after dark. Let's play this out a bit longer. Gabriel will be busy for a while yet, collecting evidence and scouring the forest around my hogan. He won't allow anything to sidetrack him from that now, so my disappearance won't be holding him up yet. After we're done here, we'll go directly to the station, or if he's not there, to his home."

Agreeing reluctantly, she followed Joshua's directions and parked in a secluded area that overlooked the road into Four Winds. "It's getting too dark to see anything clearly."

"That's the killer's advantage, and ours, too, now. Don't worry, our eyes will adapt in a few minutes." He kept his gaze on the road ahead, but out of the corner of his eye, he saw Nydia rub her arms as if cold, then reach behind her to the rear bench.

She pulled out a Navajo rug and threw it over her shoulders. Then, with a hesitant smile, tucked the other edge around him. "I know men never admit to being cold, but it is, so humor me."

Joshua felt the warmth radiating from her body. He longed to brush a kiss over her lips, to feel the velvet texture of her skin, to hear her sigh with longing. His fingers coiled around the rug in a tight grip as a flash of heat traveled down his body.

He had to focus on something else. He looked at the rug, noticing the designs. "This rug was woven with great care. Is one of your relatives a weaver?"

"No. This is a gift from someone I helped."

"Even in this light, the details are so clear. The colors

must be bright." He turned his gaze back to the road, watching for approaching vehicles.

"They are. That's why I liked it. Fortunately, I can appreciate it without letting superstition spoil it for me."

"What do you mean?" The first thing that went through his mind was that for some crazy reason, Nydia had accepted the personal property of someone who'd died, a rug contaminated with the *chindi*. But surely no Navajo, no matter how modern, would do something like that. Instinctively, he slipped it off his shoulder and pushed it away from himself.

"The person who gave it to me said the rug didn't have a flaw incorporated into it. Although I respect the story about Spider Woman, I don't share those beliefs, so that lapse in tradition doesn't bother me."

His eyes narrowed. "No flaw?"

"Well, that's what he said. I haven't personally examined the weave. For all I know, it was made in Mexico, and he said that just to make the gift seem special."

"*Who* gave it to you?"

She hesitated. "You're not going to like my answer," she said, then told him about the peddler and his van.

"Knowing about him, about the bowl and all we told you before, you still accepted his gift?"

Nydia took a deep breath, then let it out slowly. "I regret lowering my guard around him so he could play his little trick, but I do love this rug. It's so soft and well made, like the blankets our ancestors used to weave."

He studied her carefully. "What kind of trick did the peddler play on you?"

"I think he used some form of hypnotism." She told him about the inner voice she had heard before the murder. "But in retrospect, maybe that had nothing to do with the peddler. It seems far more likely that it was my own intuition. Perhaps I saw or heard something that I pieced together subconsciously.''

"Maybe, but it's also possible that your beautiful rug is as cursed as the skinwalker bowl was.'' He forced himself to keep his eyes on the road, though he was beginning to worry more about the woman beside him than himself.

"If this rug, or any other like it, had a curse and history like that of the bowl, I would have heard about it. I research folklore like that. It's my job. I document and study Navajo beliefs and artifacts.''

"Yet you discount the traditional warning to weavers. Out of respect for our customs, if nothing else, you should not have accepted this rug.''

"I respect our customs, but this is an exquisite piece of work. I was thinking of donating it to the department that funds my research. The college would love a valuable Navajo rug like this for its museum, if it's authentic.''

"You can't pass something like that on to anyone,'' he said. Nydia obviously had some knowledge of Navajo ways, but to her, it was all just another primitive philosophical concept. To him, it was the foundation of his life. His gut wrenched. As always, he found that the journey he'd chosen as a singer kept him on a lonely path. Although he admired Nydia on many counts, the beliefs that separated them seemed unsurmountable.

"Don't discount what you don't understand,'' he insisted. "The rug has already had its effect. It talks to you, it influences your actions. So far, it has helped you. Have you asked yourself why? There's nothing in the legend to account for that. You can't trust anything that comes from the peddler. Didn't you learn anything from your research into the skinwalker bowl?''

"It's not the same thing at all. I've already given you two possible explanations for the inner voice I heard.''

Joshua lapsed into a long silence. He'd warned her. That

was all he could do. There was no point in arguing. That rug wasn't his concern now. He had other problems to handle, and the first of those was getting Nydia out of the danger that nearness to him might involve.

"Do you realize that you're risking your life by insisting on staying with me? My father's killer tried to frame me, but things went wrong. It's possible he'll come after me again, and you, too, since he doesn't know if you can identify him."

Nydia considered her reply, determined not to let him out of her sight until he was safely in his brother's custody. Lost in thought, she looked past him, peering into the darkness. "We've got company," she said suddenly, her voice steady but as taut as a bowstring.

He followed her line of vision and felt his pulse quicken. Someone was walking toward them. The man was holding something, a weapon, like a rifle perhaps—he couldn't be sure.

When she reached down to start the ignition, the man quickened his pace.

The engine sputtered, then died. Joshua knew they wouldn't get away in time. "I'll divert him," he said, throwing his door open and ducking out.

By the time the engine purred to life, Joshua saw that what he'd mistaken for a weapon was only a couple of fishing poles. With Nydia's headlights illuminating the area, he could see it was old man Simmons.

"Heard you're having some trouble, medicine man," Simmons said, approaching as if he didn't have a care in the world.

"What have you heard?" Joshua answered.

"I've been walking around quite a while today. Went to my favorite fishing spot, and couldn't decide whether to use my spinning outfit or my new fly rod. On the way back, I heard people talking, and I'm sorry to say some are pretty sure that you had something to do with your father's death."

"You don't believe that. You're not frightened," Joshua observed.

"No, but *you* should be worried. Rumors like this bring out the meanness in people. It could be dangerous for you until the real killer is caught. You need your family now, my friend, especially the sheriff."

"That's good advice, old friend. I intend to follow it." Saying goodbye, he returned to Nydia's truck.

She sat ramrod straight, her breathing quick and harsh. "I gather you know him."

"Did you hear our conversation?"

"Enough to know that it's time to go find your brother."

He had to admit his quarry had slipped beyond his grasp, and for the moment, it was pointless to put off the tests Gabriel wanted him to take. "It's time to go see my brother, but let's take the long way to his office."

"Why?"

He hesitated. "I don't think there's anything to gain by being careless now. Somebody besides Gabriel might figure we'll be showing up there soon, and be watching the place."

"Okay. Give me directions."

"We'll have to go through the residential area south of Main Street. And while we're there, we might as well do one last check on the vehicles parked outside. Most of the folks there own the type of all-terrain vehicles that would have no trouble making a speedy exit out of the forested area around my hogan."

"We won't be able to see a thing in the dark."

"The dark will work to our advantage now. We'll go in silently on foot and take a closer look. Have you ever hunted?"

"Only with a camera. But I can move quietly, if that's what you're asking."

He nodded. "Looks like we'll have the chance to put your skills to a test."

AS THEY ENTERED the private neighborhood, Nydia glanced around. "There are only a few lights coming from those houses. Looks like people go to bed early here, like on the reservation where they're up at dawn or close to it."

"They're not up at dawn here, but there's not much to do after nightfall, except when there's a game at the high school or a dance."

She parked in the shadows of a giant elm. "There are vehicles parked near each of those houses. If we get caught, someone might just shoot us, especially if they know a murderer has just struck in their community."

"You don't have to come with me."

"I'm going."

Joshua suspected that she was worried that he'd give her the slip, but he had no intention of doing that. Rather than argue with her, however, he decided to let her help, knowing an additional set of eyes and ears would come in handy.

They worked their way down the row of driveways using the rising moon to guide them. His gaze was sharp even in the night. What surprised him was that hers seemed to be a match for his. She walked with confidence, and didn't stumble or fumble in the dark. As he moved down a side street with a truck in almost every driveway, he studied the tires of each vehicle, not just the body, and noticed she was doing the same.

They'd nearly reached the end of that cul-de-sac when he turned and realized that Nydia was no longer near. She'd gone down the driveway that led to Olivia Farrell's detached garage. The old woman had a dog of legendary proportions. Even the high-school kids were afraid of him.

Some of the younger boys claimed that the dog was trained to pin any intruder to the ground unless he stayed rock still.

He had no doubt that Olivia herself had started that story to keep the kids from cutting across her yard. But rumors like those grew and took on a life of their own after a while. Of course, it didn't help that Danger was black, and at night his most clearly distinguishable features were huge white canines gleaming with saliva.

Joshua hurried to catch Nydia before she walked past the hedge. "Stop!" He whispered as loud as he dared.

The warning came too late. Danger rushed out from behind the hedge, blocking Nydia's path. "Okay. I stopped," she answered in a harsh whisper. "Now do something before this mongrel decides to turn me into a chew stick."

Chapter Three

Joshua came up behind her slowly, then whistled two low tones, repeating them once, like a birdcall.

Nydia gasped with surprise as the huge black beast lay down, then rolled over on his back. She'd heard of *hataaliis* performing apparent miracles, but she'd never seen this particular demonstration.

"I've studied our singers and their abilities, but this is a new one on me," Nydia said, backing slowly out of Danger's reach. Her knees were so weak she could barely stand. She liked dogs, but this monster was to a dog what a grizzly was to a teddy bear. "If he's just an ordinary doggy here in Four Winds, I think I can get a few biologists interested in the water."

As she reached Joshua's side, she took a long, shuddering breath. There was something about being with him that made her feel safe. Maybe it was his confidence or his ability to command the situation no matter how badly the odds were stacked against him. As her eyes met his, she sensed his silent assurance that nothing would ever hurt her as long as he was near. "What's with that bird whistle? Where did you learn that?"

"Danger's a dog Mrs. Farrell found wandering around looking for a home. He was just a pup back then, but he kept right on growing. Must be the Newfoundland blood in him. I dog-sit him whenever she goes out of town, so he knows me."

"And you taught him a few commands, like what to do when he hears your whistle," Nydia concluded. "Pretty good training. Impressive, actually. For a minute, I was ready to say it was some kind of magic trick."

"Not everything a singer does is a trick, my skeptical friend."

"Most of what I've seen has been."

He started to argue, then stopped. There were other, more-important matters facing them now. "Why did you decide to come up this particular driveway?"

"It seemed like a good hiding spot because it's so far off the road. And I was right to check. Take a look," she added, pointing ahead.

A standard-sized pickup was parked way in the back, on a graveled section of the driveway that led up to the detached garage. Even in the semidarkness, it wasn't hard to see that the pickup was splattered with mud. Only the area of the windshield the wipers covered had been cleared, leaving just enough room for the driver to be able to see.

"That's not Mrs. Farrell's vehicle, so I have no idea what it's doing here, but it does look kind of familiar. Let's get closer so I can wipe the mud off the license plate and get a good look at it."

As they started toward it, the neighbor's porch and yard lights came on. "We better get out of here," Joshua whispered, stopping in midstride. "That's Mr. Gonzalez's home, and I've seen his gun collection."

As they hurried back to Nydia's truck, she added, "Do you think that is the killer's vehicle?"

"I think that's a possibility worth checking out. Let's get over to the police station. This is one piece of information my brother should have immediately."

THIRTY MINUTES LATER, after finding the sheriff's office dark and empty, they arrived at Gabriel's home. Nydia couldn't help but admire the attractive adobe house. In the glow of the porch light, red roses on either side of the doorway welcomed guests.

Joshua looked around for others who might be watching the house, then gestured to the other three vehicles parked beside Gabriel's home. "Looks like both my brothers are here, along with Lanie. They've undoubtedly been expecting me."

She started to comment, but there was no time. The sheriff came out onto the porch and glowered at them.

"Things may get a bit tense," Joshua warned, walking with her toward the door. "Give me a chance to talk to them."

Gabriel met Joshua halfway up the sidewalk. "Do you realize the stupidity of what you've done, Tree?" Gabriel snapped.

Nydia saw another man appear in the doorway, and recognized Lucas, the middle Blackhorse brother. His face was as grim as the sheriff's had been.

"You both knew I'd come back," Joshua replied calmly. "That's why you've been waiting."

Lucas shrugged. "That's not the point, Tree. We knew that you'd eventually do the right thing, but you've made matters unnecessarily complicated for yourself by taking so long."

"I was certain that I could find a lead, and I did," Joshua said, telling Gabriel about the pickup they'd spotted. "Sorry I can't tell you what color it was because it was too dark. But it definitely wasn't Mrs. Farrell's."

"There are several state policemen out now patrolling the county. That was one of the concessions I was forced to make to the mayor, who felt I was too close to the case to handle it effectively. I'll get one of those officers to check out the truck."

"You better warn the officer about that monster dog, Danger, too," Nydia added. "He might be a problem."

Gabriel nodded once, then looked at her sternly. "We'll talk about your part in all this later. Meanwhile, come inside the house. I need to radio this in and I don't want everyone standing out here silhouetted by the house lights. No need to turn the lot of us into targets."

As Nydia sat down in a comfortable-looking chair in the living room, she could feel the tension in the room. Lanie, Gabriel's dark-haired Anglo wife, smiled and brought her and Joshua cups of hot coffee. She then returned to the sofa where some papers, probably schoolwork, were scattered about.

Nydia quietly appraised each of the Blackhorse brothers. They were all undeniably handsome and strong, but there was a gentleness about Joshua, despite his size and powerful build, that she found particularly appealing.

She thought back to a lifetime ago, to the time she'd met and married Frank, her late husband, and blinked back the tears. She had loved him, but she'd been a different person then, so very young and impressed by the high-impact maleness of a rodeo cowboy.

Years alone with the responsibility for their son had taught her to look beyond appearances and posturing, however. What drew her to a man these days was a kaleidoscope of traits that attested to confidence and strength. She looked at Joshua. Right now, sadness covered him and the other Blackhorse brothers like a shroud, but Joshua drew strength from within himself, making him appear the leader, though he was the youngest. He spoke quietly, yet authority flowed from him, giving courage to those around him. There was a power in him that seemed to come from his roots and his connection to the People. But there was more to the man and to her feelings. Even the sound of his voice made her heart beat faster.

Joshua looked at Lucas, who was staring pensively into his coffee cup, then at Gabriel, who had just hung up the phone. "I'm here now, and we have matters to resolve. Let's not waste any more time assigning blame."

"We have a problem, Tree," Gabriel said. "It's been several hours since you left the crime scene, so gunpowder-residue tests are going to be inconclusive, basically useless. Cops don't even bother to conduct them this long after the crime was committed, even if the suspect hasn't cleaned his hands."

"He still has your father's blood on him," Nydia argued. "It's obvious he hasn't had a chance to wash up."

"Too much time has passed for the test to be conclusive, washed or not washed," Gabriel said.

"All right, let's move on to other matters, then. What clues were you able to find at the site?" Joshua asked.

"I recorded the tracks left by a pickup that wasn't yours or Dad's, and was too wide to be Nydia's. We found some shell casings, too, that I think will match ejection marks from your rifle. There are only two sets of fingerprints on the rifle, so the shooter must have worn gloves. You both admit handling the rifle, so those fingerprints, if they're yours as I suspect, will be easy to explain. I also have a cast of footprints that are definitely too small to be yours, and too large to be Nydia's."

"If you know there was a vehicle that's unaccounted for, and you've recorded an extra set of footprints, doesn't that support your brother's claim of innocence?"

"Support, yes, prove, no," Gabriel answered. "It could be argued that the footprints and the vehicle tracks were left by someone not connected to the crime, and that Joshua's fingerprints are there because he fired the rifle." He glared at his younger brother. "And some will say that you ran away in order to make sure the gunpowder-residue tests couldn't be used against you.''

Joshua sat up, his back straight. "You know better than that." Though his tone was quiet, the disdain in his voice made Nydia flinch.

Gabriel simply shook his head. "We all lost our father and share in that grief, but by leaving, you've given me another family member to worry about. New Mexico *does* have the death penalty, Tree." Gabriel stood and paced like a caged tiger. "I know you're innocent, but the way things are now, I have to prove that, as well as catch a killer. There are those who judge you by your actions, and running away made them believe you're guilty. The mayor has already said that he wants someone else working on the case in addition to me. He told me that the state police will be sending a detective as soon as they can spare someone."

Nydia felt her spirits sag. The murder investigation was really complicating things, and she couldn't afford the time that straightening it out was likely to take. She'd come looking for the *hataalii* at her son's request, hoping he could come with her immediately, but now it looked like she was destined to go home without the medicine man at all. Even worse, she truly feared her father-in-law's belief in the old ways was so strong, he really would die unless Joshua performed the life-giving ceremony that only he knew. If that happened, her son would certainly blame her for failing them all.

Finding her coffee cup empty, Nydia joined Lucas, who stood by the sideboard across the room pouring himself more of the steaming brew.

"You're the medic here in Four Winds, aren't you?" Nydia asked him.

"Yes. Is something wrong?" Lucas reached over and filled her cup with coffee, too, studying her with a professional eye.

The question almost made her laugh. It wasn't so much a matter of something being wrong as it was of nothing being right. "Tell me this—can someone who believes himself to be dying actually cause his own death? Is that really possible?"

Without looking back, Nydia felt Joshua's gaze on her. She hadn't asked him, because she'd known what he'd say. But he looked disappointed that she hadn't asked.

"People have died of psychosomatic illnesses. I remember a case years back. A person got locked in a railroad car he believed was refrigerated. He died of hypothermia, even though the unit inside the car hadn't been working. It was the force of his belief that killed him."

"Tell me what's wrong with your father-in-law," Joshua said, coming up to join them. "Is it possible another *hataalii* can help him?"

"I don't know. He and my eleven-year-old son, both traditionalists, insist that you're the only one, that the ancient life-giving song passed to you by your teacher is my father-in-law's only hope. You see, this started when my father-in-law was taking care of his sheep and lightning struck a tree near him, setting it ablaze. He said he inhaled those fumes and that's why he became so sick. He had a shooting chant done but, according to my father-in-law, he'd waited too long so the ceremony didn't do him any good. He continued to get worse.

"I was really worried, so I had two doctors from the medical center go take a look at him. They verified that he's dying, and much too weak to travel, but they can't find any medical reason for his condition. He's at home with family now, but grows weaker every day."

"You seem to know quite a bit about the prayer my teacher passed on to me," Joshua commented.

"My son wants to be a *hataalii* like you. He often visited your teacher. That was how he learned that the chant had been passed to you and to no one else. When my father-in-law heard that you alone possessed it, he became convinced that his one hope lay in having you brought to him."

"My brother can't go anywhere, not until this matter is settled," Gabriel told Nydia, joining the group by the coffee. "It's part of the compromise I had to work out with the mayor to keep myself on the case."

"I know it's difficult for you right now, but try not to worry too much. Four Winds called you here, and you came. Things will work out," Lucas added.

She looked at Lucas, bewildered. "Four Winds didn't 'call' me. I came here in search of help. This isn't 'The Twilight Zone.'" Nydia saw the way the brothers exchanged glances, and a shudder ran up her spine. It was as if they shared a secret.

Nydia pushed back the thought. She was tired, hungry and upset. Now her imagination was working overtime. "Would it be possible for me to use your telephone?" she asked Lanie, who was now looking at her as strangely as the brothers had been. "I need to make a long-distance call, but I'll use my credit card."

Lanie nodded, and rose from the sofa. "There's a phone in the kitchen. You'll be able to talk privately there."

Nydia dialed her mother-in-law's home, dreading the cool reserve that was always present between them when they spoke. They'd never been close, and things had deteriorated even more after Frank's death, when Nydia had chosen to go to college and pursue a career instead of following a more traditional path.

The moment Lucille recognized her voice, Nydia felt the temperature drop twenty degrees. "My husband is no worse, but he's no better, either. He's in the hogan. He stays there all the time now. My grandson is with him. Has the *hataalii* consented to come back with you?"

"There are...complications." The silence at the other

end spoke volumes. "I'm doing my best. But it may take a few days."

"My husband needs the singer. Bring him soon, or it will be too late."

Nydia heard the dial tone, and her heart sank. Lucille didn't have to say it. They were all counting on her. If she didn't bring Joshua back, her in-laws, and maybe even her son, John, would always wonder whether she'd failed because she hadn't seen the value of the singer, and had not tried hard enough.

Taking a deep breath, and wiping tears of frustration from her eyes, Nydia returned to the living room.

"Can I get you something to eat?" Lanie asked. "You don't look well."

"I'm fine," she assured. "It's my father-in-law I'm worried about."

The sound of a car arriving captured everyone's attention. Gabriel walked to the front window and glanced outside. "It's the state police. I'll go talk to the officer. Joshua, go to the door so he can verify you're actually here. My word might not be good enough for their records. But don't come outside unless I call for you."

Joshua nodded, and walked over by the door as Gabriel went outside.

Lucas came over to stand beside him. "I'm here, little brother. Whatever happens, we'll face it together."

"I know."

"I hope I find the killer first," Lucas said softly, though a deadly intent resonated with each syllable.

"Talk like that is dangerous," Nydia warned.

"I can't help the way I feel," Lucas said, the bitter dregs of sadness coloring his words.

"Nor can I," Joshua admitted.

She sensed the crushing weight of sorrow that filled

them, and her heart went out to them, though there was nothing she could do.

After several minutes, the eldest Blackhorse brother returned, and the car outside drove away. "The state police officer can't find the truck you said you spotted at Olivia's. Tree, are you sure that's where it was? Maybe you got turned around." Gabriel returned to the sofa, sat down beside his wife and draped his arm around her shoulders protectively.

"I didn't get turned around. And neither did Danger. I know where that pickup was parked."

"There weren't any tracks. The officer checked after he had Olivia take Danger inside the house." Gabriel rubbed the back of his neck, trying to ease the tense muscles. "Olivia, by the way, didn't see or hear anything tonight. But that's no surprise. She doesn't wear her hearing aid to bed. She only spotted the policeman because the flashing lights woke her up."

"Maybe it *was* the killer's truck, then," Nydia said. "He parked it there temporarily, thinking that no one would suspect Olivia or risk getting Danger's attention. The dog must have known him, too, or he'd still be there. He obviously came back for the truck after we left."

"We'll keep checking. The officer went to talk to neighbors now. Maybe someone else saw something."

Joshua stood up. "It's time for me to go. I want to return to the new hogan. I need to make a hole in the north wall. Although our father didn't die there, his death took place only a few feet away. I won't use that hogan again. After I finish what I have to do at that hogan, I'll go back to my old home."

"That's out of the question. For one, it's not safe for you to be out alone," Gabriel said. "Once word gets out and people start talking among themselves, there's no telling what'll happen. Vigilante law is not unheard-of in this town.''

Nydia knew he was referring to the legend of Flinthawk. The medicine man had almost been lynched back in the 1800s by an angry rancher and his cohorts, who'd believed him guilty of murder. The townspeople of Four Winds had saved Flinthawk, however, coming to his rescue and standing beside him, refusing to allow vigilante law to prevail. In return for saving his life, the medicine man had rewarded the town by doing a special blessingway that had assured Four Winds of safety and prosperity for its citizens forevermore. She'd studied and documented the tale as part of her research on the skinwalker bowl.

''Where would you have me go?'' Joshua's voice rose slightly. ''I'm not guilty of anything and I won't run and hide.''

''The deal I cut with the mayor, which is all that's allowing me to keep you out of jail, is that one of us will remain with you at all times. So, for now, you can stay here. No one will make a move against you as long as you're under this roof,'' Gabriel said.

Gabriel was about to say more when the telephone rang. He picked up the receiver, visibly annoyed at the interruption. As he spoke, his voice seemed to become more and more tense.

Joshua and Lucas exchanged glances, but neither said anything.

Nydia overheard enough to know it was the mayor and new rules were being set down. A shudder traveled up her spine.

At long last, Gabriel replaced the receiver and glanced at his brothers. ''That, as I'm sure you've realized, was the mayor. We have a big problem. He spoke to the state police and heard about the truck you claimed you saw. He's worried that you're guilty, and somehow all this is going to cost him his job. He doesn't want you running around free, and he doesn't think having either Shadow or me sticking with you when we can is good enough. For one thing, we're both pretty likely to be called away on emergencies, leaving you unguarded.''

Joshua narrowed his eyes and met his brother's gaze with a steely one. "You're going to throw me in jail?"

"No. I've been ordered to deputize a citizen, someone who is not related to you, and that person is to be with you when we can't be."

"Then deputize me," Nydia said. "I'm the logical choice. You know I wasn't involved. I'm also the closest to a witness that you've got. You need me here, which is fine with me since I'm not going anywhere until the singer can leave with me."

Gabriel stared at her, eyebrows raised. "You're not trained for any of this."

"This town only has one full-time cop, so neither is anyone else. The singer isn't trying to escape—all you need is someone who can testify as to his whereabouts, right?" Seeing him nod, she continued. "Well, then when neither you nor Lucas can be with him, I'll be there like I was tonight."

Gabriel nodded. "You'll have to take an oath, though I don't have a badge to give you. The town only owns one."

"No problem."

Gabriel swore her in quickly. "That's done. You're officially deputized."

"Do you know if Marlee has a room at the boarding-house, Sheriff?" Nydia asked. "I'll be needing a place to stay until the singer is free to leave town with me."

Lanie cleared her throat. "I figured you'd be staying, one way or another, so I called Marlee earlier and told her you might be coming by. She's got a room ready."

"Thanks."

Lanie walked with Nydia to the door. "It looks like Four Winds wants you around. It needs a new resident from time to time," she said with a knowing smile.

"Resident?" Nydia shook her head. "No way. I've got a life and a son waiting for me back on the reservation. I have no intention of staying here any longer than necessary."

Lanie said nothing, but there was a look in her eyes that bothered Nydia. A chill wrapped around her, filling her with a sense of impending danger.

As Nydia drove to the boardinghouse, she glanced down at the beautiful rug on the pickup seat beside her.

Fate comes in many guises, a voice said within her mind.

Nydia blocked the uneasiness spreading through her. She was exhausted. Tomorrow, things would look better. Holding on to that thought, she hurried down Main Street to Marlee's.

"YOU CAN'T KEEP ME from leaving, Fuzz," Joshua said. He wouldn't lose his temper with his brothers; they meant well. "I have my own home and I need a chance to be alone to think. I admit I lost it for a while today. Anger blinded me, and now I need time to deal with those feelings, to regain harmony. You have the luxury of hate. A *hataalii* doesn't."

"Okay, so you're not perfect," Lucas piped up. "We knew that already. Live with it. But none of that changes the situation."

"Stay here tonight," Gabriel repeated. "Tomorrow, we'll see how things are shaping up in town and how safe it'll be for you in Four Winds. Agreed?"

Joshua considered it. His brothers obviously wouldn't let him leave, not without a full-blown confrontation. The set look on Gabriel's face was one he recognized. Lucas would back Fuzz up, too. He always did. Joshua considered his

options. He didn't want to take on his brothers right now.
They might get hurt, Lanie would get in the way and he'd
probably have to take a few punches for his trouble. And
all for no good reason. They'd all just lost their father and
were under an incredible strain. They couldn't afford to be
taking their anger out on each other now. "All right. I'll
stay tonight." Joshua looked down at his hands. "I'm going to need a shower, though, and some clean clothes.
Yours won't fit me."

"He has a point," Lucas conceded. "How about if I
promise to keep an eye on Tree at his cabin? You stay here
with Lanie, and keep an eye on each other. And that way,
you'll be close to town if you get called out on police
business."

"Living up to your name again, Shadow? I don't suppose I can talk you out of it," Joshua asked.

"Not a chance," Lucas answered.

"I think it's a good idea, too," Gabriel added. "You
two be careful."

"Let's go, little brother," Lucas said, looking up at
Joshua, who towered over him. "Big brother is going to
take care of you."

"'Big bother' is more like it, shorty," Joshua retorted,
drawing comfort from the banter they'd shared for many
years, and followed Shadow out the door.

NYDIA SAT ALONE in her room at the boardinghouse. According to Marlee, it was the same one Lanie had used
months back, when she'd first arrived in Four Winds. She
remembered part of the story Lanie had told her when she'd
come to document the story about the bowl. When she'd
first arrived, Lanie had truly believed her stay in Four
Winds would be a short one. Maybe Marlee was used to
hearing that, too. She'd smiled so strangely when Nydia
had asked for the daily instead of weekly rate.

Or maybe Marlee just didn't believe that the murderer would be caught quickly. But in a town this small, how many suspects could there be? Of course, the killer could have been another new arrival in town. But if that was true, surely he would have stuck out among the residents.

A knock sounded at her door. As Nydia opened it, Marlee came in with a cup of hot cocoa and a sandwich. Since Nydia had seen her last, Marlee's brown hair had been restyled so that it fell toward her face in short bangs that framed her oval face and partially hid the scar that ran from her left temple to her chin. "To help you settle in," she said, placing the food on the bedside table. "I used to put herbs in my cocoa that helped people relax, but nowadays I don't do that unless people ask. Would you like something to help you sleep?"

Nydia sipped the chocolate. "No, this is fine. Thanks."

Nydia suddenly realized that she hadn't eaten in hours, except for the coffee she'd had at Lanie's, and she was starving. Taking large bites of the sandwich, she finished it quickly.

"Would you like another sandwich?" Compassion was mirrored in Marlee's hazel eyes.

"No. This was fine. Thanks for fixing it for me."

"You know, we didn't really get much of a chance to talk last time you were in town. I'm glad you came back."

"I wish the circumstances were different. I need the singer's help, and I can't leave without him. How well do you know Sheriff Blackhorse? Will he be able to clear up this case soon?"

Marlee considered it. "With his family so closely involved, he may not be allowed to work much on the case officially. I've already heard some talk about that. But I guarantee he won't rest until his father's murderer is caught. None of the Blackhorse brothers will." She stood up. "But don't you worry about any of that right now. Fate brought you here. You'll be okay."

"Fate? I came on an errand."

"That doesn't discount fate. Think about it," Marlee said, and shut the door behind her.

Nydia sighed, turned off the light, then walked to the window and stood there pensively, staring outside. The moon was almost directly overhead now. Silver gossamer sheets of light filtered onto the backyard, accentuating the bed of wildflowers that Marlee obviously tended very carefully. It was peaceful here. Only one sound drifted into her room—the soothing drone of the night insects dancing around the darkness like winged messengers of some far-off god.

There were touches of warmth and life everywhere, but beyond that exterior was an inescapable core of corruption. Somewhere in Four Winds tonight, a murderer walked free.

As her thoughts drifted from that back to Joshua and the loss he'd suffered, a hawk shrieked overhead, its cry slowly fading into memory. The Blackhorse family had a merciless enemy out there, hiding. To kill the father and frame the son required a unique form of hatred.

She remembered the pain on Joshua's face as he saw his father's life slipping away despite his best efforts. The anguish had been that of a strong man hammered by blows that transcended the physical. Yet within that sorrow, she'd sensed a deep well of strength and power.

Her pulse quickened, and her body quivered as she saw him clearly in her mind's eye. His grief had touched her deeply, and she'd longed for a way to soothe his pain. She shook her head. He was not for her, though he filled her with emotions she'd thought she'd never feel again. Those intense feelings in the face of the danger and darkness surrounding them both seemed odd and out of character for her. But they were oh so real!

Nydia stared up at the moon, and wondered where Joshua was now and what he was thinking.

JOSHUA PACED AIMLESSLY around the old cabin he'd shared with his father. His father's most valued possessions would be discarded in a few days. The few pieces his brothers and he would keep would need a blessingway done over them. As he stared at his father's favorite chair, he felt such a biting hurt he wanted to cry out. But he could not. His insides knotted with the anger he would not give in to. Finally, the emotion passed and left a great echoing emptiness.

He stood by the window, lost in thought, listening to the sounds of the night. Lucas was sleeping, but rest eluded him tonight. As a night bird screamed shrilly outside, he remembered what Rudolph Harvey, his teacher, had taught him. The Way meant maintaining the inner stillness needed to ward off chaos. Strength came through harmony. Peace through inner balance. Without those, he could do little to help anyone, including himself.

The memory of his father, and the loss they'd all suffered, would have to find its place somewhere within each of them where the burden could be carried. Life went on.

He thought of the woman, Nydia Jim, who had spent the evening with him. It was clear to him that Four Winds had called to her, but to what end? Her fate touched his; that was certain. As it was now, though, he could do nothing to help her or her family until he found himself again.

"Four Winds brought her back for you," Lucas said, coming up silently to stand beside him. "I noticed the attraction between you two when you met months ago. But you let her just drive away. It looks to me like Four Winds is going to be tougher to argue with this time."

Joshua shook his head. "She came in search of a *hataalii*

who may not exist anymore. I'm not the man she thought I was. I'm not the man I thought I was.''

"Yes, you are. You just have to accept the two sides of your own nature, and find the balance point between them.'' Lucas gave his brother's shoulder a squeeze. "A singer is only a man, little brother. Unless you come to terms with that, you *will* lose your way, and everything that you've fought so hard to become."

As his elder brother returned to bed, Joshua remained by the window. He sensed somehow that before this was over, he would be tested and the woman along with him. He would have sent her home, and spared her the violence and anger that was yet to come, but it wasn't his call to make.

He watched as the moon slipped behind a cloud, leaving only the faint glow of what it had been. Haze could obscure the brightness for a while, but it would not win over the inevitable.

As the cloud slowly slipped away, and the moon once again illuminated the forest, the singer murmured, "Good night, Nydia. Sleep well."

Chapter Four

The sun was still below the horizon when Joshua left the log home his father and he had built so many years back. His brother Lucas was still asleep, so Joshua slipped away silently, intent on walking to the hogan to do what needed to be done there before Lucas got up.

The long walk was pleasant, though the duty ahead weighed his spirit down. Lost in his own thoughts, he was scarcely aware of his surroundings until a flash of light between the pine branches caught his attention.

Focusing ahead, he saw his father's truck, still parked where he'd left it. A knife edge of loss cut through him. Taking a long, deep breath, he allowed the sorrow to flow, releasing it with a burst of will. Even in death, there was a purpose, and in accepting it, he would find harmony.

His own truck was parked a bit farther down, under a tree. Taking a sledgehammer from the back, he began his work, making a hole in the north side of the hogan to allow the spirits inside to exit in the required direction.

Time slipped away from him, and the sun was above the trees when Lucas pulled up in his pickup. His face was grim, and it didn't take any special talent to know that Lucas disapproved of his brother's decision to come down here alone. Joshua felt a twinge of remorse, but he had no intention of allowing either Lucas or Gabriel to start running his life.

As Lucas approached, and he saw the concern etched on his brother's face, Joshua was glad he hadn't told anyone about Nydia's run-in with the peddler. That was one concern he could spare his family, though he wasn't sure how long the secret would remain hidden. He couldn't assume that no one else had seen the man yesterday.

"I'm finished here, Shadow. There was no need for you to come."

"I promised Gabriel I would stay with you. You aren't supposed to be out on your own. And we need to talk before I turn you over to Nydia and leave for my rounds. I'll be asking questions, like Gabriel, and I need to know what to ask. When I spoke to Gabriel this morning on my cell phone, he asked again that you stop investigating on your own. Otherwise, we'll all be tripping over each other every time we turn around. If Gabriel or I find out anything, we'll let you know. But it's not safe for you to be poking into this."

"I won't hide out, or run from this," Joshua reaffirmed. "Today, I'll go see the woman as agreed, and also make a stop by Charley's." Joshua gestured toward his father's truck. "I'll use mine to tow that one and ask Charley if he'll sell it for us. Any objections?"

Lucas shrugged. "Gabriel will understand, and I have no objections."

"Thanks." He knew neither of his brothers paid the slightest attention to the laws that warned about the *chindi*'s attachment to a dead man's favorite possessions, but they would agree to sell their father's vehicle out of respect for Joshua's beliefs. It was enough.

"On second thought, Tree, let me be the one who tows the truck in later," Lucas said. "We still don't know the mood of the townspeople. This is something that may be viewed more favorably if either Gabriel or I take care of it.''

Joshua thought about his options. He suspected Lucas was right, but it still didn't make it easier to accept the need for someone else to assume a duty he considered his. He nodded once.

Joshua took one last look around. It was time to move on, to find answers and meet whatever the future held.

Joshua drove his own truck directly to Marlee's, Lucas following all the way. Despite the circumstances, he was glad for the opportunity to spend time with Nydia. He visualized her in his mind. He wanted to remain distant, but the warmth of her gaze and the softness of her voice overcame any barriers he set up. She brought out feelings he'd never had before. Being saddled with a deputy had seemed like a sentence in itself, until he learned it would be Nydia he'd have by his side.

As he reached the door and Nydia opened it, Lucas waved and continued down the road.

''Good morning.'' With a casual gesture, she invited Joshua inside. ''Has anyone learned anything new since last night?''

''No, it's much too soon yet. I just wanted to tell you that, if you want me to, I'll do my best to find another *hataalii* for your relative. I know we are few these days, but—''

Nydia shook her head. ''My mother-in-law has had people searching everywhere within the sacred mountains for another who might know the chant. They've all been told that you are the only one, until the day you choose to pass it on to another.'' She walked into the kitchen with Joshua. ''I was just having breakfast. When's the last time you ate?''

He saw the flash of concern in her eyes and felt her warmth wrapping itself around him. She glanced back at him, waiting for his reply, and that look was like sunlight shining through dark clouds. "I haven't eaten since yesterday," he answered.

"Then we'll have to fix that." She checked the refrigerator, then the cupboard. "Marlee said I could help myself to anything here. Scrambled eggs with chili, okay?"

"Sounds fine." His gaze remained on Nydia, watching the fluidity of her movements as she went from one task to another. As she bent down to retrieve a pan from the bottom cupboard, he felt a flash of heat corkscrew down his body. He glanced away, but he couldn't resist the temptation she posed and soon looked back. She was so beautiful, so graceful as she moved, totally unaware of what was going through his mind.

Several minutes later, she set a plate of scrambled eggs in front of him. "Would you like something to drink with this? Marlee brewed some really good coffee earlier."

"No coffee, thanks." As he ate, Joshua watched her moving about, cleaning up. Desire coiled through him, stronger than he'd ever felt.

"You don't look like you're enjoying your food. Did I add too much chili?" Taking a fork from the counter, she took a taste from his plate.

He watched her take the food into her mouth and flick her tongue over her lips. He knew he should let it pass, but he could not.

He stood and swept her against him, savoring her mouth. It was more than a kiss; he'd never imagined such power coming from touching a woman and feeling her respond to him. It was as if he'd found a new world in her arms that waited to be explored.

An eternity later, he released her, knowing that either he stopped right then, or he'd take her on the closest surface.

Nydia was trembling as she took a hesitant step back, staring at him, completely disoriented.

He smiled, glad to know that he'd affected her as strongly as she'd affected him. "I won't apologize. I'm not sorry, not at all."

She took a deep breath and gave him a shaky smile. "Neither am I, but don't do it again. Neither of us can afford to get sidetracked like this."

Her words brought reality crashing down on him. That heaviness of spirit that had become his companion returned.

"I want to help you find your father's killer," she said, her voice firm, though her hands trembled. "We both have a vested interest in this."

He nodded slowly. "My ways of working to find out the truth are not based on police procedure—that's Gabriel's job. What I can do is use my own strengths, my knowledge about people. For example, I can usually tell when someone's holding something back, and even when a person is lying."

"I have skills, too, which will be useful. Anthropology is a science that teaches discernment. I can help you by applying what I've learned in my work. I'm very good at talking and listening to people, that's part of my business. And I excel at sifting important facts from feelings and gossip that can't be substantiated. I can help you make sure that gossip and rumors don't win."

He weighed her offer carefully. They had worked well together yesterday. In many ways, their skills complemented each other. It was almost as though it was destined to be. More important, he was in no position to turn down her help. She was the only one not trying to keep him out of the investigation—not trying to prevent him from doing what he felt called to do. Even more than that, she was offering her help. Truly their fates were bound together.

The situation, too, was far more complex than his personal wish to find his father's killer and clear his name. He was honor bound by his chosen path to find a way to help her father-in-law. And even more important, her young son's involvement concerned him. A youngster who was interested in the ways of a *hataalii* was a rare treasure these days. For the sake of the People, he couldn't afford to fail this family.

He thought of the song that had been entrusted to him. It was such a powerful prayer that it couldn't even be said twice on the same day. He'd mastered it for the sole purpose of helping those in need. Now, he was failing to live up to the trust his teacher had placed in him. He wouldn't accept such failure.

"We'll work together," he said at last, "but you better understand that Gabriel won't thank either one of us for it. Depending on his mood, in fact, he may try to toss us both in jail for obstruction."

"One of my best traits is that I never take 'no' or 'get lost' for an answer."

Joshua smiled. Nydia couldn't have come into his life at a worse time, but he was glad to have her on his side. She was irresistible.

"Let's start at Rosa's grocery store," he said. "Everyone goes there. It's Sunday, but she's open noon to four. She feels she has to open every day since she's the only food store in town."

Joshua parked in his usual spot in the alley and entered the grocery store through the side door. Rosa was behind the counter speaking to Sally, who ran the diner. Both women stopped speaking abruptly the moment they saw him. It didn't take a genius to guess that he was as welcome as the plague.

"Ladies," he greeted quietly.

Rosa's face became pinched looking, and Sally refused to look directly at him. "I'm really surprised to see you here," Rosa said at last. "We've all heard about the…problem you're having. Everyone really respected your father, you know."

"A death is never easy to accept," he said, avoiding mentioning his father directly, as was Navajo custom.

He was aware of the way Sally watched him, as if studying a frog she knew was about to jump. "I'm sorry about what happened to your family. If there's anything Gabriel needs, tell him not to hesitate to ask. I owe him one. I won't forget what he did for my boy."

"What better way to repay the sheriff than by helping his brother?" Nydia suggested. "Could you answer a few questions for us now?"

Sally's eyebrows lifted. "I remember you from a few months ago. You're the anthropologist studying the tribes of New Mexico. What's your involvement in this?"

Nydia hesitated. She hated to share personal information with a stranger, but a personal approach could generate goodwill and help her far more than explaining she'd been deputized.

After describing the reason she'd sought Joshua's help, Nydia added, "Now will you help us?"

"I was serving customers here in town when…it happened. How can anything I know possibly help you?" Sally said.

"A very mud-splattered, dark-colored truck came through town last night. Is it possible you were working in the diner after you closed and saw it passing by?"

"How late?"

"Nine, or shortly afterward."

"Well, I was in the kitchen about that time, but my attention was on cleaning up. To be honest, between that and all the pans rattling in the dishwasher, I doubt anything except a bomb could get my attention."

Darren Wilson, the owner of the feed store, came in just then. As he saw Joshua, his smile froze on his face and he stopped in midstride. "Seems to me, Joshua, you'd have more-important things to do today than buy groceries—like maybe turn yourself in?"

Joshua stared at the man he'd known for years but who had suddenly turned into a stranger. "I met with the authorities last night. Until this is cleared up, they've asked me to remain in police custody." He glanced at Nydia, then back at Darren. "This woman has been sworn in and deputized."

Darren gave Nydia a skeptical look. "Like she's going to be able to stop you from escaping?"

"He's here, isn't he?" Nydia replied. "Or are you questioning my character?"

"Ma'am, all I know about you is that you're an anthropologist. If you're trying to study murderers among the Navajo, then I guess you're in the right place."

"The evidence the police found proves there was someone else there where the murder occurred. I'm being framed by the real killer," Joshua said flatly.

"I don't interpret things that way, and neither do some other people. I was at the mayor's house this morning attending an emergency town-council meeting. I know Bob Burns has asked the state police to provide a special investigator to handle the murder. Jake Fields also gave us an interesting perspective on the crime. He told us about the legends of your people. Skinwalkers do some pretty crazy things to gain power, and let's face it, no one had a better opportunity than you. If anyone but your brother was handling the case, you would be in jail now, not traipsing around town with a pretty, untrained deputy."

"I think you should let the police and courts decide how to interpret the evidence," Nydia said brusquely. "Of course, you could try to make a citizen's arrest, if *you* have evidence you've been withholding from the authorities." She glanced at Joshua, then back at Darren. "It doesn't look like your 'suspect' is making any attempt to flee,'' she added as if as an afterthought.

Joshua met Darren's gaze and noted with satisfaction that the man flinched. "I didn't kill anyone, but the murderer is almost certainly somewhere in this community. He won't be able to hide forever, and he won't escape justice. My brothers and I will see to that."

"Brave words for a man whose profession is to play mind games," said Bill Riley, the trucker who brought in supplies to Four Winds, stepping out from behind some shelves. "You say you want justice, but so do a lot of other people in this town. Your father was highly regarded here. We won't let his death go unpunished."

"Are you making threats?" Gabriel asked, sauntering into the store and taking the situation in at a glance. There was an innate confidence about him that made Riley and Wilson take a prudent step back.

"No threat, Sheriff, more like a prediction. Your father was sheriff here for many years, and we intend to help you catch whoever murdered him."

Gabriel nodded with a deceptively casual air. "I'm glad to hear it. No one wants this solved more than me and my family. I trust you'll cooperate fully with the police on this. In case you haven't heard, as soon as the state police can spare him, a detective will be sent here from Santa Fe. He'll be taking over responsibility for the case, although I'll still be assisting. If you really want to help, you can start by asking yourselves who might have had a grudge against my father *and* our family."

"Your family?" Rosa asked, then nodded thoughtfully. "That's assuming someone intended to frame Joshua for killing your father. But what if your theory is wrong? Maybe the answer is a lot simpler than that."

Gabriel's gaze was rock hard. "I'll find the truth, wherever it leads." Gabriel glanced at Joshua, and gestured toward the side door.

Once they were out in the alleyway, Gabriel glowered at his brother. "Damn it, Tree, you're only making things worse. I asked you not to meddle in this investigation. You're as unsuited to police work as I would be to giving a blessingway ceremony."

"The law is your business, Sheriff," Nydia snapped, "but the man who was murdered was as much Joshua's father as yours." Her voice trembled with anger. "Even more to the point, you can't refuse a man the right to clear his name."

Gabriel stared at her in surprise. "So, he's roped you into helping him?"

"Nobody *ever* coerces me into anything, Sheriff. I'm doing what I have to do, and you already know my reasons. And there's something else you should be aware of. I've studied people and I've dealt with all kinds, but there's something very wrong in this town. People who have known your brother for years are awfully quick to believe the worst of him, that he's a killer. My guess is that someone's fanning the flames, stirring up the fears that come from half truths and superstition."

Gabriel glanced at his brother. "She's right. I've noticed that myself, but I haven't found out yet who's behind it. If you insist on coming into town, you'll have to stay on your guard." He looked over at Nydia. "There's no animosity against you—yet, so you may be able to help me with something. Go talk to Ralph Montoya. He covered the meeting at Mayor Burns's house this morning for his newspaper. I've noticed that when you argue your points, you rely on logic, not emotions. He'll respect that. If you can make Ralph see that the law needs to handle this, he might decide to use his newspaper to help calm people down.

Without his backing, I have a feeling Four Winds could become a powder keg with a very short fuse."

"Just point me in the right direction, Sheriff. I'll take care of it," Nydia said.

"I'll go with her," Joshua said. "Ralph has known our family for years. I can't believe he would think me capable of a crime like this."

Gabriel's expression was doubtful, but he nodded his assent. "Don't assume anything, Tree. Four Winds has always been an unpredictable town."

Joshua fell silent as he led the way toward the newspaper office. Nydia didn't say a word until she saw the wooden sign announcing the town's paper, the *Last Word.* "It would really help if you could give me a handle on this man. The right approach is important."

"I hate the idea of manipulating anyone," Joshua replied. "Just tell him what we're here for."

"I intend to do that, but if he's already made up his mind against you, or even if he's convinced he should write an inflammatory article screaming for justice, I'm going to have to do my best to change his mind. Knowing a little about him would really help."

"I can tell you that he's a man who operates by his own rules and moral principles. That's why he's here running his own paper instead of pursuing a high-profile career elsewhere, which he apparently did at one time. When Ralph goes after a story, he pulls out all the stops, don't get me wrong. But he also knows when to pull back and bide his time, like when my sister-in-law had that skinwalker bowl."

"Thanks. Knowing that should help."

Nydia walked into Montoya's office. In comparison, the tribal newspaper offices were huge.

Joshua introduced Nydia, and Ralph waved them to the seats in front of his desk.

"I can guess why you're here," he said. "You want to know what happened this morning, and what stand the paper's going to take." Seeing them nod, he leaned back in his chair and regarded them for several seconds. "I don't believe in vigilante justice or inciting the public. My article will call for justice, but it'll call for fairness and caution, too. I intend to remind everyone how Four Winds became the town it is, and of your family's connection to our history."

"You mean about my ancestor, Flinthawk?"

"Yes. I'll remind everyone how since that time, in accordance with the blessing he bestowed on our town, evil of any kind eventually has incurred its own punishment here. Also, I'm running a separate editorial about the terrible price acting prematurely out of a need for revenge will exact."

Joshua watched the newsman carefully, wondering what had happened in Ralph's past to explain such caution. There was something broken inside this man, something that had never quite healed. But respecting the Four Winds custom of not bringing up anyone's personal history, he said nothing.

"Should my friend fear the townspeople's mood?" Nydia asked, avoiding Joshua's name out of respect to the singer.

"Yes. Even my assistant, Alex, who is normally very mild mannered, wanted the *Last Word* to take a much different approach. Many have already convicted you, Joshua, I'm sorry to say. They're afraid, you know."

"But why? People here have known me for years. Some have even come to me when Lucas was unable to help them."

"Yes, I know that. When people are desperate, they open their minds to new ideas. But right now, they're acting out of the kind of fear that closes the mind. If you have turned to evil and killed your father, none of us are safe, you see. A man your size is pretty intimidating, and if you've added a skinwalker's power to that, who here would stand a chance against you? That kind of fear can turn people into an instant mob. I wouldn't turn my back on anyone until all this is cleared up. And although I'd like to believe what I've said will make people stop and think a bit, I expect men like Darren Wilson will still want your hide on the wall. He's not long on thought, and he's not the only one around here with that affliction," Ralph said.

"Tell us about the meeting this morning," Nydia asked. "Was anyone in particular speaking out against Joshua? And what was the gist of the meeting?"

"Most folks want Joshua out of town or in jail until this is cleared up. They fed off each other's fears, so it's hard to say who started the ball rolling. They were hoping that the mayor would run Joshua out or have him arrested immediately. Some spoke of burning him out, too, which is not all that unusual for small-town mentalities. But of course, the mayor really came down hard on that kind of talk. In fact, he was the voice of reason, though I think he lost a few votes in the process. Apparently, the special investigator from the state police won't be available for a week to ten days, so the sheriff will be on his own until then. The mayor promised, however, that he'd monitor every step of the investigation himself and that the sheriff would be required to submit daily reports. Those would then be handed over to the special investigator when he arrives.

"We also learned that you'd been deputized." Ralph gave Nydia a hard look. "A word of warning for you. If you choose to ally yourself publicly with Joshua in any way, you can expect trouble. Talk has already started, saying you might be Joshua's accomplice."

"That's ridiculous."

"Is it? Then tell me what the truth is, and I'll print that, too."

Nydia told him the story of her father-in-law's illness, and the reason she had come to Four Winds. She only omitted the fact that her son was depending on her to help his grandfather and there was no way she'd ever let him down. Some things were simply too personal to share with a stranger.

As she finished, a young man wearing jeans and a sweatshirt came in. He greeted Ralph, then shot Joshua a venomous look.

"This is my new assistant, Alex," Ralph said, introducing the young man.

"I've got the material you requested, Mr. Montoya," Alex said stiffly. "Are you finally going to let me do an editorial? We talked about it two months ago."

"Only when I'm sure I can trust you with the responsibility that entails. At the moment, I'm not convinced."

Alex scowled. "You mean I won't get to do an editorial unless I happen to agree with your views?"

"It means this paper won't be a party to irresponsible journalism. You've still got a lot to learn."

"What if I do a short one on something I heard today?"

"Elaborate."

He glanced at Nydia and Joshua. "Now?"

Ralph rolled his eyes. "I guarantee they won't steal your story."

"There's a rumor that Four Winds's infamous peddler made an impromptu visit yesterday."

Ralph sat up. "When? He didn't come down Main Street, or I would have known. Where was he seen?"

"That I don't know. Mrs. Stephens, who lives in that adobe cottage near the road junction leading out of town, told me she was sure she'd seen him driving by. She was really excited about it."

Ralph exhaled softly. "Wait a minute. That same Mrs. Stephens also saw a UFO last spring. She claims that aliens hovered over her vegetable patch and that's why none of the pumpkins were growing this year."

Nydia struggled to suppress a grin after seeing the warning look Joshua shot her.

"That doesn't mean she didn't see the peddler," Alex argued.

"True, and I can't prove she didn't see aliens, either. What it does mean is that you need at least two people to verify what she saw before you can print a word of it. From the research I've done myself on the peddler and his habits, I can tell you that he usually comes right into the middle of town, and sticks around for several hours, usually longer."

"So maybe he changed his rules. Some say he's a free spirit. He comes and goes as he pleases," Alex argued.

"Fine, go find someone else to back up the story. I'm not telling you that we can't run it—I'm just saying that you need corroboration."

Alex's deep eyes burned with frustration. "Okay, okay. I'll see what I can do." He shot Joshua an icy glare. "If I were you, I'd watch my step out there. People are putting two and two together. You're not very popular around these parts right now."

Ralph rolled his eyes. "As I said, this town's in an ugly mood, Joshua. Be careful."

With a quick word of thanks to Ralph for his cooperation, Joshua left the newspaper office. As he went down the street, he read the flashes in people's eyes, emotions so clear he had no trouble interpreting them. There was fear, and anger, too. The revelation hurt him more than he would have thought possible. He'd counted these people as friends. Fear was a powerful enemy.

They had just reached his truck when, out of the corner

of his eye, he saw something flying toward them. He reached out and grabbed it in midair before it could hit Nydia. The rotten tomato burst in his hand, and he dropped it onto the sidewalk. A barrage of other rotten vegetables followed, pelting the truck and them.

He heard insults coming from the group of high-school kids who were throwing the fruit as he pushed Nydia into the cab and quickly drove away down Main Street. "I've never seen the people here act like this," he said. "Nydia, I'd like you to reconsider your decision to stay, for your own safety. I give you my word that I'll come to help your father-in-law as soon as I am able."

"No. People are depending on me not to come back without you. I won't disappoint them. Besides, I can be of more use here. I'm not afraid. We won't let anything happen to each other."

Her confidence filled him with pride and a sense of protectiveness so fierce, he pitied anyone who tried to harm her. "You *are* safe with me."

"We have work to do together," she said simply.

He could sense her drawing into herself. Nydia seemed to realize, on some level, that their beliefs were so far apart, they'd never be able to have any kind of future together. He tried to assure himself that it was just as well. He had chosen another path, and the People needed him. A modern woman was not what he wanted, but he couldn't quite rid himself of the hollow ache in his gut.

As they pulled up in front of Marlee's, they saw her cleaning the windows. Rotten fruit and vegetables littered the lawn.

Marlee gave them a tight-lipped smile as they approached. "Well-wishers," she said, trying to make a joke out of it, but not quite succeeding. "I spoke to Lanie. It was worse over there. Someone threw a rock through their living-room window."

Joshua expelled his breath in a rush. "This shouldn't have happened. I'm going to have to handle this before it goes any further."

"Wait a minute," Nydia protested as he started to walk away. "What do you have in mind?" He didn't answer and, aided by his giant strides, he was already by his truck, the door open, before she caught up to him.

Before he could start the engine, Gabriel came up in his Jeep and double-parked beside Joshua, blocking his way. "Where are you heading off to?"

"To my home. Alone. I can take care of myself, and I won't endanger anyone else if I stay there."

"Too late. I just came from there. Someone reported seeing smoke, so I went to check it out. The cabin is nothing more than rubble and smoking embers. Jake Fields took out the fire truck, and between him and some volunteers, they made sure the fire didn't spread."

A futile rage swept over Joshua. He'd done nothing wrong and now, while people destroyed his home and threatened him and those he cared about, the real killer got to enjoy his handiwork. Frustration knotted his fists into lethal weapons. He was far from the peacemaker now.

"Tree, let it go. There's nothing you can do about it now. Come to my home. That way, Shadow and I will be around to back you up if there's more trouble."

Joshua weighed the matter. "No. I'll go to our mountain retreat instead. Only the three of us know where it is."

"Then you'll have to let me in on the secret, because I'm going with you," Nydia added. "That was our agreement. I'm staying with you until this is over, then we're leaving to go help my father-in-law."

"You can't come with me now. There's no purpose to it, and it would be far too dangerous." Under different circumstances, he would have enjoyed having her with him in that secluded cabin, but now she was a distraction he couldn't afford. He needed to bring himself under the same control he'd always valued, not have this woman's softness beckoning his hands and mouth.

Nydia lifted her chin and met his gaze. "You say that there is no purpose in my coming. Let me propose one. When you learned our chants, you also took on the responsibility to pass them on. Teach me. There are women singers, so this won't be against our Way. You can teach me the chant my father-in-law needs first. That way, we'll ensure that it can't be lost, and I can use it to help the ones you're not able to reach."

Joshua remembered what she'd said about her son wanting to be a singer. If becoming a *hataalii* or learning the chants worked the way she suggested, it wouldn't have been a bad way to ensure the continuity of the prayer. But things weren't that simple. "You don't understand," he said slowly. "The chant takes months to learn."

"I may surprise you. I'm a fast learner. And I'll follow whatever rules you set down. If you can't come back with me, this is the only acceptable alternative."

"What you ask is impossible. You can't be an 'almost' singer. It takes dedication, not just determination. And you must *believe* in what you're doing."

She exhaled softly. "All right. How about this, then? The Navajo Community College is just starting to offer courses in ceremonial rites. The songs are being preserved before they're lost. Will you entrust me with the song so that I may preserve it?"

"This isn't like copying down a letter. It wasn't our way to have a written language. Written Navajo is a modern invention and an imprecise one, and the song you want is from ancient times." He didn't want to refuse her. Her soft voice compelled him with its desperation. Some said that he had a will of iron, but when she pleaded with him, the hard resolve in him melted away.

"We can record it on videotape at the same time I write it down," she insisted. "The song can then be placed in a storage vault until another *hataalii* can learn it."

Joshua shook his head. "I don't know about any of this. There's more to a sing than just words or drumbeats."

"You're my only link to the song I need. Where you go, I'm going," she said at last.

"All right, then. Come with me." She was a fascinating blend of steel and softness—a woman with the courage and tenacity of a warrior and a core of gentleness that sliced his resolve to ribbons. It was easier standing up to his two brothers and their fists than fighting the soft warmth in her voice.

"You can't just drive out of town now," Gabriel grumbled. "Anyone can follow you. Wait until the early-morning hours when most people are asleep or too groggy for clear thinking. Then go."

Joshua nodded.

"Shall I follow you in my truck?" Nydia asked.

Gabriel answered for Joshua. "No. Wait a day. Let people find out that Joshua is not around anymore. I'll say that I've placed him in protective custody. Maybe that will cool them down. You use the time to buy supplies. You'll need them out at the cabin. He doesn't keep much out there. But make a point of bringing everything you buy to Marlee's. Say you're shopping for her. Then, when it gets close to dawn, I'll come by and take you out to where my brother is."

"All right," she agreed.

Joshua watched Nydia. There was a fire in her that continually drew him. He shook free of the thought. Four Winds was having its say, despite his protests. Heat twisted and coiled inside him as his gaze traveled over her. The woman and he would face their destiny together and, if the gods were kind, neither would ever look back on this day with regret.

THE NEXT DAY SEEMED to drag for Nydia. Joshua had left just before dawn. According to Marlee, who'd been to the post office this morning, the town was already buzzing with the news of his absence. Some people were angry with the sheriff, despite the mayor's promise of eventual state police help, while others talked in hushed tones about conspiracy.

Deciding to delay shopping for supplies until the end of the day, when people were ready to go home, Nydia spent the day helping Marlee, who spoke incessantly about Lucas. Marlee seemed happy to have a woman to chat with, perhaps comforted by the fact that Nydia was a stranger. Sometimes it was easier to confide in someone who would not be around to divulge secrets later on.

By the time it was six, Nydia was eager to leave and carry out the plan that would enable her to join Joshua. She drove to Rosa's store and went inside. As she stepped through the doors, she saw Rosa speaking to two men she didn't recognize and one she did, Darren Wilson. She watched them carefully, listening as she went about her business. They were unaware of her. As she heard Joshua's name being mentioned, she ducked behind a display of canned peaches. In a burst of inspiration, she reached for her tape recorder and turned it on.

Another man came and joined the group talking. It was clear that they felt Gabriel was more concerned with protecting his brother than he was with carrying out his duties as sheriff. But it was obvious they wanted more than Joshua in jail. With a little prodding, this crowd would be screaming for a lynching.

After placing her tape recorder back in her purse, she walked around the group in the aisle and set her groceries on the counter, ready to settle the bill.

Rosa glanced at the supplies with open suspicion. "You stocking up for a trip?"

"Actually, most of this is for Marlee. I'll be leaving soon to go back to the reservation. I need to check on my son and father-in-law."

Rosa nodded, but her eyes didn't lose their gleam of skepticism. "I read about your family in the morning paper."

"Then you'll understand why I can't stay much longer," Nydia said. Uncomfortable under the scrutiny of the men's hostile gazes, Nydia settled her bill, picked up her grocery sack and walked quickly toward her truck. She'd just set the bag down on the seat when someone grabbed her from behind, clamping a strong hand over her mouth. Moving fast, her assailant kicked the pickup door shut, and pulled her into the alley.

Nydia struggled to break free, but the man, wearing a white pillowcase with cut-out eye holes over his head, held her in an iron grip that made it impossible for her to even draw a full breath. As she fought to break his hold, three other men appeared, all wearing similar makeshift hoods.

Fear swept through her. Prejudice was something that went beyond the reach of logic. No matter what these men thought they were doing, she had a feeling that at the root of their actions was an instinctive distrust of someone who chose a way of life unlike their own.

She stepped down hard on the instep of the man holding her, but instead of breaking his hold, the man simply lifted her up in the air and shook her hard. "Stop fighting, or it'll just get worse. Just tell us where he is," the man demanded in a harsh whisper.

"He...who?" she managed to say as he lifted his hand from her mouth slightly.

"No lies!"

Another hooded figure came up, holding a long-bladed

lock-back knife. Nydia twisted hard, trying to free herself, but the effort was useless.

The man pressed the side of the blade to her throat, then edged it up slowly until it rested below her ear. "I don't have to cut you if you cooperate."

Using the grip of the man holding her as leverage, Nydia kicked the knife wielder in the groin.

He staggered back and fell to the pavement in agony, but recovered more quickly than she'd hoped. "That was a mistake. Now you've made me mad, and you're going to pay for it."

The man holding Nydia forced her down to her knees and kept her there. She couldn't move her head. She could only lift her eyes and watch the gleaming blade in horror as it captured the last rays of the setting sun.

Chapter Five

Nydia's senses were painfully alert as she searched for an opening that would offer her an escape. Each second counted. She forced back her panic, struggling to see things clearly, paying attention to every detail.

Suddenly and inexplicably, she felt Joshua's presence. The feeling was strong, and no amount of logic brushed it aside. She couldn't see him—she couldn't even lift her head—but she knew he was near. She felt it as clearly as the iron grip that held her steady.

"Very brave, terrorizing a woman," she heard Joshua say.

The men stepped back, but the hand that held her never eased its hold.

"That it took four of you to accomplish this doesn't say much for you, does it?"

She couldn't see his face, but she could hear the utter contempt in his voice.

"Let her go now, unless you want to take me on instead," Joshua's voice thundered.

Nydia wasn't at all surprised when the man holding her suddenly let go. She almost fell forward, he'd released her so quickly. As she rose to her feet, she saw Joshua facing the four hooded men.

"If you're all so convinced I'm the killer, then face me

now like men. Take off your hoods and confront me with your accusations.''

Nobody spoke, but they exchanged glances and took another step back.

"Nothing to say? Why am I not surprised?" Joshua mocked.

Her original captor lunged forward, thrusting out with his knife, but Joshua easily kicked it out of his hand. "I'm not an easy target. If you plan to use knives, then you better plan on pain.''

His gaze challenged them one by one. "Attack me now, or back off. The choice is yours.''

The man who'd wielded the knife scooped up his weapon and sprinted toward the far side of the alley. Close on his tail were the other three.

Joshua went to where Nydia stood and laid his hands on her cheeks. "Are you all right?''

Nydia's pulse fluttered. "Yes. If you hadn't been here…''

"But I was." He drew her against him, holding her tightly. "You're okay now.''

She sighed softly as he tilted her chin and drew closer and closer until their lips touched. His kiss was filled with such tenderness that she yielded to him, encouraging him to continue.

Her surrender added fuel to the fires within him. His kiss, at first reassuring, blazed white hot as he feasted on her mouth and invited her to do the same with his.

When at last he eased his hold, she pressed her lips together, tasting him there, and wondering how something so simple as a kiss from Joshua could shatter her world.

"Nobody will threaten you like this again,'' he said fiercely. "You'll stay by my side as you wanted. No one will dare harm you while I still draw breath.''

They stood heart to pounding heart for what seemed a

heavenly eternity, then gathering her courage, she finally stepped away. "It's not safe here. We should go."

"They won't come back. They're cowards—they've proven that by their actions."

"Well, if it's all the same to you, I'd still rather leave the area."

Joshua walked with her down the street to her truck. Without touching her, he remained so close to her side that she could feel the warmth of his body. It comforted her and gave her courage. "How did you find me? I thought you'd gone out of town," she asked finally.

"That was the plan, but things went awry. Shadow and I were driving out to the cabin early this morning when he got called away on an emergency. He refused to let me go up alone, so he dropped me off at the sheriff's office and told Fuzz to meet me there. Shadow figured I'd be safe there until Fuzz arrived, and if anyone found out, they could be told that I'd been placed in protective custody."

"But how did you happen to see what was happening to me? You couldn't have had a clear view from the sheriff's office."

"I promised Fuzz I'd keep a low profile, but since I knew you were scheduled to buy supplies today, I've been watching for you from out near Marlee's. When you left the boardinghouse, I followed. Although I stayed out of sight on the side streets and alleys, I was never far away."

Had anyone else as big as Joshua told her he'd been sneaking around alleys, certain he wouldn't be spotted, she would have laughed out loud. But she'd seen Joshua melt into shadows as silently as a cat. "Does Gabriel know where you're at now?"

He shook his head and smiled. "He never saw me leave. He was wading through a report for the mayor, muttering to himself."

"Let's get you back there before he notices and comes looking. I've also got a tape I want you both to hear."

Gabriel's glare was as dark as a moonless night when they walked in the door. Nydia flinched, but Joshua gave her a reassuring smile.

"I should have handcuffed you to my desk, Tree," he said, stepping out of his dispatcher's office. "Where the hell have you been?"

"Cleaning up your streets, since you're too tied down with paperwork to take care of that." When Joshua told him what had happened to Nydia, Gabriel's face grew cold.

"I'm glad you were there, Tree, even if you shouldn't have been."

Nydia interrupted the tense exchange between the brothers with a description of her experience in the market, then added, "I have this tape recording I think you should both hear." She reached into her purse to retrieve the tape recorder.

"As soon as it's dark again, we're leaving," Gabriel said as she rewound the recorder to the beginning of the conversation she'd overheard. "People know you're here by now, Tree, and I'm not equipped to handle an angry mob. I have enough firepower, but not enough manpower to even the odds."

"Your brother did quite well without violence, and was outnumbered four to one," Nydia said proudly.

Joshua smiled at her. "My training as a *hataalii* gave me an edge. We learn to control situations that might lead to violence."

Nydia clicked on the recorder. "Okay, here we go."

As they listened to the tape, Gabriel and Joshua exchanged glances. They had recognized the voices; Nydia was sure of it and she was glad. Maybe that would help Gabriel identify the troublemakers and keep an eye on them.

When the segment ended, she shut off the recorder, ejected the tape and handed it to Gabriel. "I could see from your expressions that you recognized the men speaking."

"Yes, one was Manuel Ortega, our mail carrier, and the other might be Alex Green, Ralph's assistant, or Bill Riley, the trucker who brings supplies into town. Those two sound very alike. But the tape doesn't give us anything to indicate that they're the ones responsible for what happened to you in the alley," Gabriel said. "I can't arrest them on the strength of this. They're entitled to whatever opinion they choose to voice."

"I knew what they thought of me," Joshua said, "but I had no idea the tide would turn against you, too," he added, looking at Gabriel. "That worries me."

"They may think I care more about protecting my brother than I do for my job," Gabriel reiterated, "but they're wrong. I work on the side of justice, not mob rule."

"They'll come around—give them time. Lies have a tendency to make things flare up like dry kindling on a fire, but they can't withstand the test of time. Truth is the only thing that has the power to endure." Joshua walked to the window and peered out the side. "It's almost dark."

"And time for you to be on your way." Gabriel motioned for Joshua to move back as he opened the front door, stepped outside and looked around.

Nydia felt a stab of fear. "Do you think they'll try to stop us?"

"No," Joshua answered. "They'll want to, but they won't go up against the sheriff. They know he can call in the state police and reinforcements from other communities. My guess is that they'll regroup, then come after us later on when they build up their courage again."

Nydia felt her throat go dry. "But we'll be alone out at the cabin. It's not a good defensive move."

"That cabin is almost impossible to find even when you

know where you're going. We should be safe there as long as we aren't followed."

Gabriel returned before she could question him further. "Okay, let's get moving now while things are quiet."

"In separate vehicles?" Nydia asked.

"You go with Tree. I'll drive your truck and tail you both, hanging back to make sure nobody follows you up," Gabriel said. "Shadow will meet us halfway. I spoke to him a short while ago. I'll ride back with him. In the meantime, I'll keep my truck here, parked in clear view, to throw off anyone who might be thinking of following me to get to you. My dispatcher works from home at night, so I'll make sure she's aware of what's going on and knows to reach me on the hand-held or through Shadow, if necessary."

It took about forty minutes of covering some of the roughest terrain Nydia had ever traveled across, before she finally spotted a rustic log cabin in the middle of a small clearing. The dwelling was nestled between two steep ridges, hidden from the view of anyone more than a hundred yards away. It was dark now and barely visible at half that distance.

Suddenly, she heard the sound of another vehicle approaching up the canyon. Nydia bolted upright and stared into the forest, bracing herself for trouble.

"Relax, it's only Shadow."

Nydia sat on her hands so he couldn't see them shaking. "I thought that maybe you'd been wrong, and the townspeople had found us."

He shook his head. "You can trust me. I'm seldom wrong."

"Arrogance?" She smiled, taunting him. "Is that a quality of a *hataalii*, too?"

"As my brothers are fond of reminding me, a *hataalii* is

just a man who possesses ritual knowledge. He's not above being human,'' he added with a grin.

She saw the moonlight dancing in his eyes, and felt the impact of his gaze all through her body. A shiver coursed through her. Fearing the strength of her reaction to him, she turned away and assured herself that he hadn't noticed anything. When she glanced back at him, however, she realized that she'd only been fooling herself. "Just remember we're here on business."

"Of course."

She had the feeling he wasn't at all sorry to be stuck in this secluded cabin with her. She took a deep breath and let it out slowly. The problem was, neither was she. Those feelings meant trouble unless they both kept their guards up and used their heads.

Neither of them had room for romance in their lives, particularly now, and she'd never been the type to go after hopeless causes. And hopeless it was. The last person she wanted to be involved with, or more to the point, to allow her son to draw close to, was a *hataalii*. John was already influenced enough by the old ways, living with his grandparents so much of the time.

As Joshua parked his truck, his brothers approached. "I'm going to check out the perimeter," Gabriel said, "though I'm virtually certain we weren't followed."

"I'll take a look from the high ground," Lucas added.

After they'd left, Nydia walked with Joshua over to the cabin. "It's a pretty place. Did you come here to hunt and fish?"

"No, not really. It's mostly a place each of us uses when we need to get away. Building it was a family project for all of us, and we share ownership of it."

As she stepped inside, Nydia was surprised to see how large it was, and how homey. "Did Gabriel's wife help with the interior?"

"It shows that much?" He laughed, glancing at the short gingham tie-back curtains. "Fuzz uses this place more than Shadow or I do. It doesn't have a phone, and there are too many narrow canyons for a cellular, so it's the perfect place for him and his wife to come and relax."

"What if he's needed back in town?"

"He usually arranges for the sheriff in the next county to loan him one of his deputies for a few days to take care of things. Fuzz has to have time off every once in a while just to keep his thinking clear," Joshua said. Then he added, "We all do."

As Joshua unloaded the groceries, Nydia walked around the cabin. There was only one bedroom with a full-size bed. She glanced out at the living room. The couch didn't look like the type that could pull out into a bed. A tingle of apprehension sizzled through her.

"It's all clear," Gabriel called out from the front door.

His booming voice brought her back to the tasks at hand. She went into the living room and met the others there. "So, we're safe for now."

"Yes," Gabriel answered, his expression somber. "I'll leave a cellular phone with you, but you'll have to climb up one of the ridges before you can use it. If you're in trouble, Tree will lead you into the forest. My brother knows this area like the palm of his hand. No one will ever corner or trap him here." He gestured for Nydia to come outside with him while Lucas spoke to Joshua. "Sooner or later, Tree is going to get restless and want to go back into town to investigate. But you've seen firsthand how dangerous it is there. For everyone's sake, try to keep him here."

"I can't force him to do anything he doesn't want to do."

"True, but you can be very persuasive when you want to. You're here, aren't you?"

"I'll do my best, but I can't guarantee results."

"Just remember, he needs you and you need him. You're each other's backup."

"You can count on me," Nydia said, then remembered the last time she'd said those words. She'd spoken them to her son when she'd promised to bring Joshua back to the rez.

Determination filled her. She wouldn't fail any of them, including herself. "I won't allow him to endanger himself uselessly. Believe that. I need him alive and well so he can return home with me and help my family."

IT WAS CLOSE TO EIGHT when Joshua came into the kitchen with a load of firewood. "Have you ever used one of these wood-burning stoves before?"

"Frequently. My mother-in-law isn't big on modern conveniences," she said, her thoughts turning to the people she'd left behind on the reservation.

As if sensing her worries, he placed a hand on her shoulder. Although Nydia knew it had been meant only as a gesture of comfort, the fires his touch created left her feeling deliciously weak.

"I will find a way to help you," Joshua said, but before she could respond, he stepped back into the living room.

Ignoring the supplies she'd set out for dinner, Nydia stumbled back onto a chair and sat down heavily. What on earth was the matter with her? They were embroiled in a life-or-death situation. She had no time for these crazy feelings. She needed rational thoughts, not confusion.

Needing to keep busy, she warmed up a can of beans and cut up some fresh vegetables. It wasn't a feast, but it would do.

A short time later, Joshua came in with more wood and placed it next to the stove. Sitting down at the rough-hewn wooden table, they ate dinner together.

"I'm tired, do you mind if we call it a night?" Nydia asked. "I want to talk to you about your work, but only when I know I can concentrate." At the moment, she could hardly keep her eyes open.

"No problem. After what you went through today, it's no surprise that you're beat. Take the bed."

She shook her head. "I've thought about that, and it isn't right for me to be the one who gets it. I'm smaller and I'll fit just fine on the couch."

"You have the same look Fuzz gets on his face when he's determined not to take no for an answer, so I'll speed things up and offer you a compromise. We'll take turns using the bed. Tonight, you get it. You need it more than I do."

"I'm too tired to argue, but I have no idea how you plan to fit on the couch. It's against the laws of physics."

"I'm sleeping on the floor in a sleeping bag. I've done it many times before. To be honest, I prefer it to the bed. Tomorrow morning, you'll understand," he added with a wicked grin.

"Oh, great. Sour my victory." She walked through the living room and took the Navajo rug she'd brought in from her pickup. "Good night."

He looked at the rug, disapproval etched clearly on his face. "You don't need to bring that thing here. There are sheets and plenty of blankets in the chest at the end of the bed."

"I'll help myself if I need them, but I'm keeping the rug. It's warm, and soft, and I intend to put it to good use." Not giving him a chance to argue, she went in to the bedroom and shut the door.

Nydia dropped down heavily on the bare mattress and glanced wearily at the chest. The bed had been stripped, ready for whoever would use it next, but no new linens had been set out. She sighed, too tired to care about niceties right now. Her body still ached from the struggle with the men in the alley. She'd been terrified, certain she was about to be cut to pieces, or worse. In all her life, she'd never felt such terror. Then Joshua had appeared out of nowhere, like one of the mythical heroes of Navajo legend. His courage and inner strength had given him all the power he'd needed against his enemies. She'd known that nothing would hurt her then. His presence had filled that darkened alley with a magic all its own.

Grabbing the pillow, she lay back, intending to rest for just a moment before getting back up and making the bed, but soon she was asleep.

A loud peal of thunder that rattled the windows woke Nydia up sometime after midnight. Reaching for the rug to cover herself, she turned over onto her side, determined to go back to sleep. The storm was noisy, but she could sleep through it if she tried.

As pleasant gray mists began to close in over her again, she heard an insistent voice from within herself, nudging her back to full consciousness.

The sheriff and his wife are in danger. They need your help.

Nydia's eyes snapped open. Sitting up, she gave the blanket a vicious glare. "I'm getting fed up with this nonsense. If this is due to a hypnotic suggestion, then I'm too tired to deal with it in the middle of the night. Shut up." She dropped back and tossed the blanket aside, deciding she'd rather be cold than awake.

The voice repeated its message two more times before she rose to a sitting position, cursing. She couldn't ignore this, not when the voice had been right in its warnings before. She chided herself mentally. She was losing her mind for sure if she started listening to voices. The premonition had to be coming from something she'd heard or seen somewhere. And considering that *she'd* been right before, she was probably right not to ignore it now.

Nydia scrambled out of bed, and went to find Joshua. As she entered the living room, she saw him lying half in and half out of the sleeping bag. His jeans lay in a crumpled heap on the floor, and his chest was bare.

Her breath caught in her throat. Moonlight fell on him like a lover's caress, and her fingers tingled with the need to touch him. She crouched beside him and laid her hand on his chest, waking him gently.

He smiled, his eyes still closed, and placed his hand over hers. "Does the storm bother you? I'd invite you to share my sleeping bag, but then we'd find that lightning is not the only dangerous force that can light up the night."

His muscles rippled beneath her palm. She fought against the temptation to lean against him. She'd dreamed of a night like this, alone with him, more than once in the past few months.

But this was not why she'd come to him. Gathering her wits, she took a deep, jagged breath. "I came to tell you something."

Somehow, he sensed her urgency. He sat up. "What is it?"

"My instincts haven't been wrong so far, and right now they're telling me that your brother and his wife are in danger."

"The voice?"

"*A* voice, from within me. Don't read more into it than there is."

"Get your jacket. We're leaving right now."

By the time she returned to the living room, he was dressed and waiting by the door. Together, they hurried across the muddy ground to his truck.

"We'll take the fast way back," he said as they followed a pair of tire ruts through the trees.

"But what about the townspeople? What if someone spots us near Four Winds? At this hour, they're likely to shoot first and think about it later."

"My brother's home is outside town. His nearest neighbor is a quarter mile away. No one will see us."

Twice the truck nearly struck a tree, the muddy roads proving treacherous. The shortcut Joshua had selected turned out to cost them time, the storm having turned the forest floor into a bog.

As they finally reached a real road, dawn broke over the horizon. "Fuzz's house is right over that rise. We'll be there in three minutes."

As he accelerated, Nydia tried to keep her hands from shaking. She couldn't explain it, but she knew the danger was growing, like an evil creature whose power increased in proportion to the fear it engendered.

A short time later, as they cleared the rise, three sharp bangs echoed down the canyon, filling her with terror. Her heart hammered against her ribs. "Were those—?"

He nodded. "Gunshots. And they're coming from my brother's house."

Chapter Six

Joshua parked behind a cluster of boulders fifty yards away from Gabriel's house. "I'm going in on foot, but I'm staying close to the stream that runs behind his house, just in case. Stay here."

"No way. I may be able to help. You don't know what you're up against."

As Nydia left the truck and headed toward Gabriel's house, Joshua stifled a curse. She surely knew how to test a man!

To her credit, she stayed low and to his right, moving with agility and speed. When they neared a clearing, he stopped and held up a hand. Peering ahead, he struggled to pinpoint the precise source of the gunshots, which had continued at regularly spaced intervals.

"I don't get this," he said at last. "What's my brother trying to do?"

"What's going on?" She stepped up next to him and followed his line of sight.

"Look for yourself," he said, gesturing ahead. "He's shooting at the wood pile."

"Target practice?"

"From inside his house? Hardly. And nobody's hiding behind the firewood. We can see both sides from here."

"Maybe he's had one drink too many...."

"My brother doesn't drink. None of us do. I'm going to get closer and see what's going on. I think he's trying to signal someone—he's firing three shots at a time. That means there's trouble."

He wasn't surprised to hear her right behind him as he jogged ahead. Stopping short of the house, Joshua yelled to his brother. "I'm here, Fuzz. What's going on?"

"Be careful! Don't either of you come any closer to the house. During the night, while the thunder covered up his sounds, someone crept up and taped trip wires to the doors and windows. If they're opened, what looks like a big pipe bomb placed between the screen door and front door will go off. And cutting the wires isn't going to help, either. That bomb could still be set to explode."

Moving cautiously, Joshua stepped closer and studied the wires. "How did you happen to discover all this before setting it off?" he asked Gabriel, who stood behind the partially opened window.

"I tried to use the phone early this morning and discovered it was dead. When I glanced outside the window toward the telephone wires, I noticed the trip wires and the bomb at the door. I've been waiting for a chance to signal someone. When I saw your headlights, I started shooting the three-shot distress signal, hoping to draw your attention. I'm sure glad to see you."

"What about your hand-held radio? Can you call for backup, or did you do that already?" Joshua asked.

"The radio's not working. Whoever did this must have disabled the receiver in the Jeep, which relays from the hand-held."

"Bombs are out of my league. Tell me what to do."

"I've moved as much furniture as I can against the living-room wall to create a barrier between us and the bomb, but what we really need to do is disarm it. Get Jake Fields and Shadow out here. With their military experience, especially with Jake having served as an army Ranger, those guys are the best chance we've got. Go to my Jeep and see if you can figure out what's wrong with the radio. If you can't start it up, then leave Nydia here to warn off anyone who might approach, and go find those guys."

"I have a better—and faster—idea," Nydia interrupted. "There's an ax leaning against the wood pile. I'd be willing to bet that your big little brother could cut a hole in the side of the house you could climb through."

"Yes, I believe I could," Joshua said.

"Go for it, then. I want Lanie out of this place as quickly as possible," Gabriel called out. "The house is expendable. She's not."

Joshua picked up the ax, but then, on a hunch, went to take a closer look at the bomb itself A cold chill swept up his spine as he crouched by the door.

"Tree, what the hell are you doing?" Gabriel called out to him. "Get away from that thing!"

"I've got bad news, Fuzz. We've all got a *big* problem. This thing has a timer on it, and it's counting down. We have less than five minutes."

His brother's violent oath was loud, and summed up the situation well.

"That about covers it," Joshua said ruefully. "Care to give me more-useful instructions?"

"Describe the bomb to me, Tree."

Joshua did his best, then had a suggestion. "It should shut down if we can disconnect the wires leading to the power supply, which is a lantern battery."

"Okay, do it."

"I can't. I'd have to open the door to reach the bomb, and that would pull a pretty tight trip wire."

Another expletive followed.

"Your brother is too big to reach in there, but I can fit my arm through without moving the door," Nydia said.

"Then I guess you're elected," Gabriel answered, sounding regretful.

"Be careful out there, please," Lanie called out, her voice trembling.

"I will be. Think good thoughts, okay?" Nydia rubbed the perspiration from her palms by brushing them against her pant legs, but nothing could stop her hands from shaking.

Joshua noticed it. "Take a deep breath and let it out slowly. You'll be okay," he whispered so that he wouldn't alarm his brother's wife.

She gave Joshua a grateful nod, then called out to Gabriel. "Do you have wire cutters? I'm going to need them."

"In the garage, on the peg-board rack." Gabriel answered. "Only make sure there are no surprises there before you charge in."

"I'll go," Joshua said.

Joshua went around the back to the detached garage and studied the area before approaching it. The windows and door showed no signs of tampering. This building hadn't been touched. There were no tracks on the muddy ground surrounding it, either. Satisfied that it was safe, he took the wire cutters from the peg board and jogged back to Nydia's side. "Here you go."

"You're the only one of us who can actually back away from here," Nydia said. "Why don't you stay as far away as you can in case things go wrong? We might need your services." She glanced down at her hands to show him that she was still trembling.

Instead of doing as she said, Joshua started to do a quiet sing. He felt the power of the ancient chant leaving him and weaving around her distrust, finding a way inside her. Benevolent forces were gathering, responding to his cry for help. Although he could see that she didn't understand what was happening, her hands stopped shaking.

Nydia reached through the small opening in the screen door, then froze, fear rising again, holding her captive.

Joshua increased the tempo of his chant. Power flowed through him, filling the air. The sing became a cry against the injustices that had brought them to this point and a demand for the right to restore harmony.

Scarcely breathing, Nydia held the clippers to the wires, then looked up at him.

There was nothing he could do except reassure her that they would share the same fate. He placed a gentle hand on her shoulder, then closed his eyes and focused all his energy on the chant. His senses were so acute it was almost painful. He heard the snip of the cutters, then her sigh.

He opened his eyes, but his relief vanished as he heard her gasp. "What's wrong?"

Even before she could speak, he heard a low, rhythmic electronic beep. "There's a second clock," Joshua called out to Gabriel.

"Find what it's connected to," Gabriel answered. "Quickly!"

Nydia bent down, trying to look beneath the bomb without widening the opening between the screen and the door. "The second timer is beneath the bomb. It's not connected to the top wire, but it's counting down! Only seven seconds left!"

Joshua shoved her roughly aside, grabbed the bomb and yanked it free. With a mighty heave, he tossed it toward the stream.

The bomb splashed into the water and exploded. The blast knocked Joshua to the ground, and water rained everywhere.

Nydia scrambled to Joshua's side as he managed to rise to his knees. Sinking to the ground before him, she threw her arms around him. "I thought we were all dead!"

He held her against him. As he felt the softness of her

breasts against his chest and her slim thighs against his, passion exploded inside him. Mouth to mouth, they strained against each other, seeking comfort in that union that spoke of fires and life.

His fingers sank into her hair, slanting her head, devouring her sweetness with a wild, reckless hunger.

"Hey, little brother," Gabriel said, rushing out the front door with Lanie. "Don't take advantage of this poor woman. You're a hero, but don't push it, okay?"

Joshua felt his brother jab his foot playfully against his side. The mood was broken, but he didn't release Nydia, more out of principle than anything else.

"Time out, guys," Gabriel said, laughing.

Joshua glared at Gabriel as he helped Nydia up. "You're lucky I don't believe in violence, Fuzz."

Gabriel grinned. "Yeah, I've told myself that many times." He glanced at Lanie and Nydia, who were both walking away, talking at once. "Hey, it's my job as big brother to keep you from getting in way over your head," he said quietly. "Be careful, Tree. That woman is not for you."

"Really?" Joshua managed to say through clenched teeth. He'd never allowed his brothers to butt into his personal life, and he wasn't about to let it happen now.

Gabriel shrugged. "The beliefs you treasure are ones she spends time recording, much like a biologist tracking something that crawled out from under a rock."

Joshua's hands curled into fists. His brother's words cut through him like a knife, mostly because they were true and he knew it.

"It would be different if you were the type who was just out to get laid, but that's not you."

If he'd ever truly considered punching his brother's lights out, this would have been the time. Not for his own sake, but for Nydia's. Instead, Joshua turned and walked away from Gabriel.

Nydia moved toward him, but out of the corner of his eye, he saw his brother stop her. Gabriel was right to do so. Right now, he needed a few quiet moments to think. Gabriel was right—and yet, so wrong. He couldn't explain it, but things felt...right...when he was with Nydia. Glancing back, he saw Nydia slip around Gabriel, ignoring him, and come toward him anyway.

"Hey, what's going on? Was big brother giving you a hard time?"

Joshua managed a smile. "It doesn't matter. My life's my own. And I can assure you, I've done my share of razzing back." He returned with her to the house. "Let's see what else needs to be done here."

"Has Gabriel asked why we happened to come by?"

"No, but he will. And now that you've brought it up, have *you* thought about what's been happening? The rug is helping both of us. At the worst time of my life, it suddenly surfaces and reaches out to me through you. That makes for interesting speculations."

"It's not the rug that's at play here. It's my own good instincts and intuition, which are seldom wrong."

"And in the middle of the night," Gabriel said, joining them, "you suddenly got a gut feeling that I was in trouble?"

"Don't look a gift horse in the mouth. Ask Joshua or Lanie if I was right. Who knows? Maybe in that mess in the alley, I heard something, or got some indication of this."

He nodded slowly. "It's possible, but I don't suppose you remember anything more specific?"

"No, but I'll try to think back, and if I recall anything else, I'll let you know."

"Did you check out your Jeep?" Joshua asked. "I'm curious about what happened to your radio."

"It's been trashed," Gabriel answered. "My next step is to take a walk around the house and check out the tracks. The mud is going to make it easy for us, harder for the son of a—" he looked at Nydia "—frog, who did this."

Lanie joined them. "I'll stay out of your way, but I'm coming along. This is my home, too."

Gabriel nodded, his jaw clenched. Sensing his outrage, Joshua placed a hand on Gabriel's shoulder. "Control your anger. Unless you do, our enemy will win."

"That works for you, Tree," Gabriel snapped back, "but not for me. Right now, I'd like to put the person who attacked me and my family in intensive care."

As they reached the side of the house, Gabriel held up his hand. "Stay back," he said, crouching by the giant footprints that led around to the porch. "These weren't here last night, and neither of you came over to this side."

Lanie gasped. "Those prints look like Joshua's! He's the only person in the community with feet that big!"

"You're right," Joshua said. "But those aren't my footprints."

"Joshua was with me last night. He didn't go anywhere," Nydia said staunchly.

"I'm sorry, I didn't mean to imply—" Lanie looked at Gabriel helplessly.

"Don't worry," Gabriel said. "I know darned well this isn't your work, Tree."

"Look closer at those tracks and you'll see they *prove* it wasn't your brother," Nydia said, crouching just behind Gabriel. She gestured to where Joshua had walked. "His tracks sink deeper into the mud. The person who wore these shoes to implicate your brother wasn't nearly as heavy."

"Few are," Gabriel replied. "And for the record, I noticed that tidbit, too, Deputy," he added with a smile.

"I was sure you had. It's no reflection on you. I just have a hard time keeping quiet when I've got a point to make."

"Really? I hadn't noticed," Joshua said, chuckling.

"This attempt to frame Tree may result in this person's downfall," Gabriel observed. "There are only a few stores who carry shoes this big."

"Here's your camera," Lanie said, handing it to him. "I figured you'd want it."

"You're starting to anticipate me," he said with a smile. "That makes life easier. Thanks."

Joshua saw the look that his brother gave his wife. He envied him, despite what had just happened to them. His brother had found a mate to share his life with; he had no one. He glanced at Nydia, knowing that she couldn't be his, that Gabriel had been right about that much.

"I'll be busy here for some time," Gabriel said. "I've got to photograph the prints, then the booby trap setup and the wiring. Why don't you all just go inside the house. Just don't touch anything on your way in."

Hearing running footsteps coming toward them, Gabriel turned, automatically reaching for his holster. Suddenly, Pete, the diner owner's son, appeared from behind the pines that bordered the north side of the property.

"Sheriff! Boy, am I glad to see you! My mom and I heard the explosion. Heck, we *felt* it! She sent me up here, but our truck got bogged down in the mud, so I had to run the rest of the way. Is everybody okay?" He leaned over, resting his hands on his knees and gulping for air.

"Take it easy, son," Gabriel said. "It's over. Nobody's hurt."

"The volunteer fire department is on their way with the pumper truck."

"There's no need," Gabriel said.

"Then you'll have to use your radio to recall them, because they're already halfway here."

"I don't have a working radio or phone, so we'll just wait for them," Gabriel said. "You relax now and catch your breath."

Joshua saw the look Gabriel gave him, and without words understood what his brother was thinking. Others would soon know what had happened here. Once the news of the footprints got out, if Gabriel didn't get a chance to explain, the situation in Four Winds was bound to take a turn for the worse. Things would soon become even tougher for him and his two brothers.

"You should get out of here now," Gabriel said quietly, taking Joshua aside. "The skinwalker connection and the footprints could create problems. I don't want someone getting the bright idea of trying to follow you back to the cabin." He'd just finished speaking when they heard the powerful whine of the old fire truck.

"Too late," Joshua said. "But maybe it's better that I am here. It makes no sense that I'd be risking my life to help you if I'd been responsible, and we can point out the difference in the footprints."

"True, but I can't swear that folks will be logical about any of this."

"Sooner or later, they'll understand." Even as Joshua said it, he wasn't sure if he believed it anymore. Anger shot through him, but he pushed it down. He couldn't afford to let that blackness overwhelm his spirit. Others, like Nydia and his brothers, were counting on his stability. They depended on it, in fact. He'd knowingly accepted the pressures of being a *hataalii*, but nothing he'd studied had ever prepared him for something like this.

He watched as the fire truck arrived. Whatever came, he'd face it squarely. Running away from trouble was not his style.

Chapter Seven

Joshua was standing a few feet away from his brother as the mayor's four-wheel-drive pickup pulled up right behind the old pumper. Bob Burns emerged from the mud-spattered vehicle, cast a suspicious and hostile look at Joshua, then turned his attention to Gabriel. "Are you and your wife all right?" he asked. "We heard the explosion in town, though you're out here on the outskirts. On the way, I tried to call your brother in case a medic was needed, but he's an hour out of town with a patient."

"We're all fine, thanks to Mrs. Jim and my brother."

Burns's gaze took in Joshua and then Nydia. Distrust and contempt were mirrored clearly in his eyes. "What have *they* got to do with this?"

As Gabriel explained, Nydia came up from behind Joshua and joined him. The half-dozen volunteer firefighters had climbed down from the truck, and were staring at them openly.

"Maybe I'm jumping the gun, but I have a feeling that we should have tried to leave before everyone arrived," she said softly. "They're looking for a way to blame this on you. I can see it on their faces."

Anger lay heavily on Joshua's chest, an almost suffocating pressure. It was a struggle for him to remain calm, to keep indignation from overcoming his control. "Yes, I can sense that, too."

As Gabriel warned the men to stay away from the sides of the house where the bomber's tracks were, Joshua spotted Darren Wilson, the feed-store owner, following a trail on the ground. As he made his way to the porch, Joshua knew he'd seen the tracks that had been left there to implicate him.

Darren looked up as he reached the end of the trail. His gaze met Joshua's, his eyes narrow. Finally, shaking his head, he scowled and looked away.

"Now we're in for it," Nydia said.

As if sensing trouble, Gabriel moved closer to where his brother stood. Bob Burns followed, seemingly unaware of what Gabriel was doing.

"Who could have placed a bomb here? Who wants you dead?" the mayor asked, shooting one question after the other, and not giving Gabriel a chance to reply. "Is someone after all our sheriffs now?"

"You want to know who did this, Mayor? Well, here's your man," Darren yelled, grabbing Joshua by the arm. "His footprints are the only ones around the windows."

"Is that true?" Bob Burns looked at Gabriel.

"Not if you look closely," Gabriel answered.

"I just checked, Sheriff. I *know* what I saw," Darren said. "Go see for yourself. Heck, this is as plain as the nose on your face. The medicine man is out to kill his brother now. And I think I've got this figured out. I saw the peddler driving around the same day Mrs. Stephens did. He never came into town, but maybe that's because he found the medicine man and went no farther. A skinwalker bowl like the one that caused the problems in Four Winds last time would be a disaster in the hands of someone like this man," he said, shaking Joshua's arm.

Joshua pried Darren's fingers off his arm one by one.

Then, lifting Darren a foot off the ground by the waist, he set the feed-store owner beside Gabriel.

Darren sputtered, but the words were so caught in his throat that none made sense.

The sheriff smiled mirthlessly. "Don't you *ever* disobey a lawful order of mine at the scene of a crime. I told everyone to stay away from the house. If I find your footprints have disturbed any of the evidence, I'll throw you in jail for obstruction. And I strongly suggest that you don't annoy my brother. He may interpret your action as an attack, and remove your arms. You want to unload feed bags with your teeth?"

"Now wait a minute, Sheriff," the mayor interrupted. "Darren's made a good point here. If your brother's footprints are the only ones in the mud, that naturally points to him. Nobody could have avoided leaving tracks on this ground, not the way it rained last night."

"The person who did this was wearing shoes that were meant to implicate my brother, but he was careless about details. Check the depth that those prints sink into the ground," Gabriel explained. "The bomber wanted us to think it was my brother, but whoever wore those shoes was a much lighter man. The evidence proves my brother's innocence." He glared at Darren. "And that nonsense about the peddler is beneath even you."

"We know when he comes around—he always leaves trouble behind. Why should this time be different?"

"I haven't seen the peddler," Joshua said, joining them. "And I can assure you that I would never accept or purchase anything from that man."

"So you say," Darren snarled.

"I have no reason to lie to you. Your opinion does not matter to me."

Darren's eyes grew wide, and his face turned puce. "Of all the low-down—"

Nydia took Joshua's arm, but despite her gentle pull, he stiffened, holding his ground.

"Come on. Nothing will be gained by this. His mind is closed to reason."

Joshua studied the people gathered there, then let Nydia lead him away. Though there was no need for the old pumper to remain, curiosity kept the crew there. But that curiosity was a good sign. It indicated an opening of their minds, one that could lead them to the truth.

A moment later, Gabriel approached them. "Jake Fields is going to stay and help me gather evidence. Whatever we find will be turned over to the FBI. For now, though, I want you two to clear out. Most of these folks heard the arguments about the footprints, but it may not be enough to convince them, especially while you're still around stirring things up."

"I'll go away, but the problem you're facing won't. They're not going to let it all drop just because I'm not around."

He nodded. "I know, so watch yourselves. I can't leave here, and Shadow's gone, so there'll be nobody to cover your tail. Use all the tricks Dad taught us, Tree."

"I will," Joshua assured. "Now I have one favor to ask you. Will you bring me some of Alma's books on Navajo artifacts?"

Gabriel's eyes narrowed. "You *do* know something about the peddler?"

Joshua shrugged. "I didn't see him. That's the truth. And I'd never accept anything from him, not in a million years. I just need to research something."

"What?"

"It'll take too long to explain," Joshua answered.

"Okay, I'll take your word for it," Gabriel said, "but if I find out that you're holding back evidence, Tree, I'll pound your face into the ground."

"You can't even reach it."

"I'll get a ladder," Gabriel said with a scowl, and strode back toward the house.

As Nydia and Joshua reached their truck, Jake came up to them. "I overheard what you said to Gabriel about Alma's books. Since Alma's death, her most valuable books have been placed in a locked section of the library." He handed Joshua the keys. "You can get in using the back door. It looks like everyone from Four Winds is either here already or on their way, so nobody's likely to spot you in town," he said, gesturing toward the vehicles filled with curious citizens still arriving. "You'll be safe. Just go in and take what you want, then lock up and leave the key inside. I have a spare set of keys hidden in my truck."

"Thanks," Joshua said, touched by the man's show of faith. "It's good to know I have at least one friend."

"I am that. I've got to tell you, if there's one thing I learned in the service, it's how to judge people. Murder just isn't your style. And nothing can ever convince me that you've changed that much, because I don't believe that people do. Good luck."

As they got under way, Joshua noticed that Nydia was unusually quiet. "What's wrong?"

"What's right?" she muttered, then shook her head. "I just resent the heck out of what the peddler did to me."

"You accepted that blanket freely. And so far, it has helped us."

"You've chosen to credit the blanket instead of my own intuition. That's your choice. But if it is as I suspect and the warnings are triggered by a posthypnotic suggestion that he planted in my mind, the peddler is insulting everything I pride myself in. I'm a scientist, not a believer in the paranormal. His little mind games work constantly to undermine me."

"Are you sure it's all just a mind game?"

"Definitely. And you know what? I think he planted a suggestion that's triggered not only by my viewing the rug, but also by any similar pattern. It's the only logical explanation for the odd times I hear the voice. But what worries me most is that the peddler was probably involved in your father's murder in some way. He must have known it was about to happen for him to cause me to hear the voice when I did, though he certainly couldn't have done the shooting himself because of the time frame involved. Also, he would have had to have known of plans to plant a bomb here way in advance, or was responsible for it himself."

"The peddler is part of this town's legacy," Joshua said. "He does bring trouble, but he's never directly responsible for it."

"So maybe he changed his M.O."

"The problem with you is that you feel compelled to try and explain everything away with scientific, logical arguments. There are powers that defy objectivity and training. Your intuitions are coming from a legacy of our people, not from the peddler's trickery."

"That's why you wanted to research Navajo artifacts? You're looking for a more detailed explanation of the rug's powers and why it's helping us? I can save you some time. If this rug was part of a legend like that of the skinwalker bowl, I would have heard about it. That's my area of expertise."

"It may not be as well-known, but we're dealing with a powerful object. You know that as well as I do, though you're not willing to admit it."

"What's your theory? Why do you think I'm getting such helpful warnings?"

"I believe the weaver's spirit needs my help and is reaching out to me through you. But I should look into it more before I make any judgments."

"I wish life were as simple as the Navajo Way says.

Then all problems could be solved by finding the right chant or ceremony that would compel the gods to help us."

"Not all troubles can be solved that way, but many can be," he answered patiently. "There's peace in our Way. There isn't any in the one you've chosen," he said sadly.

"But at least it's a path where there are no false trusts."

"The sciences are full of false trusts," he countered. "And it's a solitary path where pride and knowledge compete, and often to the betterment of no one."

Nydia's silence spoke more loudly than words ever could. It proved to him that, despite the strong feelings between them, there was too little common ground. He'd known all along that she was not for him, but each little proof stabbed at him like a knife reminding him of the high price of his choice to be and remain a *hataalii*.

Joshua went into the library by the back way, but the precaution seemed unnecessary. The town was nearly deserted, just as Jake had predicted. As they entered the special-collections room, Joshua looked around. There was one tall, glass-front bookcase that was locked and separated from the rest of the collection.

He used the key and opened the door. After handing to Nydia the books that looked most promising, he relocked the case and they hurried back to the truck and slipped out of town.

IT TOOK ABOUT FOUR TIMES as long this time to reach the cabin because of all the precautions Joshua took to prevent anyone from following them. When they finally reached high ground, Joshua surveyed the area below.

"We weren't followed," Nydia said. "You doubled back so often, the person would have needed a helicopter to stay with you."

"I had to make sure it was safe for us to go to the

cabin.'' He glanced over at her. "But why are you so impatient? We're not on a time clock."

"I hate wasting time. If we're going to research what's in these books, I want to get to it."

"You hurry too much, just like the Anglos."

"And that's what you don't like about me, isn't it?" She studied his expression.

He took a deep breath, then let it out slowly. "It's not about liking or disliking. It's simply a fact, something I have to accept as part of you."

"And also the safety line that keeps us from getting too close," she finished for him.

"Is that how you see it?" Joshua shook his head. "I wish you could value the same things I do, but the truth is that what we want plays almost no part in any of this. There's more going on here than you know. There's a sense of...fate working on both of us. Don't try to tell me you haven't felt that."

"Maybe fate's just having a laugh at our expense."

"Maybe."

They each withdrew into the privacy of their own thoughts, but alone there, Nydia found only questions and loneliness. By the time they reached the cabin, she was eager to immerse herself in the books, anything to focus her thoughts elsewhere.

They remained quiet as they sat on the floor and sorted through the collection they'd borrowed. Nydia found nothing useful, despite her efforts. When she finally glanced up, she saw Joshua intent on a passage in the leather-bound volume before him.

"What have you got there?" she asked.

"It's information about Spider Woman and stories about the traditions of our weavers. The background information here has helped me verify what I believe is at the bottom of everything you've experienced."

She sat back, leaning against the cool log side of the cabin wall. "I'm listening."

"The artisan who crafted the rug you now own was a great weaver, but foolish because she didn't follow the precautions taught by our gods. When Pretends-To-See-People, the Navajo prophet, was taught about sandpainting, he was shown pictures on clouds. The gods warned him that earthly people couldn't be trusted with permanent pictures, so only sand was to be used to create the paintings, and those were to be wiped out the same day. Spider Woman also warned that a line was needed from the center outward in any weaving, particularly one depicting the Holy People, otherwise the spirit of the weaver would become trapped."

"I remember those legends," Nydia said. "Not just learning about them in books, either. My grandmother would tell me stories like that on cold winter nights." But now the myths were taking on a more somber meaning. She wasn't so sure anymore that they were just folklore, despite her staunch words to Joshua.

"From what I've learned from other *hataaliis*, and what I've read here, I believe that the woman who made your rug went blind, then insane within three years of weaving that blanket. She broke two of our taboos when she depicted an image from a sandpainting, and also left the weaving flawless."

"My grandmother told me many stories, but I recall one in particular about a weaver who was too proud for her own good."

He nodded. "She ignored the warnings and paid a price for her foolishness. Her work is said to bring bad luck to whoever owns it because her spirit is still trapped within the rug and does whatever it can to call attention to its plight."

"I respect your beliefs, but I won't destroy or damage

the rug. I just can't. It's an exquisite antique that belongs to the *dineh* and is part of our history. But maybe, out of respect, it should go on exhibit with no one owning it outright."

"You refuse to understand what I'm telling you."

"It would be a crime for me to destroy what is a part of our heritage, especially out of fear. But don't get me wrong—I'm not ignoring the danger. I'm going to put the rug in the back of my truck and I'm going to avoid even looking at it just in case I'm right about a posthypnotic suggestion. And in case you're right about its magic, it'll also be safely out of our way there," she added with a gentle smile.

He nodded once. "All right. I'll accept that compromise for now."

Hearing trucks in the distance, Joshua scrambled to his feet. "We have to go see who is approaching before they get any closer. Come with me. If we have to get out of here fast, it'll save time."

They were already climbing up the ridge behind the cabin when Joshua stopped and held up his hand. "It's my brothers. I'm sure of it. Did you hear that squeal when the driver shifted gears? That's the trademark of Shadow's truck." He crouched behind a tree and looked down. "I was right, it's them. Shadow's had that truck fixed a bazillion times, but it always reverts. I think it's his driving, but whenever I point it out, he just offers to go get a baseball bat and pound me into the ground."

Nydia knew the same threat coming from Gabriel or Lucas would have given any other man pause. Of course, the brothers were close, and although she had no doubt that Gabriel and Lucas had tangled more than once in their lives, she couldn't imagine Joshua ever getting involved in one of their scuffles. "I have a feeling you broke up more fights than you ever participated in."

"That's true. Fuzz and Shadow have always enjoyed hassling each other. I never understood it, but I have to admit there were times when I wanted to crack their skulls together. I figured one big brain would work better than two separate ones with them."

When they reached the cabin, Gabriel and Lucas were waiting by the door.

"Good going, Tree," Gabriel said. "You heard trucks and headed for cover. You can't be too careful now."

"What's going on in town?" Joshua asked.

Gabriel filled them in as they went inside.

Nydia watched the brothers, aware of how different the three were. Yet together they constituted a formidable force. Being in the same room with them was like standing next to a generator at the regional power plant.

Lucas paced while Gabriel stayed by the window. "I'm all for patience when I'm working a case," Gabriel said, "but this one has pushed me to the edge. Someone wants our family down for the count, boys, and I'm not getting answers fast enough. Every time I turn around, the killer is throwing another curveball at me."

Lucas stopped and leaned back against the wall, regarding them with an expression that did little to disguise the violence in his thoughts. "Let's just find out who it is. I'll end his game—permanently. I'm not planning on sitting through any murder trial."

"Then it's a good thing that neither of you have solved the case," Joshua said, his voice harsher than Nydia had ever heard it before. "Our father's killer is destroying more than he ever dreamed. And we're helping him. Do you see what's going on here? We're defeating ourselves."

"Forget it, Tree. Sermons or not, someone's declared war on us. It's eye-for-an-eye time, brother," Lucas answered.

"Shadow's got a point, Tree," Gabriel said. "This isn't

some morality play we're debating. This dirtbag killed our father.''

Joshua looked at his two brothers, then spun around and slammed his fist hard into the log wall. The cabin shook, and two pots fell from the mantel.

Joshua's action took Gabriel and Lucas by surprise. Gabriel jumped to his feet, and Lucas stepped back, his eyes wide.

Joshua turned and looked at Shadow first. His brother held out his hands and took a step back. "I'm not arguing with you.''

Joshua met Gabriel's gaze, then gave him a quick half smile.

Gabriel expelled his breath in a rush, and then sat back down, shaking his head slowly. "Okay. You've now got our attention. Say what you have to.''

"Wait a minute! You did that for *effect?* Tree, for future reference, there are other ways to get my attention. It's not necessary to give me a heart attack.''

Joshua's gaze was filled with understanding as he regarded his brothers. "I'm capable of anger and pain, too, but if we let those twist us up inside, then we'll never find that balance that we need to live our lives. We're Navajo. We have to walk in beauty, because it's part of who and what we are. It's when our people leave that path that chaos follows them. We can't allow this killer to take our father, and then destroy us all from the inside out. If we do, his victory will be complete.''

Gabriel nodded. "You're right, but it's hard to keep a clear perspective when they've attacked my wife and me in our own home.''

"Which is probably just why our enemy did that,'' Joshua said.

"He knows us, guys. We probably see him every day,'' Lucas added.

Nydia remained quiet. In her opinion, Joshua had the most to contend with. *Hataaliis* had been warriors at one time, and great fighters, but without the inner peace they had to maintain, without that certainty that they were acting in the right, they lost the part of themselves that they valued most. Even when they had to serve as warriors, they had to retain the sensitivity that would also destroy them if they couldn't master the need for violence within themselves.

"Do you have any possible suspects in the bombing?" Nydia asked Gabriel.

"None that I like," Gabriel answered. "These are people all of us know. It's difficult to imagine anyone in Four Winds hating us this much."

"But the answer has to be there," she insisted.

"The only person besides Shadow who I know is familiar enough with bombs to build one is Jake Fields, but I can't imagine what motive he could have for the crimes. He didn't even know our father that well."

"Then it's got to be someone else," Nydia said.

"I'm doing background checks now, and hopefully we'll know more soon. Shadow and I just came by to make sure everything was okay here. I also wanted to tell you that I think you both should be armed. I have a shotgun and rifle in my truck. You're already deputized," he said, looking at Nydia. "Which would you prefer?"

"Neither, but I'll take the rifle."

"I'll leave you with enough ammo."

"But even with a rifle, without the ability to call for help, we're sitting ducks if we're caught in here," Nydia said. "The cell phone won't work unless we climb the ridge."

"This place is far from perfect in a tactical sense, but Tree knows this country. He can find hiding places you'd never dream of. And nobody knows about this cabin. Together, that gives you a considerable advantage."

Gabriel went outside, then returned with a box of cartridges and the rifle. "This is all I can spare."

"It's more than enough," Nydia said. "If I have to fire more than a few shots, then we're in too deep for gunfire to get us out."

Gabriel looked at his youngest brother. "I can't give you a weapon, not one that belongs to the town, but I can lend you my shotgun."

Joshua shook his head. "Personally, I don't think that even your deputy," he said, looking at Nydia, "should have one. If we respond with gunfire to any challenge we get here, the situation will escalate. We can't hope to win in a situation where firepower is the deciding factor. Using a gun is an absolutely last-ditch option as far as I'm concerned."

Gabriel thought about it, then finally nodded. "Okay. That's your call, I suppose. Can I count on you to stay here?"

"No," Joshua answered. "Tomorrow, I intend to pay Jake Fields a visit."

Gabriel's eyes narrowed. "You think he might actually be involved? If you do, tell me, because I'm counting on him to help me out. He's going to try and track down the places where the bomber could have purchased bomb components."

"I don't know if he's involved or not—that's why I need to talk to him. I have the books I borrowed from him, so I've got a perfect reason to go see him. What I intend to do is sound him out on all this. If he's innocent, I'll know it soon enough."

"Are you sure you want to go back into town?" Lucas pressed. "You might get jumped—or worse."

"Nobody will attack me face-to-face, and nobody will ambush us in broad daylight. You can count on that."

"I hope you're right. I don't suppose you'll let me talk you out of this," Gabriel asked.

"No."

After both of Joshua's brothers left, Nydia sat down on the sofa. Joshua joined her. "I can tell there's something on your mind. What's wrong?"

She exhaled softly. "I've been at odds with the traditionalists for quite some time. To turn away from medical science and hold to ways that, to me, were as outmoded as the horse and buggy seemed incredibly foolish. I wasn't at all sure it was good for my son to continue learning about traditionalists' ways. But now..."

"Something's changed your mind?" He leaned forward, regarding her closely.

"After what I saw today, let's say I'm thinking it over. The way you held it together, despite the way the situation was tearing at you, and in the face of your brothers' outrage—the old ways have given you strength, not weakened you."

"Yes," he answered, leaning back, almost as if disappointed with her answer, "but they demand much, too."

"I don't doubt that for a moment. I'm sure there are times when you're tempted to chuck it all, and act with your heart instead of your head, like your brothers."

"I've had second thoughts, but I've chosen the right way for me. The old and the new can coexist, you know. Medical science, for example, takes care of the body, but a *hataalii* treats the person. We take into account the effect that harmony gives the body. Our people need both the old and the new. Do you know that many of the *dineh* are using both doctors and *hataaliis* now as a matter of form? A few months back I was called in to do a sing for a man who'd been in the hospital for appendicitis. The doctors removed his appendix, but the patient wanted me to do a lifeway to heal the wound the knife had left behind. Both methods support each other.''

Nydia brought out her tape recorder, ready to work. ''Will you tell me more about a *hataalii* and what the work demands?''

He stood up and shook his head. ''Not now. We both need rest. Later today, at sunset, we'll go down into town, but I need to be alert then.''

''Take the bed, then—I had it last night.''

He shook his head. ''I'll sleep outside. I can't stay in this cabin with you anymore. I have to keep an eye on the area, and I've trained myself to sleep, but not so soundly that I miss danger. Only I need to be outside since the cabin mutes the sounds and dulls my senses.''

''The bedroll?'' Nydia asked, pointing.

''No, I won't need that until after nightfall. It's too warm right now. Get some rest yourself,'' he said as he left.

Though they'd had precious little sleep the night before, Nydia lay awake in the bedroom. Restlessness held her captive as her heart listened for his in the silence.

JOSHUA LAY BACK, using the trunk of a tree to rest against. Attuning himself to the sounds of the land, he closed his eyes. If anything changed, he would know, and he would awaken.

As his body relaxed, his mind drifted back to the woman now alone in the cabin. Hunger flared between them like lightning in the summer skies. He needed her, and she needed him, but some needs were better left unfulfilled. A one-night-stand would only increase his desire to possess her body and soul.

He took a deep breath, trying to banish her from his mind. He had to restore his harmony, not confuse it with other, more-primitive urges. He wouldn't be able to help anyone if he wasn't in control of himself.

As the breeze touched his skin, its warmth reminded him of the soft caress of her hands. The thought burned through him, and his body stiffened. With a groan, he shifted restlessly. It was useless. Underneath and around every thought he had, was the woman herself.

He exhaled softly, knowing the wisdom of accepting what was happening between them. He couldn't change what was; he could only control his actions.

As the cicadas filled the silence with their continuous, pulsing song, he kept his eyes closed, but did not sleep.

Chapter Eight

They arrived in town at around three that afternoon. Joshua's gaze darted everywhere as Nydia drove through the back streets in her truck, avoiding Main. A few townspeople saw them, but they didn't give them more than a passing glance. It was almost as if people were trying hard to pretend they hadn't seen them at all.

As Nydia parked in the alley beside the library, near the cover of some brambling pyracantha bushes, Joshua remained alert to anything that might signal danger. He watched Nydia out of the corner of his eye, aware that she'd stored the rug in the rear bench. Its presence made him uneasy. He forced himself to focus on their surroundings. He was aware of the laughter coming from the diner patrons, and closer still, kids near Charley's waiting to gas up their cars at one of the two pumps. Everything seemed painfully ordinary, though it was not. The reason he was here was enough to rob him of any comfort familiar patterns might have given him.

"All right. Let's get going. If we run into anyone, face them squarely. Don't show any hesitation, or that in itself will bring on trouble," Joshua warned.

"All right." She took the books they'd borrowed and, giving him half, climbed down out of the pickup.

As they reached the back door, they saw Jake busy nailing down a loose board on the back porch. "The library's closed for the day," he said without looking up.

"We know," Joshua answered softly.

Jake glanced up at them quickly, then put down the hammer, opened the door and hurried inside with them. "What in the name of all that's holy are you doing in town, boy? Haven't you caught on that it's not safe for you here?"

"Your books," Joshua said without answering his question.

"You took that kind of risk for those?" Jake shook his head. "It would have waited."

"I came to talk to you, also," Joshua said, pulling out a chair for Nydia and one for himself.

Jake swung a chair around, and straddled it. "All right. I'm listening."

"Someone is working real hard to make me look like a criminal. Planting that bomb in my brother's house means he'll stop at nothing, including more deaths, to destroy my family. But whoever it is has some specialized knowledge about skinwalkers and bombs. What's your take on this?"

"You know that I served in the Rangers. I could have built that bomb, if that's what you're thinking, and had I done it, I *might* have used a double timer to take out anyone trying to disarm it. That was well thought out. But I didn't do it."

"Who else around here might know how to build a bomb?"

"I honestly don't know. But I can tell you this—I'm keeping my eyes and ears open. The way I see it, you've got few friends and lots of enemies in town right now. Ralph Montoya and I are doing our level best to fight the rumors with facts, and make people see that going off half-cocked isn't going to solve anything. But the danger to you is real and always present. One thing you can count on is that I'll fight by your side if things get out of hand. I don't much care for vigilantes.''

Jake stopped, then met Joshua's gaze. ''But even having said that, I'll understand if you still have doubts about me. I do have the skills needed, several times over, to have committed the crimes. Only keep in mind that your brother Lucas does, too, and you know he didn't do it.''

''You have no reason to strike out at any of us,'' Joshua conceded, ''and you've proven yourself to be a friend, despite the risks. I don't suspect you.''

Joshua was aware of Nydia's gaze on him. Whatever thoughts she had, she was keeping to herself.

Almost as if sensing what Joshua was thinking, Jake turned to look at Nydia. ''You're not so sure about me, are you?''

''I don't know you, and there's no past friendship between us to confuse me,'' she said bluntly. ''I'm not saying that you're guilty, but I think I'll wait before I judge you a friend. My definition may be a lot narrower than yours.''

Jake glowered at her, then suddenly and unexpectedly laughed. ''I don't trust people easily, either, so I can't hold this against you. But for what it's worth, I *will* look out for both of you. In time, you'll see that my definition of friendship isn't much different from yours.''

They stayed and talked for a while longer. When at last Joshua and Nydia started heading for the door, Jake suddenly stopped them, and gestured toward his private quarters. ''I almost forgot! There's an issue of the *Last Word* you should see.''

Once inside the Spartan living area, he picked up a copy of the town's daily paper. ''Ralph is openly acknowledging the peddler's visit. I've kept a close ear on what people are saying, but the only thing everyone agrees on is that the peddler came for a purpose and accomplished it, or he wouldn't have left.''

"So now they're waiting for the other shoe to drop," Joshua said.

"And watching you, thinking that somehow you're involved and that you'll profit from all of this." He glanced at Nydia and explained. "The tragedy that always follows the peddler has struck, you see, but now what remains to be seen is who will benefit from the good fortune that the peddler also brings."

"But they can't have it both ways," Nydia argued. "My understanding of the legend surrounding the peddler is that no one with bad intentions *ever* profits from whatever gift he brings."

"That's also tied in to the legend of Flinthawk, my ancestor," Joshua said.

"So if they think you're the murderer, then they also can't expect that you'll profit from the crime, right? It doesn't fit the legend," Nydia said.

"You're using reason," Jake said, "but in an emotionally charged situation, people bend logic. Fear twists them up inside. The only thing that's going to settle them down and bring this town peace is finding the killer."

Joshua set the newspaper down. "Thanks for showing us the article."

As they reached the back door, Joshua abruptly stopped in midstride and held a finger to his lips. "Did you hear that?" he mouthed, looking at Jake, then Nydia.

Jake nodded once, then hurried to the side window and pulled the curtain back slightly. Looking back at Joshua, he shook his head.

Joshua opened the back door and peered out cautiously. The alley was empty.

Jake came up next to him. "It's clear now. I'm not sure what's going on out there, but if it had been harmless, whoever that was wouldn't have been lurking around."

Jake opened the locked drawer of his desk, then returned, a .45 pistol in hand. "I'm walking you two to your truck."

"No. I've involved you enough," Joshua said.

"I'm going along anyway. And then I'm following you at least to the outskirts of town."

"No. I can lose a tail better if I'm on my own," Joshua insisted.

"All right, just to your truck, then. But if you change your mind, come back, I'll be waiting. You have backup here. Count on it."

As NYDIA DROVE, Joshua kept his eyes glued on the side mirror. When they finally reached the highway that led out of town, he asked her to pull over. "Let me take the wheel. I can't see anyone, but I feel someone there."

She nodded. "No problem. You know these roads better than I do. And something *is* wrong. I feel it, too." She scooted over.

"The voice?"

"No voice. Just a feeling."

As Joshua maneuvered the hairpin curves in the road, a shot rang out. The right front tire blew out, and the truck lurched violently to the right. Joshua struggled to keep the vehicle from rolling as he maneuvered off onto the shoulder and into a shallow arroyo.

Joshua did not try to come to a stop until he reached the deeper end of the wash. The steep sides could provide cover. "Stay low," he said as they left the vehicle.

Hiding in a crevice beside the truck, they waited for several minutes, but no other shots rang out. Joshua listened to the wind, invoking its power as messenger. After an eternity, the insects began to hum. "The danger has passed."

"Passed? No way. We're being manipulated. This was

too easy and too convenient. Let's get the tire changed, fast. If anything, we're in more trouble now.''

''Intuition?''

''It's common sense. Puzzle it out. If the sniper wanted us dead, he wouldn't have shot out the tire, he would have aimed for the driver—you. Why would he bother doing something like this unless he was also planning something else?''

''Yeah, but what and where?'' Joshua muttered as they worked to change the tire quickly.

''What would we do if we were him?'' she mused. ''He wants to frame you....''

''So he would go back to Jake's and do something there,'' Joshua concluded. ''People saw us in town, and possibly at the library. So if anything happens to Jake now—''

After the last nut was tightened on the spare, they threw the jack and damaged tire into the back, and raced back to town. Joshua felt an urgency, a sense of impending danger tugging mercilessly at him. Nydia's acknowledgment that she shared his feeling had only heightened his concern.

As they parked behind the library, Joshua saw Jake standing by the window that faced the alley.

Joshua hurried inside. ''Are you all right?''

Jake nodded, his eyes narrowed, his body tense. ''Yeah. What's wrong?''

Joshua explained about the tire and the progression of logic that had brought them back. ''Has anything happened here?''

''Follow me.'' Jake led them back outside, and pointed out a trail of giant footprints beneath the window. ''So this couldn't have been your work, then.''

Nydia crouched by the tracks, studying them. ''The same person who left the footprints at the sheriff's house did this,'' Nydia said. ''See for yourself. Look where Joshua walked. The depth is different. But what's this all about? Did he set a bomb here, too?''

"No. I had just brewed a fresh pot of coffee when I thought I heard a sound outside. I came out, but all I saw were those tracks that disappear into the brush. I followed the trail, but got nowhere, so I came back."

"Maybe you interrupted his plans," Nydia said.

"Or maybe he was just casing the place, intending to return later," Jake said.

Hearing a vehicle approaching, Joshua turned around, braced for trouble. He relaxed as he recognized his brother's Jeep.

The look on Gabriel's face spoke volumes to him. The investigation was eating at his brother, eroding his confidence. One thing he knew about his eldest brother was that the more confident he appeared to be, the less so he truly felt, though Gabriel would have denied that vehemently.

Joshua filled Gabriel in quickly on what had happened. "While you record whatever you need to here, I'm going to follow the tracks and see where they lead me," Joshua said.

Jake shook his head. "Waste of time. As I said, I already tried that. The tracks disappear by the stream, about a mile from here." He glanced at Gabriel. "And both of you *know* I can track. If there had been anything to follow, I would have found it."

Gabriel photographed the tracks, then working together with Joshua, Jake and Nydia, followed the trail. It was a rugged hike, but as Jake had said, the footprints ended abruptly at the stream. "Whoever did this knows how to lose a tail," Gabriel muttered.

"I'm going to keep searching upstream," Joshua said. "The trail's got to pick up somewhere, and I intend to find it."

"You'll never be able to tell if you're tracking the same

person, because you can bet he changed shoes farther on," Gabriel said.

"I've got to try anyway," Joshua insisted.

"All right, but watch yourself," Gabriel said. "I've got to get back to town and see if I can get a plaster cast of the prints. If it rains again tonight, all the evidence will be gone."

As Gabriel and Jake went back, Nydia studied the tracks. "He obviously went into the water, and on the far side of this stream there's too much grass for him to have left a trail. I hate to tell you this, but I think we're out of luck."

"If I had been him, I would have gone up or down the stream for a long while before crossing to the other side. I'm wading to the other side, because sooner or later the trail will pick up there. I intend to keep looking as long as there's light."

"Okay. We'll cross here. Four eyes are better than two. We can come back here and continue on from this spot if we find nothing on the other side."

"You don't have to do this, you know. You can search this side now, and I can come back and meet you here later."

"Nothing doing. We're sticking together. There's no telling what other surprises this scumbag is going to throw at us if we get close. You need me."

"Yes, I think I do," he murmured provocatively. He heard the way her breath caught, and saw her eyes darken in response to his words. They did need each other, more than he'd ever dreamed possible.

Forcing himself to concentrate on the task at hand, Joshua waded across the waist-deep stream. The going was slow, but to his surprise, she swam past him, arriving at the other side just before he did.

As she stepped out of the water, he noticed the way her shirt clung to her, accentuating the softness of her breasts.

Heat slammed into him. He wanted to pull her into his arms, to feel her softness against him, to hear her crying out his name.

As if she sensed the direction of his thoughts, she looked back at him, her mouth parting slightly. The gesture almost shattered his will. He forced his gaze away, forsaking what he wanted most at that moment.

Together, they slowly made their way upstream. Nydia matched his pace, never slowing him down. After an hour, he'd still failed to find anything to support his theory or his hope of picking up the trail. It was getting close to dark, and frustration tore at him. As he turned back to look at her, he suddenly realized that she was no longer with him.

He glanced around quickly and called out to her.

"Here!" She was crouched by the edge of the stream, studying a long branch.

"What have you found?"

"I was walking along when this caught my eye. The other end is partly lodged in the middle of the stream. That's what gave me an idea. I remember playing in the Animas River as a kid and pole-vaulting across from one sandbar to the next. It was fun, and if you missed, you just splashed in the water. The way this branch was lying in the water reminded me of that."

He crouched next to her. "A pole vault," he nodded slowly. "No wonder we didn't see any footprints close to the streambed on this side. He made sure he landed in just the right spot."

"Like right there." She gestured toward the grassy area near the boulders.

Joshua walked to an area thick with vegetation and crouched down, searching the ground. Spotting a broken twig, he picked it up and placed one end in his mouth.

"Oh, please! Didn't your mother tell you not to put

things in your mouth when you don't know where they've been? That's unsanitary!"

He looked up, surprised. "The sap is fresh. He didn't cross long ago. Shall we go on?" He had to struggle not to smile. Although her observation skills were good, she had forgotten the tricks the trackers of their tribe had often used. "Old tricks sometimes work the best."

"Maybe, but I wouldn't have done it."

"I'm more worried about gunfire than I am about a twig and germs."

Nydia fell into step beside him. "So where are we heading now?"

"Right through that wooded area. He wants to avoid leaving a trail, so that's where he'll go."

As they passed a thick stand of young pines, he suddenly stopped.

Nydia ran into him. "What the heck are you doing?"

"He's anticipated me," Joshua answered, his voice taut. "Look." He walked around what seemed to be a bed of pine needles and scattered tumbleweeds. "Study the edges. It's not solid ground beneath." With the toe of his boot, he pushed the cover away and exposed the deep pit below. Nasty-looking spikes protruded skyward from the bottom. "The fall might have killed us, even if we hadn't been impaled by those sharp stakes."

Suddenly, there was a snap beneath his foot, and he knew he'd been had. In a heartbeat, a branch whipped down from a tree and swept him into the pit.

Chapter Nine

Nydia's heart lodged in her throat. Lying down on the ground, she edged forward on her stomach. "Talk to me! Are you hurt?" She avoided using his name, knowing that now, more than ever, he wouldn't wish her to do so. The *dineh* believed that names had power and, if used properly, could help a person at a critical time. At the moment, she couldn't think of any two people who could use help more, so neither could afford to waste any source of power.

"Answer me!" she repeated loudly. As she heard him groan, a paralyzing fear shot through her. The certainty that he had been impaled by a stake, and that she wouldn't be able to bring help in time, made her ache everywhere.

"I'm all right. I managed to bounce off the side and avoid getting speared. Nothing appears to be broken, either," he managed to say.

His voice seemed to be coming from the grave. Though it was dusk now, there was enough light to see the sharpened stakes protruding upward. She couldn't see the bottom of the hole, however. About the only thing she could make out was Joshua's face and that, just barely. "How deep is it? Can you climb out?"

"Not without your help."

"I can't pull you up. Your weight would just pull me in with you. I'll go get help."

"No. It'll be dark soon, and I think that whoever set this trap is waiting for that. I'm not armed, and if he comes up on me while I'm here alone, these spears won't be much of a defense against a gun. Look around and see if there are any sturdy branches you can lower down to help me get back to the surface. In the meantime, I'll pull out these stakes and throw them up and out of our way."

Nydia moved off, searching the ground and the area. "I'm going to have to look farther out. There are taller ponderosa pines ahead. One of those branches might work, but I don't know how long my search will take."

"All right. But before you go, there's something I want you to carry with you."

A moment later, a beaded pouch landed at Nydia's feet. She recognized it immediately. "That's your medicine bundle. I can't take that!"

"Yes, you can," he said. "It's all I have to give you while you search. It'll help you in ways you don't yet understand. Go ahead. Take it."

It was his way of protecting her though he couldn't be with her himself. Understanding him, she took the medicine bundle and placed it carefully in the button-down pocket of her shirt. "I'll be back soon."

Darkness settled, increasing her uneasiness. After a long search, she spotted a partially fallen branch that dangled precariously from a tall, old ponderosa pine. Putting her weight on it, she worked it back and forth until it fell with a mighty crash.

She dragged it back slowly. By the time she reached Joshua and lowered it down, her hands were scratched and bloody from the rough bark and pine needles. "This is the only one I saw that might work."

"It's fine. Hold it still while I use it to climb up."

She did her best, but the moment he put his full weight on it, the branch rolled out of her grasp. "I can't hang on to it. I'm going to have to get someone else here. It's your only chance.''

''Try once more.''

She heard him start a sing. The chant filled the darkness, and took flight into the night. It seemed as if the air itself shimmered with power as old as the woods around them. Her skin tingled, and she felt a new confidence making her stronger. She wasn't sure how long it took, but soon she saw Joshua reach up and grasp her forearm. It was then that she saw the blood that covered his shirt.

For a moment, she couldn't breathe, and her newfound strength vanished. She knew he needed her to help him climb the rest of the way, but how could she do that? He was so heavy.

His song grew stronger, wrapping itself around her. The world seemed to begin and end in the texture of the notes and the magic of the chant.

She closed her eyes, letting the power enter her. Before she realized it, he was safe on the ground beside her. A tear spilled down her cheek as they both sat gasping for air.

''No, *sawe,* my sweetheart, don't cry,'' he said, drawing her against him. ''I'm all right, and so are you. That's the only thing that matters.''

''You're hurt. You're bleeding,'' she managed to say. One of the spikes had caught his shoulder badly.

His callused finger brushed away the tear. Then, holding her face in his hands, he took her mouth with his own. His tongue caressed her intimately, searching out secret places that left her quivering in his arms.

She was aware of everything about him, his strength, the tenderness of his touch and the searing intimacy of his kiss. The wildness, the passion swept over her. She'd never imagined anything could be like this.

Joshua released her slowly and reluctantly. As she pulled

away, she saw through his partially open shirt a profusion of smaller cuts that covered his chest in a blanket of crimson.

"You need a doctor. We have to get out of here now."

"Yes, we do have to leave, but I don't need a doctor. They're all small cuts I can take care of once we get back." He reached for the medicine pouch that rested half out of her shirt pocket.

His knuckles brushed her breast, and she shuddered. What unimaginable power he had over her senses! Weak at the knees, she pulled out the medicine bundle and handed it back to him. "As soon as you're ready to go, say the word."

He stripped off his shirt, revealing his spectacular build. As she watched him, he placed some herbs on the scrapes that covered his torso and shoulder. She knew she couldn't offer to help. Neither of them could afford the distraction.

"All right. Let's get moving."

"We're going to your brother's clinic first," she said.

"I've told you it isn't necessary."

"The way I see it, a doctor doesn't treat himself, and neither should a *hataalii*."

He laughed. "I'm not sure if that's an apt comparison, but we'll go."

His grin practically tore her breath away. Forcing her thoughts to what lay ahead, she remained close by his side as they made their way back.

THE HIKE IN THE DARK was rough, but at least they were able to cross the stream on a fallen log instead of getting wet again. Both were exhausted after their ordeal. As they reached the truck, Nydia felt as if her limbs had been carved from stone. "We're here! I don't think I could have taken another step."

"You can do whatever you set your mind to," he said.

A wonderful warmth filled her as she heard that admiration in his voice.

Following Joshua's directions, Nydia drove her truck to Lucas's clinic, but the number of cars there took her by surprise. "I don't get it. How come so many teenagers are here?" she asked.

"I'd say there was a dance at the high school tonight. That means an occasional fist fight, and business for my brother."

Spotting her truck, Lucas hurried outside. His gaze traveled over Joshua quickly. "Drive around the back. I'll meet you."

As they circumvented the kids and parents waiting at the front, a few insults rose from the people gathered there. Inside, comments could still be heard even though they were sequestered in a closed room.

Lucas led his brother to an examining table. "What the hell happened to you?"

Nydia watched as Lucas cleaned out the wounds. Had Lucas dabbed that much alcohol on her, they would have had to scrape her off the ceiling. Joshua didn't even flinch, but continued to tell his brother about their adventures.

"Is Joshua going to be okay?" Nydia asked, her voice taut.

Lucas smiled at her. "Tree is built like, well, a tree. He's got the constitution of a gnarled oak. He'll be just fine."

Nydia took the first deep breath she'd taken in two hours, and dropped down into a chair. "We'll need to tell the sheriff what happened."

"I'll take care of that. He'll get a call just as soon as I'm done patching up my brother."

As Lucas worked on Joshua, Nydia heard boys' voices just down the hall. Her thoughts drifted to her son, John, and the task she'd undertaken at his request. Despite her best efforts, she was no closer to bringing the *hataalii* back.

She pictured his serious face whenever he tried to convince her he was a man not a boy. He had so many goals for himself. In his intense black eyes, she could see the strength of the *dineh*.

An anguish as black as night speared her. She missed her son. Their relationship was a close one. It had been their love for each other that had seen her through the sorrow and loneliness of her life since becoming a widow. As she watched Lucas and Joshua, she longed to be with her own family and to hear John's voice.

"I need to call home," she said. "May I use your phone?"

Joshua's gaze was filled with such compassion that Nydia knew he'd read her thoughts. "I *will* go back to the reservation with you. Assure them of that. This situation can't last much longer."

She nodded, but didn't speak, not trusting her voice.

"Go down the hall, then turn left," Lucas said. "My office is there. Feel free to use the phone as long as you need."

As she opened the door and went out of the examining room, the crowd's eyes fastened on her, and every conversation stopped almost at once. Nydia kept her eyes forward, went down to Lucas's office and closed the door behind her. She sat behind his desk and dialed home. It was late, almost John's bedtime, and she hoped she wouldn't wake him.

Her mother-in-law answered as usual, and the frost in her voice made a shudder run up Nydia's spine. "I need to talk to my son," Nydia said simply.

"It's very late. Are you bringing the *hataalii?*"

"No, not yet. There's a matter here that needs to be resolved first."

"Then why—?"

"I want to speak to my son," she repeated calmly.

There was a silence, then she heard the phone being set down. A few minutes later, John answered.

"Mom?"

"Hi." She nearly cried at the relief of hearing his voice. So much had happened, and she needed him now. "How are you doing?"

"I'm fine," he said, then added, "but you're not. What's wrong? Won't the *hataalii* come?"

"He will, but there's a complication here, some legal matters that make things difficult for everyone. How's your grandfather?"

"He's really weak. Grandma's worried about him, but I think he'll hold on because he knows you'll bring back help. You can't let us down, Mom, you just can't."

She heard the desperation in his voice, but it was the seed of doubt there that worried her most. He was losing faith in her, and that hurt her more than she'd ever dreamed possible. "If you need me for any reason, call the sheriff's office here. He'll know where to find me."

"I just don't understand...."

"About what, son?"

"I always thought I could count on the old ways and those who followed the Navajo Way to come through for me, no matter what. But maybe you were right all along, Mom. Maybe the only thing we really can count on is ourselves."

"I'll be back as soon as possible with the help we need. Hold to that."

She heard the dial tone as John hung up, and felt the aching emptiness that being away from him always left inside her. Then her thoughts turned to Joshua, and the heartache eased, filling the empty spot with warm feelings she didn't dare define.

Hearing a knock at the door, she glanced up and saw

Joshua entering. "Is everything all right?" he asked, closing the door behind himself.

She smiled thinly. "I was just asking myself the same question about you."

"That's not an answer," he said.

She shrugged. "You're needed on the reservation. What else is there for me to say?"

As he stood with his back to the closed door, angry voices filled the next room. Then something was thrown against the wall, shattering with a loud crash.

Nydia heard Lucas's voice rising above the crowd's, then there was an uneasy quiet as he spoke to the gathering.

"They're afraid and angry, but we have no reason to fear them here," Joshua assured her.

She saw the pain in his eyes, and knew that despite his calm words, the reaction of the townspeople had opened a wound no amount of medicine would ever heal.

"I don't fear them, I resent them," Nydia said angrily. "And you have a right to that emotion, too."

"I can't afford that—I have to keep my thinking clear. Among them is a murderer. And instinct tells me that he's the one who's working hardest to turn the people against me by feeding their fears. He's the one I need to find. If I allow emotions to sidetrack me, he'll gain the advantage and he has enough of one already."

A moment later, Lucas came in with Rosa, the owner of the grocery store. Joshua's expression revealed he was surprised to see her there.

Rosa looked them both over with kind eyes. "I heard what happened to you tonight. Lucas explained to all of us. I wanted to assure you that no matter what, I will continue to sell you whatever supplies you need. But if you could come by after-hours, I'd really appreciate it. After the last time you visited my store, I received an anonymous note warning me that my store would be history if I helped you any more.''

"Did you recognize the writing?" Nydia asked. "And what did you do with the note?"

Rosa glanced at Nydia. "I didn't recognize the writing, so I threw the note away. At first, it just made me angry—I don't like people telling me what to do. But then I thought of Rosita, my niece, who goes to school here. I don't want her pulled into this situation. To be honest, I'm afraid for her.''

"We understand," Joshua said.

"I'll open for you really early or really late if you need something. Or maybe your brothers can shop for you."

"We'll work something out."

Nydia felt anger tearing at her. Now when Joshua needed friends more than ever, it seemed as if Four Winds was all but deserting him. She wondered how he could stay so calm.

Seeing the warning look Joshua gave her, she refrained from speaking her mind. After Lucas led Rosa back out, Nydia stared defiantly at Joshua. "Sometimes patience is *not* a good thing. You should have spoken up for yourself. She might be worried about retaliation, but capitulating to bullies is never the answer."

"She's doing her best, and she hasn't turned me away. I'm isolated enough as it is, and to turn down her offer of help and the limited friendship she is able to give would be playing right into my enemy's hands. He wants me to stand alone."

Nydia walked to the window and stared out into the darkness. "When I lost my husband, I felt completely alone. My parents were in Europe, where my father was serving in the army. There was no one there for me except my in-laws, who don't approve of me, and my son. But even in those dark days when my world was crashing down, my fight was nothing compared to yours.''

"I choose to think of this as a passage. You came through tough times, and became stronger for it. It will be the same for me." He studied her expression. "But there's something else eating at you right now. How's your son?"

"His grandfather is growing weaker, and he's worried, of course. But it's not so much what he said, but what he didn't say," Nydia answered in a strangled voice. "He's losing faith in my ability to bring you back. He's losing faith in me. And in—" She stopped. Joshua had enough to contend with.

"And in the old ways he trusts," Joshua finished for her. "We can't let that happen. There's more at stake here, too, than the life of one elderly man and the beliefs of your boy. I know what your son means to you, and that you need him to believe in you. It's as much for you as it is for anyone else that I *will* succeed in helping your father-in-law. I won't let up in my search for the killer even if it means driving all of us relentlessly, because I know time is running out for you and those you hold dear."

She wanted to tell him that she held him dear, too, that his concern had touched her more than she could ever put into words, but just then Lucas came in.

"Okay, I've tended all the split lips and black eyes the boys who were caught in the fight came in with. Luckily, there were no broken bones this time. It's time to get you back to the cabin."

"You'll follow to make sure we aren't tailed?" Nydia asked.

"Yes, but you won't see me, so don't bother looking in the rearview mirror. Go your way, and don't worry. You'll have backup if you need it."

"Is it necessary, you think?" Joshua asked. "People surely know that I didn't dive into that pit on my own."

"I told them what happened, but many don't believe it went down the way you described. Somebody said Jake made up the story about the footprints to help you, since he's your friend."

"It'll be dangerous for him, too, then," Joshua said.

"Jake can take care of himself—you know that. You're the one I'm worried about."

"Before we get too swayed by Jake and what he's doing, I think I should point out that he's still the best suspect," Nydia said. "That man is trained to make and use bombs and he's probably a crack shot, too."

Joshua looked at Lucas and shook his head. "No, he isn't responsible."

"Maybe you're just so relieved to find someone who believes in you that you're not taking into account the obvious. Jake may be taking your word because he knows *he's* the guilty one."

"She's got a point," Lucas said. "Finding a sympathetic ear could be coloring your judgment."

"But it isn't," Joshua said flatly. "I'm seldom wrong about people—you know that," he added looking at Lucas.

"That's true. Well, it doesn't matter now. At the moment, what we have to do is make sure you get out of town safely," he said, leading them out the back door.

Nydia took the wheel, knowing Joshua was still in some pain. As they drove down Main, she glanced in the rearview mirror. "I can't see your brother anywhere."

"He told you that would happen. You can count on Shadow. He's there."

As they drove past the feed store, Nydia slowed down slightly. "Look at that truck parked in the alley."

Joshua sat up and glanced out the window. "It's Darren Wilson's truck."

"You know what? That truck could easily have been the

same one we saw parked by Mrs. Farrell's place the day of the murder.''

Joshua studied the truck as they passed by. "Yes, you're right. I never linked the two until now."

"And if you think back, Wilson's truck wasn't there that night. You noted that yourself."

Joshua kept his gaze on the vehicle as she drove by. "Our view of the pickup that night was sketchy, though. I can't say for certain it's the same truck. Can you?"

"No," she admitted dejectedly. "Still, it's something the sheriff should be told about."

"My brother will be coming later. You can count on it. Shadow has already spoken to him."

"I'll stay up and keep watch until he does. You're going to have to get some sleep. And tonight, you take the bed, no arguments."

"No. Sound sleep is still an enemy, particularly now. We need to stay on our guard."

"My night vision is as good as yours. I'll take care of that. If you don't get some rest, you won't be any good to anyone, including yourself."

When he didn't argue, she realized just how exhausted he was. And it was more than physical exertions that had worn him down. Emotional blows had wounded him deeper than the wooden spikes in the pit he'd escaped from. Nydia's heart went out to him.

Allowing him whatever rest he could get as she drove to the cabin, Nydia remained quiet. She only wished there was more she could do—and not only for him, but for those who were counting on them both.

Chapter Ten

When she finally pulled up by the cabin, she saw Lucas's truck emerge from the high ground to the north. "You're okay here," he said, parking next to them, "but I've got to go back. Fuzz and I will both stop by later."

As he drove away, Nydia and Joshua walked inside the cabin. Joshua took slow steps, then sat down on the sofa with a soft groan.

She was at his side instantly. "Are you okay?"

"Yeah, I'm just sore from the fall."

"Come on. Let me help you to bed."

He stood, and she wrapped her arm around his waist. As awareness shimmered between them, she felt the shudder that traveled through him.

"It's better if you don't help me right now," he said softly.

She nodded. She prided herself on logic and self-discipline, but around Joshua her thoughts were clouded by desires and needs as reckless as her wildest dreams. But she was an adult with too many responsibilities to allow herself the luxury of these distractions. As she watched him move slowly to the bedroom, determination shot through her. She wouldn't let him down. He needed her help, whether he admitted it or not.

Nydia strode past him into the room and tossed the

covers back. "Come on. I'll help you take your boots off. No way you'll feel like bending down to do that."

He sat on the edge of the bed, and she knelt in front of him. She could feel his gaze flowing over her.

"What else will you remove for me?" he taunted softly.

His whisper felt like warm oil poured slowly over her skin. She felt a honeyed weakness winding itself around her. Then passion's fire crept through her, making her burn with yearnings too powerful to simply brush aside.

"We are a lot alike," he said. "You and I tend to over-estimate our own willpower."

Nydia set his boots against the wall and then went to help him remove his torn shirt. His muscles flexed and bunched at her slightest touch.

"You'd better let me do this," he managed to say through clenched teeth.

He was so powerfully male, yet he needed her. The knowledge was like sweet wine. She wasn't sure what happened, but she began to tremble. Following the leanings of her heart, she rested one knee on the mattress between his thighs, then leaned over and kissed him.

His response was explosive. With a guttural cry that sent its vibrations rippling through her, he took her mouth possessively, a storm of hunger unleashed.

She cried out softly, but he drank the sound from her lips, answering with all the heat and power of the man he was.

For an exquisite moment, she allowed desire to run free. She wanted to love this man who'd haunted her dreams. She shivered when he buried his lips at the hollow of her neck. The night exploded into a million bright colors.

Her emotions were at fever pitch, but it was that intensity that frightened her. She was losing a part of herself to him, a part she'd never recapture.

Nydia pulled away abruptly. "I'm sorry. I started this, but I had no business…"

"What we feel…is difficult to fight."

She wanted to slip back into Joshua's arms, but knew she could not. Frustration tore at her. "Ever since I came to Four Winds, nothing makes sense. Sometimes, I don't even recognize myself."

"Yes, you do, and you understand what's happening just as I do. That's what scares you the most."

"And you? Does it frighten you, as well?" Bewildered, she gazed into his eyes. The white-hot passion mirrored there sent a jolt of longing all through her.

"I don't want to hurt you—in any way. I also don't want to play games. Loving you, but knowing I could never truly have you—" He shook his head. "You're not ready to lie with me, *sawe,* because for us it would mean acknowledging love."

She couldn't breathe; she couldn't think. Like a coward, she started to leave the room, but he reached out for her hand.

"No. You never have to run from me. I failed you once, but I'll do my best never to do that again."

"Failed me?"

"By not being able to leave with you—to go help your father-in-law. I failed you, them and myself most of all."

"You can't blame yourself."

"But I do, particularly when I think of your son."

Nydia nodded. "But there, *I'm* the one who failed. I should have discouraged his faith in the old ways a long time ago. Hard facts and science are more reliable than beliefs shrouded in mystery and antiquity. As his mother, I should have given him the wisdom to see that a long time ago. It's just that I wanted him to know both, then let him make the final choice. But in trying to give him everything,

I've left him vulnerable and, possibly, without anything to depend on in life at all."

Joshua grasped her shoulders, forcing her to face him. "I know how desperately your family needs me and I have a duty to honor the trust the tribe places in me as a singer. But I have responsibilities here, too, and for now, I have to stay. But I give you my word that if your father-in-law's condition deteriorates any further, we'll both go back to the reservation whether or not matters here are settled."

"If you do leave with me, it will be seen as an admission of guilt. You'd never clear your name."

"I know."

"I believe you would do this," she whispered in a raw voice.

"I need you to have faith in me."

"I do."

She moved away, knowing that if she remained where she was, they'd kiss again and this time, she wouldn't walk away.

"But we have to stop these feelings, this crazy attraction, between us," she said, her voice taut. "If we don't, we'll hurt each other more than either of us ever thought possible."

"You're so certain...."

"It's wrong between us, *hataalii*, and it's on a level too deep to fix. You're not the man I want in my life. I know only too well what it's like to have the love of a man whose heart is already given."

"There is no one else—"

"No, but there is something you have given yourself to completely. My husband was like you, only his love was the rodeo. He loved my son and me, too, but he spent most of his time pursuing his work. I could never count on him. Whenever I needed him, he just wasn't there. I won't put myself through that again. Your first loyalty is to your way of life, to your path as a singer, and that will never change.''

''Love isn't depleted by giving, *sawe*. It's something that needs to be nurtured, that's true, but with care it sustains itself and feeds the spirit.''

Nydia shook her head, avoiding his gaze. ''I don't believe in love anymore. It brings betrayal, disillusionment and pain.''

As she left the room, she felt an unspeakable sadness filling her. Even though she assured herself that she'd only spoken the truth, she felt hollow inside. There was safety in never surrendering her heart, but with that safety came loneliness, and sorrow for what would never be hers.

Nydia stood outside the cabin, letting the night breeze console her. As she listened to the rustle of the wind through the pines, Joshua's whisper-soft voice reached her ears. ''I will be there for you and your family.''

She shook her head. No, it was impossible. It was her imagination. Joshua was inside the cabin, and too far away for her to hear.

NYDIA SLEPT LIGHTLY, never truly surrendering to the weariness she felt. A part of her remained alert even as she rested, listening to her surroundings, just as she'd always done whenever John had been sick. It was an ability that came naturally to most mothers.

Close to dawn, an out-of-place sound roused her. She sat up quickly. A truck was coming. As she looked down the hillside, she saw two vehicles and recognized them as those belonging to Joshua's brothers.

She hurried down to the cabin and went inside. Joshua was standing by the window watching.

''You heard my brothers?''

''Yes.''

"They'll be here soon, and I'll tell them then about the truck at the feed store."

She nodded. "I'm also going to push the sheriff into letting us get more involved in the case. He's been gathering clues and should have leads, but he's only one man. He needs all the help he can get. I've got to convince him to use me, at least."

"By now, he may be more amenable to help. We all tend to want to handle things alone. But sometimes, that just isn't possible."

She listened to the approaching trucks for a moment. "I'm going to wash up, then check our supplies. With luck, we'll have enough coffee for everyone. I sure need it. How about you? Did you sleep?"

"I'm rested."

"Are you still sore?"

"A bit, but it's not bad. I can move around freely enough."

She wanted to smooth the lines of concern from his face, to tell him that he never had to put up a front for her and that if he hurt, she wanted to know and help him. Instead, only too aware of the dangers that followed the slightest touch between them, she turned and walked away.

JOSHUA MET HIS BROTHERS outside, looking closely at their faces. Fuzz looked worried, as he often did these days. Shadow's tense anger also seemed to have become a part of him.

As they walked inside, Gabriel spotted Nydia, wearing a T-shirt and jeans, going down the hall to the bedroom. He gave his brother an appreciative wink. "Good thing the situation here isn't too rough for you."

Joshua answered him with narrowed eyes and silence.

"She's a pretty woman," Lucas said with a grin. "Bet that's why you're not too concerned with those bruises you took when you fell. A woman like that can make a man forget almost anything. If, after this is over, you still haven't decided whether you want her, I think *I'll* ask her out."

"Do, and I'll redesign your face," Joshua warned in a lethal whisper.

Shadow laughed. "So much for the nonviolent *hataalii*. See how a woman changes a man? That's why I'll never get into a serious relationship. I like myself too much the way I am."

"Too bad nobody else does," Joshua countered.

As Nydia came back into the room, Joshua shot his two brothers a warning look.

"Sheriff, I hope you've got some good news on the case," Nydia said. "We could use some."

Gabriel straddled the wooden chair next to the fireplace. "I managed to get an FBI man to come in and search the bomb site. He was passing through our area and called me with an offer to help. Jake and I were thorough, though, because he wasn't able to find any additional pieces of either the bomb or the detonator. Tests are still being run on the parts Jake and I uncovered, but I was warned that it'll be a while before the state lab gets any answers for us."

"Did you find *anything* that will point to a suspect?" Nydia asked.

"No, not yet. There were no fingerprints where the booby trap was set up, and except for the detonators, the materials used could have been obtained almost anywhere. The explosive was made from common smokeless powder, the type used in modern firearms, and available to gun owners who reload their own ammunition."

"Any of that powder available around here?" Nydia asked.

"No. Most reloading supplies are purchased in sporting-goods stores in Santa Fe or Española. I'm checking into those now," Gabriel answered. "The timers were pretty simple. The first one, the one Nydia disarmed, was the kind found on water sprinklers. It was modified to complete an electrical circuit when the desired time was up. The second came from an electronic egg timer. Directions for making bombs like this are available in any number of books and on the Internet via a computer. But to be honest, anyone with high-school science or industrial arts could have done this. Anyone with a detonator, that is."

As his brother grew silent, Joshua spoke. "I have one interesting speculation for you." He told them about Darren's truck at the feed store.

"I'll check into that," Gabriel said, then once again grew silent.

Joshua watched Gabriel as he paced restlessly. He knew his brother had something to say that he found difficult, so he waited, knowing that his brother would get to it in his own time.

After several long minutes, Gabriel stopped and sat down. "I need help. This town normally doesn't require more than one law-enforcement officer, but right now things are far from normal. The mayor is breathing down my neck. He wants daily reports and instant answers that I just can't give him. I have leads, but not the manpower to follow up on most of them until I get some relief from the state police. And who knows when that will be."

"How can we help, Sheriff?" Nydia asked.

Gabriel's gaze took them all in. "I need all of you to search for people in our area who have used explosives or have had access to detonators. Mining companies, engineering firms and contractors are the most likely sources."

"I think you and Lucas, particularly if you deputize him, are more likely to get answers from companies like those than we are," Nydia said thoughtfully.

"We would have better luck focusing on people who

may have had dealings with those kinds of companies,"
Joshua said. "For example, we can talk to anyone who has
had construction work done within the past year. We can
also check out sites where explosives have been used in
the last six months or so."

"Good angle," Gabriel said.

Shadow stood up. "I've got to check on my patients,
especially if Fuzz is going to need me later. I should get
going."

"Me, too." Gabriel stood. "Will you start your end of
this today?" he asked Joshua.

"Yes. I'll be leaving here shortly."

As they stood at the door, Joshua caught a whiff of
smoke in the air. "There's a fire somewhere. Not too close,
but in the direction of Four Winds."

Shadow inhaled deeply. "Your senses were always
sharper than anyone else's. I can't smell a thing. Let's go
uphill. Maybe we'll be able to see something from there."

As they reached the top of the hillside behind the cabin,
Gabriel used high-powered binoculars to scan the area. Finally, he gestured to a section of land close to town.
"There's a faint trail of smoke there. It looks to be close
to the highway. Where do you think it's coming from?"

"The hogan behind my old home," Joshua said, scram-
bling back down toward his truck.

Chapter Eleven

Joshua's gut knotted with anger as he drove Nydia's truck, which had been parked closest to him, toward the old hogan. "I hope I'm wrong. That hogan was the last thing that connected me to the days with my father, learning from him, and becoming a man. If they destroyed that, then they've left me with precious little."

"You have memories no one can take from you," Nydia said. "Those will always be beyond their reach."

As they passed by the burned-out shell of his home, he was overwhelmed by rage and that familiar darkness that tore at his restraint. Like a drop of rain on a windowpane, it moved through him slowly but inexorably, leaving only pain in its wake.

He drove past the old, giant cottonwood and saw it, too, had caught on fire, probably when they'd torched the house. His hand tightened around the wheel. "That tree defined what I am. At one time, it gave me comfort simply by being there. Its roots went deep into the soil, as I imagined my roots went into the heart of everything that was Navajo. That tree stood for strength and continuity, but in the end, man defeated it. Now it's only a hollow shell that speaks only of death."

"Nothing lives forever," Nydia said gently. "That's part of our Way, too. Remember the story that tells why we still have death. When the Hero Twin, Slayer, met Death, he thought of destroying it, but Death reminded him that he was really not the enemy. That without death, there would be no room for the young men or their dreams which would shape the future."

Joshua smiled slowly. "I remember. In that story, Death says that he is a friend, though few really understood him. I'm glad you reminded me of that," he said, but his mood remained somber. Even now, his knowledge was deserting him. Instead of drawing from it as he should have for comfort, he'd needed Nydia to remind him.

As they entered the clearing where his old hogan had once stood, a faint trail of smoke still curled into the air. Only a pile of smoldering rubble remained. "So this is finished, too," he said.

Nydia touched his arm. "*This* part is finished, but that's all it means."

He felt the warmth of her touch as it reached and banished the coldness he felt within. "Let's go take a look."

They were walking around the burned-out hogan when Lucas and Gabriel joined them.

"This fire was never a threat to anything except the hogan. The brush was cleared away," Gabriel commented. "Whoever set it must have counted on our volunteer fire department not spotting anything this small. We probably wouldn't have, either, if the wind hadn't blown just right for Tree to pick up the scent. He's better than a bloodhound sometimes."

"It hasn't been smoldering long, either," Shadow commented.

"This is strange," Joshua said, crouching by a section of the hogan that had been reduced to ashes.

Gabriel joined him and followed his line of vision. "Someone took some of the ashes from here and scattered them all about. It doesn't make sense."

"Yes, it does," Joshua said. "In our tradition, ashes scattered after daylight is an insult to Sun—spilling them makes a trail for Poverty, who was avoided by the Holy People."

"So they want you to lose all your earthly possessions?" Lucas asked. "But that assumes that whoever did this knows a great deal about the *dineh*. I think it's far more likely this was done by accident. Maybe they were searching through the rubble for something of value. That makes far more sense to me."

"To me, too," Gabriel said.

Joshua walked to what remained of his father's blanket. Only bits and pieces had survived, but the ashes had been disturbed here, too. "We'll have to wait and see to be sure of his intent, but our enemy will show his hand soon."

"Yes, I think you're right about that," Nydia said slowly.

It was her tone that alerted him. He glanced back at her, studying her expression. Her slight nod told him all he needed. She'd heard the voice again.

As they gathered back at their vehicles, he could see his brothers were eager to go. Gabriel, in particular, seemed even more restless than usual. He also had taken this incident to heart.

"I won't let them get away with this, Tree," he said after Shadow drove off. "I know what this hogan meant to you, particularly now that the other is gone."

"My enemy is our enemy, true, but this isn't up to you alone to solve."

Gabriel nodded slowly. "I know that we all share the loss of our father, but it's hard to maintain the detachment I need to do my job as sheriff when things like this keep on happening."

"It seems to me that you each have a source of individual pride in your lives," Nydia said, approaching. "That's where you're most vulnerable, and that's where he's choosing to attack you. Can you see it? With Tree, it's his abilities and credibility as a *hataalii*." Somehow, for the first time, it seemed right to use the nicknames the brothers shared, as if sharing their grief made her somehow part of their family. "With you, it's your authority and duty as sheriff of Four Winds. With Shadow, it's his responsibility as this area's only medic. By forcing Shadow to keep an eye on you two, the murderer is diverting him from his duties and placing him in an awkward situation with the townspeople. This person doesn't want to just get away with his crimes. What he really wants is to destroy the Blackhorse family."

Joshua and Gabriel stared at her as the truth dawned over them slowly.

"Good insight," Gabriel said at last. "I'll keep it in mind as I continue to investigate the case. But no matter what our enemy tries to do, I can guarantee this. No one ever takes on the Blackhorse brothers and wins."

As Gabriel left, Joshua turned to look at her. "That was a valuable observation about our enemy and his motive. Your own?"

"If you're asking if it was based on that odd inner voice I've been hearing, it wasn't. It was simply a matter of piecing together what has happened. I'm taught as an anthropologist to sift through information, discard what can't be substantiated and formulate a logical theory. That's what I did."

"Your talent will be useful this morning. We have work to do. Mr. Langdon's property is at the edge of town. I know that he used dynamite to level some old buildings that were on his property. His kids were playing in them, and he was afraid that sooner or later they'd get injured. The blasting went on for a couple of weeks, on and off."

As Nydia drove, following his directions to the farm,

Joshua saw her tensing up. Her fingers were curled in a death grip around the wheel. "Are you feeling all right?"

She said nothing, then at last nodded.

"You sure?"

"I'm okay, I just—" She shook her head. "It's crazy."

"What? Are you getting one of your...intuitions?"

"Maybe. But it's different this time. There's no voice, just this feeling, as if ants were crawling over me. I can't shake it."

"Is the blanket in the vehicle?"

"Yes. It's in the back so I could avoid looking at it."

"A warning's a warning. We shouldn't ignore it."

"If the peddler's involved as I suspect, he'll allow us to depend on these warnings he has planted in my head, then eventually use them to make sure we hang ourselves."

"So we'll be skeptical, but still it's foolish to ignore the entire thing." Joshua watched Nydia carefully. She didn't want to do this because she hated admitting that she had been influenced. "You shouldn't close your mind to the other possibility, either. The *dineh*'s history is filled with magic. The Anglo world sometimes calls them miracles, but science can't explain everything away. I know you resent these warnings, seeing them as an intrusion into your being instead of an attempt to help—"

"That's exactly what they are. The peddler tricked me, and I resent the heck out of it."

"Why can't you accept any other possibility?"

She remained silent for several moments. "Beliefs that are based on coincidental incidents or even hearsay have their place. They can give courage to people when they have exhausted their own, but they're not for me."

"Yet you see how the Navajo Way strengthens me. It doesn't take anything away."

"Yes, it *is* a source of strength for you. I never disputed that. I chose a different path than yours, because it's one that I feel comfortable in.''

A heaviness of spirit settled over him. If he could just find a way to show her that the peace he'd found through the old ways could also be hers to share, if she'd only reach out for it.

"I'll tell you what. I'll take out the rug and hold it. Let's see if this creepy feeling I'm getting has anything to do with its influence. Who knows? I may just be coming down with the flu.''

"Do you honestly think that's it?'' he scoffed.

"Don't push it.'' Nydia pulled over, stepped out of the vehicle and took the rug from the rear compartment of the cab. She stared at it for several long seconds, then shook her head. "Nothing. No warnings, no intuitions. Maybe it *is* the flu,'' she said with a thin smile.

As they got under way, Joshua kept a watch on her. Suddenly he saw her eyes narrow and her face became drawn. "What's wrong?''

"Someone's going to come after us before too long. I know. I...heard it.''

"All right. We'll stay on our guard.''

"But we were going to do that anyway! This is silly. It's not exactly an apocalyptic warning of major proportions. It stands to reason that the more we investigate, the more someone will try to stop us before we get any answers.''

"True.''

"Maybe I'm just nervous about going to ask questions. It's going to stir up a hornet's nest, and you're still pretty banged up. Your body needs rest and time to heal, but the situation isn't allowing you time for that.''

Nydia was more worried about him than herself. He felt a rush of tenderness, then a flash of familiar heat. If he could have, he would have made her his here, in these woods, beneath him under the sun, as a man would have taken his woman in bygone days. He could have shown her then, in the most primitive way of all, that she had no reason to worry. He was not hurt. She was the only person who truly had the power to hurt him.

Silence stretched out between them as they traveled to Tony Langdon's property.

"Tell me something about this farmer we're about to see," she said.

"He's reclusive, living at the edge of town. He stays pretty much on his own at the ranch, except for his two little boys and his wife."

"Will he answer our questions?"

"I think so. He has no reason to be hostile to us. He doesn't know my family very well, and he has no particular allegiance to anyone."

As they started down a long driveway that led to a ramshackle farmhouse, Joshua gestured to a man near a truck parked by the barn. "There he is, fixing that corral."

Nydia pulled to a stop beside Langdon's truck, and Joshua got out. The farmer stopped hammering a wooden brace and came toward them. "What can I do for you?" he asked.

Joshua started to introduce himself, but Langdon shook his head. "I know who you are, but I've got work to do. What do you need?"

"You used explosives to clear away some old buildings several months ago. At any point, did you notice any of your detonators were missing, or any of the explosives themselves?"

"I used dynamite, blasting caps and safety fuses. If one stick or cap had been missing, I'd have known. My budget's always tight. If you want fancy explosives, then you've got to talk to the principal at the high school, and the contractor. They built that new gym right on the same spot the old one had been."

"Thanks for reminding me," Joshua said.

"I've told you what I know, so there won't be a need for you to come back, hear? I've got a family to watch out for," he said in a flat voice.

"Do you think that by helping us, you'll place your family in danger?" Nydia asked.

Langdon shrugged. "Don't know, but I don't gamble where my family is concerned."

As they drove off of Langdon's property, Joshua's fists clenched and unclenched on his lap.

"You can't blame him," Nydia said. "If he's reclusive, as you say, then the fact that he helped you at all counts for something."

"I wonder how many others are being terrorized by the gossip and lies being told about me in town," he said, his voice taut.

"I don't know, probably quite a few, but all we can do is continue to investigate." As they reached the road, she looked around. "Where to now?"

"The high school."

They'd only traveled a few miles when Nydia slowed the truck down almost imperceptibly. Joshua noticed it right away. "What's wrong?"

"Something's up on that ridge." She gestured to her right. "I saw a flash of light, nothing more, but—"

"Don't go to the high school, then. If there's trouble following us, we don't want to lead it in among the kids. We'll take another route. When you get to the crossroads, turn north. I know that stretch of land like the back of my hand. We'll have the advantage there."

"Unless whoever it is knows that area, too."

"Even then. A few miles ahead is a shrine. It is my family's place, started by Flinthawk, our ancestor. Finding himself so far away from the reservation, he placed his prayer sticks there and invoked Changing Woman's protection. Since then, it has been a place my family has gone to whenever we're in trouble.''

As they continued north, her eyes darted back to the high ground often. "I can't find any sign of anyone up there now."

"We'll leave the truck here," he said as they reached the base of a low hill. "It won't be easily seen, and we can hike up on foot. If someone is around here, we'll see his tracks."

She did as he asked, but he could feel the tension within her as keenly as he could his own. Nydia stayed right behind him, though she had to struggle to keep up as he climbed. When they reached the tree-covered summit, he turned, taking in the area, then crouched to examine something on the ground. "Someone has been here."

He followed a trail of footprints until they disappeared into the scrub oak and hard-packed earth. "I can't track him from this point, but he's going in the direction of our shrine. I'm going over there to check things out."

He wasn't sure exactly who warned whom, but Nydia stopped in midstride just as he grabbed her hand and dived to one side.

"That sounded like a pop. What was it?" Nydia asked.

He raised a finger to his lips, listening. He could feel a trickle of warmth running down his arm, just below the cuff of his T-shirt. Glancing down, he saw pieces of a hard white material embedded in his skin.

His enemy had found another way to fight. Revulsion filled him as he pulled the tiny fragments out of his arm, oblivious to the pain.

"What is that?" Nydia asked, eyebrows furrowed. "Did you pick up some splinters when we dove to the ground?" She reached for her handkerchief and gently dabbed at the shallow wound.

He jerked away. "Don't! It's bone ammunition, a skinwalker's weapon."

Chapter Twelve

Nydia's breath caught in her throat. She'd heard of skinwalker weapons, of course, but she'd never actually witnessed their use. "You can't be sure that's what it is."

"But I am. To shoot human-bone fragments into a person is to invite contamination with the *chindi*."

She exhaled softly. "And what better way to destroy a medicine man than through his own beliefs," Nydia said, finishing the thought.

"Spoken like an Anglo," he said with a tight smile. "The danger is real, I assure you."

"Do you still want to try to reach your shrine?"

"Yes. Now more than ever. There I can begin a prayer to Lightning and Snake." He reached into his medicine pouch and handed her a tiny sliver of black flint. "Flint armor, the circle of protection created by the light and sound it produced, protected the Hero Twins when they battled the monsters that preyed on the land. The *chindi* fears flint. This will protect you, too, whether you believe it or not."

He reached inside his medicine bundle for another tiny sack and placed it on the outside of his belt. Then, taking a piece of charcoal from the pouch, he drew a line from his left ear to his right, along the front of his chin. "Evil can be brought under control and bent to the will of a *hataalii*. Let me go do what I was trained for.''

She kept up at the pace he'd set, though it was often difficult for her since his strides were so much longer than hers.

''Why did you do that with the charcoal? I know it's part of a rite, but I can't remember which, or its significance.''

''The charcoal was taken from a lightning-struck tree and mixed with the fat of a certain animal. That transforms it into the essence of lightning and the bearer of all its powers. Evil fears it, so we will both be protected.''

''You know that's the greatest advantage of the Navajo Way.'' She realized a second too late that she'd spoken the thought out loud.

His expression darkened slightly. ''Explain,'' he said in a clipped tone.

She hesitated, then measuring her words carefully, continued. ''The Anglo world is filled with troubles of all kinds, but more often than not, there are no counters for their people to use as a weapon against fear. The *dineh* perform a rite and afterward they're left with a feeling of safety and well-being that's enviable. I've got to tell you, I wish I *did* believe, because I could use some of that confidence once in a while.''

''I don't understand you sometimes. It's as if in your heart you're a traditionalist, yet you're still desperately trying to wear the trappings of the Anglo world you've adopted.''

''That's not true. I'm a product of the new more than I am of the old. I would never put my faith in anything that I don't fully understand.''

''Like love?'' he asked softly.

His question took her by surprise, and for several seconds she didn't answer. Finally, she nodded. ''Yes, even love. I hadn't thought about it in that way until now, but it's true enough.''

"Your beliefs imprison you far more than you realize. Even the most ardent traditionalist has freedoms you won't allow yourself.''

Nydia felt the rift between them widen a little more. Sorrow filled the emptiness within her.

Suddenly, he stopped and pointed ahead. "There. The shrine is just beyond that stand of pines." He led the way forward and, as they drew near, he slowed down. "Even here, he challenges me.''

Nydia watched him crouch down by ashes that had been piled before a three-foot cairn of rocks topped with a turquoise bead. "These ashes came from the hogan, and the piece of cloth trapped in it came from the medicine bundle I gave my father a long time ago. I recognize the material.''

Rage filled him. "He desecrates what I value, and insults me at every turn. Yet I'm expected to control my emotions, to be in harmony.''

"You don't have a choice." She wanted to touch him, to soothe away his hurts, but nothing but the truth could do that now.

Joshua said nothing for a long time as he stared at the remnants of the medicine bundle. "He won't win. Black flint and Lightning will give me strength and protect me. Through them, *I* will win." He stood up and faced her squarely. "But to you, it's nonsense, all a false trust?''

"I don't share your beliefs, but I do have one belief that is stronger than even your own." She held his gaze. "I believe in *you,* and nothing can shake the power of that.''

Her words sparked a flash of vulnerability in the eyes of the man who stood before her, and she saw that the power to comfort his wounded spirit was in her hands.

"I am with you in this," she said softly. "Whatever happens, we are a team.''

"That we are." He brushed her face with his palm. "Maybe we were always meant to be, and we're just too stubborn to see it."

As the cry of a coyote rose in the air, he glanced around. "We have to go. But before we head back to find my eldest brother, I need to make one more stop and confirm something."

IT WAS MIDAFTERNOON by the time they reached the cemetery outside town. "This is where you wanted to go?" she asked, surprised. "Why?"

"It's not the type of place I'd normally go near, but we have our protection and I need to know how far my enemy is willing to go. If one of these graves has been disturbed, then we know that he used human bones to make bone ammunition. We'll also know just how motivated he is if he's willing to risk desecrating a site just about everyone around here considers sacred."

As they entered the graveyard, a burning sensation filled Nydia's mind. Disturbed by her own reaction and blaming it on superstition, she tried to brush it aside.

She glanced at Joshua, figuring that because of his beliefs, it had to be even worse for him. Yet, instead of fear or hesitancy, he walked around confidently, bolstered by the rituals and the power of the magic that was at the root of his beliefs.

As they approached the low wall that bordered the back of the graveyard, she spotted a mound of freshly dug earth next to a large spruce. Her breath caught in her throat as she drew close and saw the unearthed coffin next to it. Its simple lid had been pried open to reveal the skeletal remains inside.

She tore her gaze from the coffin, swallowing back her disgust, and saw the large footprints that had been left in the soft earth.

Joshua approached and stood beside her. "If someone else had found this, the story would have spread, and soon people would have been even more convinced that I'd become a skinwalker."

"We'll go find the sheriff and bring him here. He's got to be told about this as soon as possible."

As Nydia drove back to town, she was afraid, more so than she'd ever been. Whoever was behind this was working hard to create the kind of panic that led to lynch mobs. If enough incidents kept happening, sooner or later the people of Four Winds would take matters into their own hands.

As they parked behind the sheriff's office, she kept an eye out for anyone approaching, but the side street remained deserted. "Let's get inside quickly."

They were reaching for the back door when Gabriel opened it, meeting them halfway. "What's happened?" he asked, looking from one to the other, and ushering them inside.

Joshua explained quickly. "We thought you should know right away."

"I'll get over there and make sure that the coffin is interred again. Walt Meyers takes care of that cemetery for the county and he lives in the caretaker's cottage out there. Did you talk to him?"

Joshua shook his head. "No, I wasn't sure who I could trust."

"I'll talk to Walt, and make sure he keeps his mouth shut. If this gets around town, then I'm going to have a panic here, and that's the last thing I need."

"Whoever's behind this knows quite a bit about our people," Nydia mused. "Who *are* the experts here?"

Gabriel shook his head. "Jake, the librarian, has access to any books he wishes, both through our own collections and through interlibrary loans statewide. He'd also know who in town has requested books on the subject. But other than that, I don't think there's anyone I've heard about or spoken to." Gabriel looked at his brother's arm. "Do you want Shadow to take a look at that?"

Joshua shook his head. "It's not necessary. I've done what needs to be done."

Suddenly, the front door of the sheriff's office flew open. Gabriel brought his hand down to the butt of his pistol, but then relaxed when he saw the newcomer was Ralph.

Gabriel gave him a steely glare. "Don't ever come in here like that again, not unless you want to find yourself staring at the business end of my handgun. Things are kind of tense around town, in case you haven't noticed."

"Tense? That doesn't even begin to describe it! I just got a real interesting but anonymous phone call. Before I run this story, though, I want to talk to you. I was just told that Joshua was seen robbing a grave for skinwalker weapons."

Nydia felt her stomach sink. As she saw the look on Gabriel's face, she realized that he, too, hadn't expected someone to use the news against them quite so soon.

"I was told to check out the graveyard," Ralph added.

"That's because this anonymous person wants you to see the footprints that he left there to implicate me," Joshua said. "You've known me for a long time. You know that I'm not a liar. Trust me now when I tell you that if you print that story, you're playing right into his hands."

"Can you make any guess on the caller's identity?" Gabriel pressed.

"No, except that it was a male voice. He was talking through something, maybe a handkerchief. I could barely make out his words," Ralph answered, then looked at Joshua. "If you're being systematically framed, then you *must* have an idea of who's behind it. Nobody makes an enemy like this without being aware of it, my friend."

"I honestly don't know who it is. If I did, I'd be at their doorstep right now."

Ralph rubbed his chin pensively, then glanced up at the sheriff. "What do you want me to do? If I hold on to this story and word gets out anyway, it's going to be even worse. They'll just say I was in cahoots with you."

"If you print it, considering the mood in this town, it's going to lead to more violence," Gabriel answered.

"I know, but if I print it, I may be able to downplay it."

"I would ask one favor of you," Joshua said. "Don't print it yet, but if word gets out, then go after the whole story. Print the discrepancies in the footprints, as well as the impossibility of my shooting myself in the upper arm like this." He raised the sleeve of his T-shirt. "I was attacked with bone ammunition, a skinwalker's weapon."

"They'll just say that Mrs. Jim did it for you." Ralph shrugged. "But I'll go along with it, if that's what you really want. For the record, though, I think this is going to blow up in all our faces."

"We'll have to risk it. We need to buy ourselves some time," Gabriel said.

As Ralph left, Gabriel turned to Joshua. "I have to go over to the cemetery to record the evidence and make sure that coffin is reinterred before people start going over there on their own to check out the rumors."

"If you need backup for crowd control," Nydia asked, "could you get it?"

"Yes, but I'm not sure how fast," he said. "That's the biggest—"

The front door suddenly crashed open, and Gabriel spun around. "Damn it, Ralph, I told you not to do that!"

"I was halfway down the street when I heard Mrs. Wilson, Darren's wife, talking to Rosa. The story's already out. Apparently, the caller made several calls, not just to me."

Gabriel walked to the front window and, standing to one

side, looked outside. "They're starting to gather in small groups. I don't like this. This is how mobs get started." He turned to Joshua. "Get out of town now. Use the back roads. I'll make sure you're not followed. Then stay put up at the cabin until I come."

Joshua nodded once. "But don't wait too long."

"I'll be there no later than daybreak."

As Nydia looked from Joshua to Gabriel, she heard the inner voice speaking to her.

The loyalty and love that binds the brothers will become their greatest strength...and the tool used to bring about their downfall.

AS NIGHTFALL ENCOMPASSED the cabin, Joshua stood guard outside beside a small campfire he'd concealed among some boulders. The warning given by the rug, which Nydia had told him about, preyed on his thoughts. Harmony required balance, and eventually he would have to do something to repay the spirit of the weaver for the guidance they'd received. Of course, it was entirely possible that the rug would become just another instrument working against them. The peddler's gifts always had many facets.

Lost in thought, he stared at the cabin from hiding, watching the light that still glowed from within. So, Nydia couldn't sleep, either. There was danger in the darkness surrounding them, and he had a hunch she sensed that, too.

As she turned down the lights, he glimpsed her outline near the window. He could tell from her movements that she was undressing, and longed to be able to see her more clearly. She was beauty, light and passion, but as out of his reach as the moon. A savage pain tore at his heart. It seemed that ever since he'd met her, he'd regretted the path he'd chosen, because it was one that would keep him from sharing his life with the woman he had grown to love.

His thoughts churned like clouds filled with the fury of

an impending storm. Then, from the edges of his consciousness, he heard a sound that brought his thoughts crashing back to the duty at hand.

Immediately, his senses sharpened, attuned to the woods. Becoming one with the night, he slipped into the shadows and peered into the veil of darkness surrounding him. Just ahead, he could make out three figures darting toward Nydia's truck.

He let out an undulating, soft whistle, like the cry of a night bird, the arranged signal in case of danger. It rose high in the night, a burst of sound that spiraled upward with tension and purpose.

There wasn't much time, but she would know what to do. They wouldn't catch her unawares inside the cabin, but now he had work to do.

Reaching into his medicine bundle and throwing some powders into the fire, he began to chant. A faint echo within the notes of the chant spoke of fear, but as his song rose, power and the essence of deliverance filled the night air.

Smoke rose from the campfire, thick and choking, but he never skipped a note. Soon everything was engulfed in a foggy grayness that swallowed even the tiniest slivers of moonlight.

NYDIA HEARD THE SONG through the dense cloud of smoke that obscured everything near the cabin as she crawled out the side window. She wasn't sure why she wasn't coughing and choking in the thick air, but she was having no problems. She could hear men's voices close by. The fear and confusion in their shouts comforted her. They would not win, not this round at least.

As she listened to Joshua's song, she felt the intensity of it surrounding her, going through her, touching her more intimately than even his touch ever could. The richness of it imparted a sense of peace that brushed her fears away.

Nydia moved uphill noiselessly, with a confidence she hadn't believed possible. She knew from the shouts of the men behind her that their inability to see clearly, and the deep timbre of the song that came from everywhere and yet nowhere, was frightening them, heightening their confusion. It was the sound of something implacable that could not be stopped. To her, that meant safety—to them, danger.

Reaching the forest, Nydia crouched behind a pine, listening. The voices of the intruders carried easily.

"It's that Navajo woman," one said. "She's to blame. She confuses the sheriff with her way of twisting things around. He wants to believe that his brother is innocent, and she's playing to that.

"Joshua Blackhorse is a murderer, but this woman is as much an enemy of Four Winds as he is. As far as I'm concerned, they should share a common fate."

"First we have to catch that slippery snake."

"Well, we left a clear message for her tonight. Turning her back on Joshua Blackhorse is her only hope."

As they moved off, their voices faded into whispers, then nothing.

Nydia heard vehicles in the distance, and then silence covered everything. Not even the rich cadence of Joshua's chant penetrated the quiet that fell around her.

For a moment, the total silence jarred her, filling her with a renewed sense of fear. Finally, the smoke began to dissipate. Hearing a sound behind her, she turned her head quickly and saw Joshua. He appeared through the pines, moonlight glittering just over his shoulders. His shirt hung open, revealing his powerful chest and muscles that rippled as her gaze caressed him. His eyes darkened as if in response, and she felt the all too familiar sizzle in her blood.

"We're safe now." He offered her his hand and helped her to her feet.

"So they've failed, thanks to you."

"Failed?" He shook his head. "No, I wouldn't say that. They've found the way to our sanctuary at last. Let's go see what other harm they've done."

As they drew closer to the cabin, Nydia remembered the words she'd overheard and recounted them. "So now I'm public enemy number one to them, along with you."

"If I could have spared you that, I would have."

As they stepped through the bramble that surrounded the east side of the cabin, she caught a glimpse of her truck. Her breath caught in her throat. The tires and seats were slashed, and the windshield shattered, but it was the spray-painted message on the hood that made her blood turn to ice. It read Go Home Or Die.

Chapter Thirteen

Nydia reached into her truck quickly, pulled down the sun shade on the driver's side and breathed a sigh of relief when she saw that her son's photo was still there, undamaged. The less her enemies knew about her, the better.

She pulled the photo loose and placed it carefully into her shirt pocket. At least John was too far away to be affected by any of this.

She then reached behind the driver's seat and pulled out the rug. It also had survived undamaged. She held it against her as she stared aghast at her truck.

Standing behind her, Joshua wrapped his arms around her and pulled her against him. "They want you to fear them. Don't give in. Nothing will happen that will leave your son without his mother," he whispered, his breath warm against her cheek. "I would lay my life down for yours before I saw any harm come to you."

Nydia shuddered and moved away. "I don't want anything to happen to you, either. You're needed by so many people!"

"And you? Do *you* need *me?*" he asked, his voice a throaty whisper.

She shook free of the warmth his voice evoked. "What I want...what I need, makes little difference. I've got too many responsibilities." Too restless to remain still, Nydia began pacing.

"There's a place I love near here, a place of peace. Leave the rug inside my truck for now and let me take you there. I've used it often when I need to gather my thoughts."

He led her some distance down the canyon, then through a narrow pass, concealing their tracks as they went. At last, they emerged in a meadow filled with bright yellow sunflowers that swayed and danced in the moonlight.

"It's beautiful," she said. "It's like a hidden garden."

"Yes. Here, worries seem to drift away as easily as the breeze that stirs the flowers."

Nydia shook her head, then smiled sadly. "Not my worries. Those never go away. You don't understand what it's like to be a single parent. I'm always wondering if I'm doing things right, if I'm good enough at the most important job a person can ever have. There are times when I'm really afraid that, ultimately, I'm going to fail John just as much as his father failed me. What I want most for my son is for him to grow up knowing love and security, but I'm afraid I'm just not doing enough."

Joshua gathered her against his wide chest. "It's your fears that trap you. Release them and you'll see that your love encircles your son and protects him even now. No matter where you are, he is a part of you." He brushed a stray tear away from her cheek with his lips. "As I want to be," he added in a raw voice.

His warm breath bathed her face, touching her senses as his mouth covered hers. He was like liquid fire melting through her skin, surging along her nerves, laying siege to her heart.

She felt reckless and wanton, and one thing she knew was she would not stop this time. She would seize the moment and take the happiness life was offering her.

A groan was torn from his lips as she slid her tongue back and forth over his, inciting him, urging him to step past the threshold of control that kept him in check. "We'll let it happen between us," she whispered in his ear. "No promises, no more fear, only love and the comfort we can give each other."

"I've waited to hear you say that for so long!" He pulled her body into the cradle of his thighs.

The air hummed and shivered, and light danced in her head as each piece of their clothing was discarded, falling to the ground by their feet. He whispered sweet words to her that spoke of tempting fires yet to be savored and left her breathless and trembling in his arms. With a husky murmur of satisfaction, he lifted her easily and guided her legs around him, letting her feel him against her center, but careful not to enter her yet.

"We'll go slow, my *sawe*. Let it be all that you ever dreamed."

"And what of your dreams?"

"Mine will all become real when I'm inside you, feeling your heat surround me."

She tasted his skin, letting her lips slide down his neck, nipping at his flesh. The shudder that tore through him left her feeling giddy with the knowledge that she could give him such pleasure.

As she slid her tongue across his heated skin, he groaned, then lowered her gently to the ground. He lay beside her, savoring the feel and the taste of her skin, building the fever within her.

"Please, my love," she moaned, her fingers digging into his back.

He swept her knees upward and, parting her thighs, sank into her body with extraordinary slowness. He rocked her gently in tune with the restless pulsings of the night. Together, they overwhelmed the outer world with a passion so strong and powerful nothing could withstand it, and in a moment of exquisite surrender they found that place where dreams are made real.

For an eternity, guarded under the canopy of stars, neither moved. When at last she stirred, Joshua moved away reluctantly. "I'm sorry. I know I'm heavy."

"It's all right. I liked feeling your body on mine," she murmured.

He cradled her against him. "I've never truly surrendered. I've always wanted to remain in control, to avoid that fall. But tonight, at my greatest moment of weakness, I found my strength with you."

She nuzzled against him. "Let's sleep here tonight. We're hidden in this beautiful place, protected by the canyon. The stars and the moon will keep watch over us."

Feeling his powerful arms around her, she found peace.

NYDIA CAME AWAKE in his arms as the first rays of sunlight bathed the meadow in a soft golden glow. Moving away carefully, so as to not wake him, she stood, stretched, then looked at the sleeping man on the ground before her. He lay naked, their discarded clothing turned into a makeshift blanket that covered very little. He was magnificent, and as untamed and natural as the desert of the *dineh*.

"Didn't anyone teach you it's impolite to stare?"

She gasped. His eyes were still closed, so how could he have known she was staring? "What makes you think I'm looking at you?"

"I felt it. I don't need to rely on physical vision to feel your closeness to me," he answered, then smiled and opened his eyes.

She felt his gaze searing over her and, with effort, turned away, gathering her clothing. She felt sadness sweep over her with the knowledge that their time had passed. What they'd shared would be a memory to treasure forever, but it was time to let go of what she'd known could only be theirs for a brief moment in time. There were other matters now that demanded their attention, lives that hung in the balance.

He stood and dressed, and before she'd even finished buttoning her shirt, was ready to go. She glanced at him, surprised. "Are you always this adept in the morning?"

He smiled slowly. "You'll have to find out for yourself sometime."

She felt the blood rush to her face, and a pleasant warmth enfolded her as gently as an embrace. "We have a lot to do today," she reminded him quietly. "Where do you propose we start?"

"My brother needs to be told about this latest incident—"

"I'm here," a familiar voice interrupted him. Gabriel stepped around the cluster of boulders that protected the mouth of the pass. "After seeing what happened to the truck, and signs of what you two went through last night, I came directly here. I figured this was where you'd go."

Nydia straightened her clothing quickly. "Someone is inciting the townspeople. This was an act of anger and hatred, the kind that doesn't usually develop without someone's prodding."

"I know," Gabriel conceded. "One thing's clear, though. We have to find a new hideaway for you."

"Do you have any ideas?" Joshua asked.

"Not yet, but I'll think of something," Gabriel said. "By the way, I spoke to Ralph late last night. He knows that someone's trying to undermine his influence with the townspeople, and he's angry at this anonymous caller for phoning his tips not only to the paper, but to other places, as well."

"I'm going to go talk to Ralph," Joshua said. "If he's angry enough, he may tell me more than he would otherwise. I have a feeling that by now he's got an idea who the caller is."

"If you go into town, you'll be making yourself a prime target," Gabriel warned.

"I'll be okay. Haven't you noticed the common denominator? Nobody wants to face me head-on. They sneak-attack and hide in the shadows. Being in town during the day may be the safest place for me."

"You may have a point," Gabriel conceded.

As they headed back toward town in his truck, silence descended between Nydia and Joshua. Without the need for words, Nydia understood his mood. They had discovered the kind of love most people never experienced in their entire lives, but despite the yearnings of their hearts, it wasn't theirs to keep. Their lives would tear them in opposite directions. Her heart had been made vulnerable by love, and now sorrow wounded her deeply.

She glanced at the blanket that lay in the rear bench. It gave her no warnings now. Only silence echoed within the walls of her hollow heart.

As they entered Four Winds, Nydia saw the townspeople starting to open up their businesses. Storekeepers hurried about, getting started on the day, and a school bus stopped to pick up students waiting by the curb.

Joshua drove to the rear of the newspaper office, parked, then walked inside with Nydia. "You look like you're ready to do battle," he cautioned. "Ease up. Ralph's not our enemy."

As a cool breeze blew against them, she reined in her temper. "You're right, but I'm through accepting evasions. If he knows something, I'm going to make sure we get it out of him."

JOSHUA WATCHED NYDIA as she spoke to Ralph. Her anger was in check, but it was clear that Ralph resented her tone of authority. She looked young and soft, and so very beautiful, but her dark eyes were direct, cutting through vague thoughts and rumors, throwing the inconsequential out of the way and systematically taking note of the valuable pieces of information she garnered. This was what she excelled at, and she knew it.

"Whoever is working against us is working against you, as well. You must have some idea who is behind the calls," she insisted.

"I don't have enough information to point a finger yet." Ralph shrugged.

"We're not asking as law-enforcement people," she pressed. "We simply need a place to start looking. Work with us, please."

Ralph started to answer when Alex, his assistant, came into the office. Seeing Joshua and Nydia there, he stopped in midstride, his gaze filled with suspicion. "What's going on?" he asked, looking over at Ralph.

"Apparently, some of our townspeople paid them a visit last night. Care to make any guesses who?" Ralph suggested.

Alex met Joshua's gaze with a level one of his own. "The possibilities are endless. Almost everyone in this town is willing to take action against you."

"Including you?" Nydia challenged.

Joshua noted the way she watched Alex, as if trying to make a decision about him. She was studying him openly, and wanted him to know it.

"I'm not a violent person. I have other tools I prefer to use against people who think they can get away with murder."

"Like inciting a crowd through rhetoric?" she pressed.

"I'm a writer, lady, not an orator," he snapped back, then glanced at Ralph. "I could do a lot with that skill for this town if I were given the chance."

Ralph shrugged. "You're not ready for that responsibility, not at this newspaper. You haven't quite learned that it's our job to report the news, not make it."

Alex glared at Ralph, then without as much as a glance toward Nydia and Joshua, walked back out.

Ralph shook his head. "No, despite what you may be thinking, he's not the one behind the local uproar. He's not very charismatic. He couldn't sway people to do the kind of things that have taken place lately."

"Unless they *wanted* to believe him," Nydia countered.

"You may have a point." Ralph stood, indicating that he wanted their meeting to be over. "I'm going to keep looking into this, believe me. When I know something more, I'll let you in on it. But until then, you'll just have to trust me."

As they walked out into the street, Nydia glanced down toward the sheriff's office. "Before we talk to anyone else, would you mind if we made a stop? I'd like to call my son and find out how things are back home."

"No problem. We'll go see Fuzz, and you can use the phone there in private." As they got into the truck, he added, "By the way, I noticed the strange expression you had on your face when you were talking to Alex. What's going on?"

She took a deep breath, then let it out again. "I don't know. Something's bugging me about that guy, but I can't quite put my finger on what it is. I need time to mull it over."

As they drove to the sheriff's office, Joshua was aware of the curious glances the townspeople gave him. He wasn't hated by all, not yet, but curiosity and suspicion, not affection, were in most of the faces. Sorrow filled him as he longed for the days when they would have just smiled and waved.

As he pulled up behind his brother's office, Nydia suddenly sat up. "I know what's bothering me. It's Alex's voice. I think he was one of the men I overheard last night."

Chapter Fourteen

Joshua waited until Nydia was in the next office using the phone. "What are the chances of my leaving town long enough to go help her family?"

Gabriel shook his head. "Forget it. You'd likely be arrested before you got to the county line. I'm having to report your whereabouts daily to the state police as per our illustrious mayor's instructions. Which brings me to another point. You may want to make yourself invisible soon. Mayor Burns is coming by this morning."

"Does he know what happened at the cabin?"

"Yeah. I'll bet he also knows what happened at the graveyard, too. My guess is he's going to ask me to put you in jail this time. That way, he'll take care of two problems at once. The townspeople will be happy, and you'll be safe from vigilante justice that would reflect badly on him."

"What are you going to do about it?"

"Play my trump card. I'll point out that we can't convict anyone on circumstantial evidence. And if he forces me to make a formal arrest now, the case will get thrown out of court. Then it'll look like he either pushed for the arrest of the wrong man, or that the right man got off because he was premature in his actions."

Joshua nodded, a faint smile on his lips. "Good one, big brother."

"Yeah, I thought so, too," he said, sitting back down. "So tell me what brought you here, besides borrowing my phone. You've got something on your mind, so spill it."

He told Gabriel about Nydia's suspicions that the voice she'd heard belonged to Alex.

"That's one lead I intend to follow up on right away." Hearing a knock, he glanced at the door and saw Jake Fields come inside.

"I thought you might like to know that there was a meeting at the feed store today," Jake said. "Most of the townspeople were there, including the mayor."

"I wasn't told about this."

"I know. I would have come to get you, but I didn't want to miss any part of it."

"Tell me what happened," Gabriel said.

"People got to sound off, mostly. Alex repeatedly called for action on the mayor's part, insisting Joshua get thrown in jail," Jake said. "But I think what he's really doing is taking a popular stand so others will follow his lead. He wants to be the voice of this town, to take Ralph's place in people's eyes. But that will never happen. He just doesn't command respect around here."

"Was Ralph there?" Joshua asked.

"Yes, but he arrived late."

When Nydia came out of the back office, her face was drawn and her shoulders slumped from exhaustion. As she faced the men, she suddenly straightened, her face becoming cold, her eyes intense. By now Joshua knew her well enough to realize that when she took such care to hide her feelings, it was because she'd been pressed to the limit. Her emotions were too raw to be openly revealed.

"Did anyone take my brother's side?" Gabriel asked.

"Believe it or not, Mayor Burns did. He fought like

crazy to calm people down and make them listen to reason. He reminded them that he has the authority to put the town under martial law if they go after one of its citizens, and that he will not tolerate mob rule.''

"He's on our side in public, yet he pressures my brother to take action against me," Joshua said. "That doesn't make sense."

"He's *not* on your side in public," Jake corrected. "Don't misunderstand me. He's only calling for right action in order to cover his tail."

"Well, at least he's not inciting people any further," Gabriel said.

"I think we have to concentrate on finding whoever is knowledgeable about Navajo beliefs, especially about skinwalkers," Nydia said. "Let's face it. Few of the *dineh* would ever tell an outsider about our skinwalkers, much less their methods and habits. If we stay on that track and don't allow ourselves to get diverted, we'll find the killer."

"As a librarian, I could get detailed information if I wanted to, so I guess that puts me high on the list of suspects," Jake said.

"Maybe, but it also places anyone with a library card right there next to you," Joshua added. His gaze returned to Nydia. He was worried about her, but he'd have to wait to ask her about the phone call later when they were alone.

Jake smiled. "Not *every* library in the region has the kind of books that would give detailed information about your tribe," Jake ventured slowly.

"Who does?" Gabriel asked.

"I don't know offhand. I'd have to check."

"We're also going to need the names of people who have accessed those special collections. They have to sign to get into those rooms, right?" Nydia asked. "Most of the libraries I've seen that have special-collections rooms keep them locked. You can't just walk in there."

"That's true," Jake conceded.

As Gabriel was about to speak, there was a knock at the door, and a moment later, the mayor stepped inside.

His gaze drifted over Joshua casually, his face polite and empty. It was the expression of a man with nothing to hide, but nothing to show, either.

"Sheriff, we need to talk," Mayor Burns said.

"Since this undoubtedly concerns my brother, I think you should feel free to talk in front of him. The accused has the right to hear from his accusers."

Mayor Burns glanced at Jake and Nydia, then back at Gabriel. "I'll accept your brother's presence, but this isn't a town meeting."

Jake stood, as did Nydia. "We'll follow up on that matter we were just discussing," Jake told Gabriel. "We'll be at the library."

Joshua watched the two of them leave. There had been no time to ask Nydia about her family. He'd promised her that if things became critical, he would leave Four Winds and fulfill his duties as a *hataalii*. He'd meant it, and even if it meant sealing his own fate, he intended to keep that promise.

"We have a problem," Burns said, sitting down. "The state police assure me it will be another week before their detective can come and take over this investigation. The way things are shaping up here, that may be too long."

"I heard there was a meeting this morning. Why wasn't I told about it?" Gabriel demanded.

"That wasn't my call. I only found out about it ten minutes before it started. Darren Wilson came over to my house and got me. But I've got to tell you, the mood in this town is getting uglier by the hour." He looked at Joshua. "I strongly suggest that you stay in jail, if not for your own sake, for that of this town. More violence will erupt unless you do."

"I can't do that. I'm not guilty. It's my right to try and find the person who's behind all this."

"To what end? If you find that person, if they do indeed exist, what will you do to them?"

"You mistake my intent, Mayor," Joshua said coldly. "I want to catch the killer and bring him to justice. My task doesn't include dispensing that justice."

The mayor held Joshua's gaze. "You realize that there's a good chance that you'll only make things worse by meddling. If you're out there, going from place to place publicly, sooner or later someone's going to go after you and succeed."

"This is a fight that needs to be fought."

"You're a holy man, a medicine man—how can you talk like this?"

"I'm *not* a holy man. A singer is only a man who possesses certain ritualistic knowledge. We are not priests or Christian ministers."

"Then all that stuff about harmony is just a slogan."

"Not at all. To fight for what is right and just is one way to restore harmony."

"How noble," Burns argued. "But in the meantime, this town's being torn apart, and everyone's answer is the same. They want justice—their way."

"You choose to manipulate and distort my words. Nothing I say will change your mind if it's already closed."

The mayor stood up so abruptly, the chair he was using nearly fell over. "I stuck my neck out for you, but now I'm beginning to wonder if I did the right thing. Maybe the townspeople are right about you. You're the one who's twisting words, but then again maybe trickery like that is the way of the singers."

As he stormed out, Joshua looked at his brother, slowly shaking his head. "I did *not* provoke that reaction. He doesn't know a thing about our tribe and our ways, yet he wants to dictate what I should do.''

Gabriel nodded slowly. "The problem is that you're tampering with the mayor's image of himself and this town. His position here in Four Winds means more to him than most people realize. Being mayor defines him—it makes Burns feel that he still has a function that's important. He needs that, particularly since the death of his son. For a long time, he couldn't come to terms with what happened, but recently, he's started to get his life back in order. Being mayor has helped him do that.''

"To be honest, I'm surprised Burns didn't leave town after his son's death,'' Joshua said. "I would have thought there'd be too many memories here for him.''

"Leave here and go where? And toward what? Here he has identity and purpose and, more important, he's close to his son's grave.''

Joshua nodded. "I'd forgotten that, unlike the *dineh*, being close to a grave gives Anglos comfort.''

Hearing the door open, Gabriel shifted, his hand drawing closer to his weapon automatically. A moment later, seeing Jake and Nydia enter the room, Gabriel relaxed.

Jake sat down, a smug look on his face. "We made progress. Nydia is quite resourceful, you know.''

"I just came up with a way to cut down our margin of error,'' Nydia explained.

"She had me find photos of almost everyone in town,'' Jake said. "You'd be surprised how many there are available if you look. We picked out shots of people like Darren Wilson, Alex, Ralph and even Rosa and me. Then we faxed them to the regional libraries that have special collections.''

"Did anyone get recognized?'' Gabriel asked with uncharacteristic impatience.

"Well, everyone knew me. I do research all the time, since I write articles for our trade journals. By keeping our town in the spotlight, so to speak, I've managed to get some grants.''

"Who else?" Gabriel asked.

"Well, two of the librarians thought they recognized Mayor Burns, but when they checked their sign-in sheets, they didn't find his name there. I did press them, but they just couldn't be sure if it really was the same person or not.''

"What reason did you give them for wanting to know?'' Joshua asked.

"Only that I needed to find out which of our residents made it a practice to utilize other library's resources, since I was planning to ask for a budget increase. I don't think they really bought it, but they didn't dispute it, either.'' He glanced at his watch. "I have to get going. I have an English class coming in today to do research for their term papers. If there's anything else I can do to help you all, just let me know.''

As soon as he'd left, Nydia looked at Joshua, then at Gabriel. "Of course, the really interesting thing is that Jake was always recognized.''

"He told you why," Joshua said.

"Yes, he had a good enough reason," Nydia replied, glancing at Gabriel. "But that doesn't necessarily mean it was his *only* reason.''

Gabriel leaned back in his chair, pushing it back until it rested on two legs. His gaze never left Nydia's face. "You don't trust him. Why?''

"He may not have an easily identifiable motive, but he has more opportunity than almost anyone else in town.''

"She doesn't know him like you and I do," Joshua told his brother.

"And perhaps that's why I see him more clearly.''

"Or why you've misjudged him," Joshua countered.

"I tend to agree with Tree, but I do see your point, too,''

Gabriel told Nydia. "I'll tell you what. I'll do a thorough background check on Jake. Maybe there's something that our familiarity with him has caused us to miss."

"I think that would be an excellent idea."

Joshua led Nydia to the door. "It's time for us to go. I need to go pay Mr. Mora a visit."

"The high-school principal? Why?" Gabriel asked.

"Remember the old gym? They had to blast it to bits before it finally came down."

"Yeah, I remember. Let me know what you find out, if anything. In the meantime, I'll continue looking for a new safe house for you."

The moment Nydia and Joshua stepped outside, they were both instantly aware of the furtive glances aimed in their direction. "Sometimes I wonder if they'll ever see me the same way again," he said.

The pain in his words was so intense, it wrapped itself around her until she could barely speak. "They will, but not until they know for certain that you're not the killer," she answered.

As her gaze fell upon him, a part of her yearned in vain for a time when he'd willingly leave Four Winds and come make a home with her on the rez. It was impossible, of course, nothing more than a wish upon a star. Yet the biggest surprise was that within her was the soul of a woman who was still capable of dreams.

"Do you really believe that their attitude toward me will go back to what it was after the truth comes out?"

"Yes," Nydia replied. "In fact, I think they will try very hard to make it up to you. Of course, whether you accept them again after all is said and done is another matter."

He smiled ruefully. "You don't think I'll be able to put things behind me?"

Nydia considered the question as they got under way. "You won't forget their distrust, I know that, no more than

I would imagine Flinthawk ever did. But it's possible you may be able to find a way to forgive."

THEY ARRIVED at the high school at lunchtime, parked and walked across the grassy expanse that bordered the school. As soon as some of the kids outside spotted them, Joshua felt the ripple of unease that went through the crowd. Yet the emotion he saw in their faces wasn't censure, as it had been in the town; it was curiosity.

"I hope they don't plan on pelting us with rotten produce this time, too," Nydia said softly.

"No, I don't think so. There's a different mood here today. Can't you feel it?"

Nydia said nothing for several moments, then nodded. "They're watching us, but there's nothing written on their faces except maybe speculation."

"They've heard what their parents are saying, but now they want to make up their own minds. It is often that way with the young." He watched them talking among themselves. Though he couldn't hear them, he suspected from their furtive glances that it wasn't him they were interested in as much as Nydia.

"They're going to approach me first," Nydia said, echoing his thoughts. "I think they're still scared of you, at least enough to be cautious."

"Yes, that's my impression, too." He'd hoped that it would be different here. The last thing he wanted was to be a source of fear to young people. He'd never done anything to merit that.

"Let them approach me, then. I'll see what I can learn from them while you speak to the principal."

Joshua agreed with a quick nod. Like their parents, the kids were bound by their instinctive distrust of whatever went beyond their understanding. It was strange how, on one level at least, nothing ever changed. He was walking the same path Flinthawk had trod, though more than one hundred years separated him from his ancestor. As it had been then, whatever was different was more often than not viewed as evil, until understanding bridged the gap between fear and reason.

the Sanchez down-draws had been beaten, there was something a pocket in the corner somewhere they could not—They looked at each other now, not understanding anymore...

Chapter Fifteen

Nydia felt a moment of apprehension as Joshua continued toward the building, leaving her alone to face the seven or eight approaching teenagers. She didn't read hostility in their expressions, but there was a certain reserve on their faces that meant things could go either way. She sat down on one of the benches and waited, ready to play it out.

One girl led the group. She had bright red hair, a rarity in these parts. "I'm Annie O'Malley," she said with a hesitant smile. "We know who you are. Do you mind if we ask you some questions?"

"No, not at all. What's on your mind?"

"Well, for starters, what are you doing here at school? With all the gossip in town, we figured you'd be off looking for another medicine man, instead of still hanging around with Joshua Blackhorse."

"He's the only one who has the chant knowledge my relative needs," Nydia answered. "But you know, I'd hoped kids your age would remain more open-minded. Too many people are judging him before all the facts are in. There's no hard evidence against him. And consider this—he's stuck it out in Four Winds, fighting to clear his name, instead of running off."

Annie nodded. "Yes, I've thought of that myself."

"If all of you are really interested in learning the truth,

not just wanting to point a finger at someone, why don't you help me by answering a few questions," Nydia added.

"What do you want to know?" the dark-haired boy with Annie asked, his eyes narrowed with suspicion.

"There was some blasting done here at this school a few years back, when they built the new gym. Do any of you remember it?"

"I wasn't here then, and just heard about it," Annie said, then glanced at the girl who stood just behind her. "Ellen, your sister was here then. Can you help?"

Ellen was a short, dark-haired girl with eyes as gray green as sagebrush. Her face was alive with intelligence.

"What exactly do you want to know?" Ellen asked.

"Was there a lot of curiosity about the construction crew's equipment or supplies while the blasting was going on?"

Ellen smiled. "You mean did anyone think about ripping off any of the explosives?"

Nydia smiled back. "Yeah."

Ellen looked pleased. "I remember a conversation my sister had on the phone back then. She didn't know I was standing in the hall, listening. I remember her saying that some seniors had broken into the contractor's trailer and found something to help start out New Year's with a real blast. That was just before winter break. I kept my ears open to hear what exactly they had in mind, but I never heard about it if anything ever happened."

"Did you ever find out who had taken the explosives, or ask your sister about it?"

"I did ask her, on New Year's Day, but she got really angry with me and we ended up arguing about her right to privacy, and junk like that."

As Joshua approached, the group said goodbye, then drifted back toward the main building, giving him curious glances but a wide berth. "I think you must have made progress," Joshua said as he reached Nydia. "They're still guarded, but their eyes are now filled with more questions than judgments."

"Maybe they'll carry some of that open-mindedness back to their parents," Nydia said, then filled him in as they returned to the truck. "What about you, how did you fare?"

"I only got to speak to the principal briefly. He acknowledged a rumor that some blasting caps had been stolen, but then told me that the contractor had denied any losses. He wasn't sure if the man was telling the truth or covering his tail, but when there was no further trouble, he let it drop."

"We should track down that contractor and see if he'll speak to us."

"He will. His name is Ricky Miller and, fortunately, I know him well. He was a few years behind me in high school, so we didn't become friends until much later in our lives, but I've helped him out a few times. If nothing else, he owes me."

"We'll see how he feels about repaying debts." She wondered how much more rejection Joshua could take. Even a strong man had his limits. As she looked at him, she noticed his face was set, a portrait of determination. He'd bear up, no matter what happened, but the price it would continue to inflict on his spirit made her ache everywhere.

She placed her hand on his shoulder. The gesture had been meant to be reassuring, but the impact of that touch went through both of them like a jolt of lightning. Feeling the shudder that traveled through him, she reluctantly drew her hand back. Desire taunted them, remaining just beneath the surface of everything they thought and everything they did.

THEY ARRIVED at the Miller Construction office ten minutes later. The title seemed lofty, considering it was nothing more than a trailer parked in the middle of a fenced-in vacant lot.

"Some firm," she muttered.

"When he's got a contract, he hires townspeople who need work, and rents whatever equipment he doesn't have. He keeps the overhead low."

"Does he get enough jobs to stay afloat?"

"He's no millionaire but, like most people here in Four Winds, he always seems to earn enough to fill his needs."

As they parked near the front door, a short and rather portly man came out the door and invited them in with a casual wave of his hand.

"Come on in and bring your lady friend," he said. "It's good to see you. I've been hearing some crazy things in town lately. If you ask me, people are acting really stupid. Anyone who knows you realizes you couldn't have hurt your father."

"Thanks for believing in me," Joshua said.

"Hey, I know you and what drives you. You really care about people. Remember when you helped me after my parents divorced and moved away? I'd just turned eighteen and decided to stay on my own, but I didn't have a dime to my name." He glanced at Nydia and explained. "I was living in an old van, and the only family I had left was that mutt over there," he said, pointing to a yellow mixed breed that was lying in the corner. "He was just a pup then, and so sick he wouldn't eat. I figured he was a goner, but then Tree came by, fixed some herbs and gave them to Tiger. The next day he perked up, started eating. After that, he was fine." He met Joshua's gaze. "I'll never be able to thank you enough for that." He glanced over at Nydia then back at Joshua. "A guy who would do something like that for someone he didn't really know and not even expecting to be paid isn't the sort who's callous enough to take the life of someone he loves.''

The dog got up, stretched, then came over and nosed Joshua's hand, asking to be petted. Joshua complied and spoke softly to the animal.

"Tiger's getting up in years, but he still goes everywhere I go," Miller said.

Nydia smiled as the dog came over and licked her hand, then went back to lie on its blanket.

"Now, tell me what I can do for you," Miller said. "Whatever you guys need, if I have it, it's yours."

Joshua explained what had led them to him. "I need the whole story. Were there any blasting caps stolen?"

Miller leaned back in his chair, regarded them thoughtfully, then finally nodded. "Yeah. I denied it at the time, because I assumed one of the local workers had been responsible and I didn't want to have to fire anyone. There's a certain amount of theft that goes on at any site, and I've learned to expect it. Also, to be honest, since the job site happened to be a high school, reporting it would have meant a lot of bad publicity for me. I really couldn't afford that, so I covered the loss with some creative bookkeeping.''

"Can you tell me what brand of blasting caps you were using?" Joshua asked.

"Not offhand, but give me a minute." He walked to a file cabinet set against the wall, and pulled out an old, worn manila folder. "Here it is." He sorted through it and pulled out a sheet, made a copy and handed it to Joshua. "That shows what was taken and when. It's a complete list. If that information gets out, it could hurt me business-wise, so I trust you to use it wisely."

Joshua stood up. "I will. Before I go, may I use your phone?"

Miller waved at the one on his desk. "I'll step outside

and give you some privacy. It's time for Tiger to go out and stretch his legs anyway.''

Nydia accompanied Miller, curious about the man. ''How can you keep a contractor's business going in a community this small? It must be an uphill battle.''

''It sounds crazy, but the truth is that whenever I've needed a job to come in, one has. Maybe it's Four Winds and that touch of magic people say protects the town.''

''Do you really believe that?''

He hesitated. ''I don't know, but I can tell you this— sometimes it's the only answer that makes sense.''

Joshua came out of the trailer, and thanked his friend, then walked with Nydia to the truck.

''Who did you call? Gabriel?''

He nodded. ''I found out something interesting. The missing blasting caps match the brand used on the bomb found at my brother's house.''

''Do you think it's possible that a high-school kid or a former high-school kid is behind all this?''

He shrugged. ''How much do you remember about the mayor's son and the part he played in the theft of the skin-walker bowl?''

''According to Gabriel and Lanie, the boy was working for the person who wanted it, and died as a consequence of their conspiracy.''

''That boy was trouble. He was responsible for the destruction of the old library. He also blew up a barn at the edge of town.''

''But he's dead. He can't be a suspect.''

''His best friend was Peter, the son of the diner's owner. He's the one who showed up first to help when Gabriel's house was wired to blow, remember? I'd like to talk to that boy. He may know something that could help us.''

''Where to?''

''The diner. He works there. But I have to tell you, unless Sally gives us permission to talk to him, we won't get anywhere. They became really close after that mess with the skinwalker bowl. In that way, Four Winds came through for them. Their relationship is one good thing that came out of that tragedy."

"You realize that it'll be only about one o'clock by the time we get back into town. You'll probably be walking in on the lunch crowd," Nydia warned.

"You don't approve?"

"Let's just say I don't think it's wise to act that publicly. Besides, I can think of something else we need to do. It's time you and I took a closer look at that troublemaker Alex. Let's find out where he goes, what he does and who he sees."

"There's a pair of binoculars in the back," Joshua said. "I use them when I help the county keep an eye out for fires during the dry seasons. I'll call Ralph and try to find out where Alex is now, then we'll pick a spot to keep watch from a distance."

They stopped to use the phone booth at the back of Charley's gas station. Nydia kept a sharp lookout for anyone who might be following them. Though she hadn't said anything to Joshua about it, she could feel trouble brewing like a tangible presence in the air.

She glanced back at the rug that lay folded in the rear bench. She stared at it for several seconds, wondering if another warning would ensue, but the voice was silent now.

"I spoke to Ralph and heard Alex in the background," Joshua said, returning, "so I didn't have to ask where he was. Let's drive up the hill behind the library. We can keep watch over the newspaper office and most of Main Street from there without any problem. And if we have to come in for a closer look, it'll be a snap. We can be right on him within a few minutes."

"Sounds good. Let's do it," Nydia said.

"You're very tense, as if you're expecting trouble. What's going on? Have you heard the voice?"

"No. If I had, I would have told you. It's been silent for a while, come to think of it. Maybe it's given us all the help it's going to."

"It's also possible the spirit of the weaver is waiting for a sign from us that we intend to repay the debt by ending the legacy of the rug."

"If you want me to turn it over to you so you can destroy it, I won't. It belongs to the People."

"I don't have to destroy it, but it will need to have an imperfection worked into its design."

"Its beauty is in its perfection, don't you see? Changing that is like defacing a beautiful work of art, or a piece of fine craftsmanship."

He exhaled softly. "The decision is yours. I won't pressure you. But if it wasn't because of the voice, why are you so tense?"

"I'm just thinking that if anything happens while we're in town today, you'll be giving the mayor more reason to dispute Gabriel's handling of the case, as well as putting yourself in jeopardy."

"Always so logical," Joshua murmured as he pulled to a stop. Shifting, he turned to face her. "Haven't you learned yet that I can take care of myself?" He brushed his knuckles against her cheek gently.

His touch set her senses on fire. No matter how she tried to deny it, there was something so very right about their being together. It was as if she'd come face-to-face with a destiny she was meant to fulfill.

Nydia pushed the thought aside and got busy with their plan. There were other matters to attend to right now. Refusing to let anything cloud her thinking, she took the first watch on the newspaper office.

"Alex and Ralph are coming out," she said after about half an hour. She offered the binoculars to Joshua.

"Looks like they're going over to the bank," he said. "No, they kept walking. They're going to the feed store. And there's Darren Wilson and some others waiting. Looks like another meeting."

"We've got to get closer. We shouldn't miss this opportunity."

Leaving the truck, they walked quickly into town, circling around to the back of the feed store. They were hiding behind a giant trash bin near the rear entrance when the sound of angry voices reached them. Nydia recognized the speakers easily.

"You can't continue to bury your head in the sand, Ralph," Darren Wilson said. "You're trying to stay on the fence, and it isn't helping anyone."

"I report the news, that's it. You're not going to use my paper as a propaganda machine for your unsupported accusations. Forget it."

"You wouldn't have to take a stand, if that's what worries you," Alex said. "I could write the pieces as editorials and use my own byline."

"If I allow you to do that, you'd bring down the standard I've set up for my paper. Editorials carry a certain amount of responsibility with them. I won't allow you to present a one-sided view of what's happened just so you can sway people over to your opinion. Not when it hurts innocent people."

"Come to one of our meetings," Darren said. "Hear all the arguments for yourself, then make a decision. Our sheriff is a good man, and right now he needs help. He's being duped by his brother and that woman. It's up to us to see to it that justice doesn't slip out of his grasp."

"Spare me the sanctimonious tripe. You want to convict a man without benefit of a jury or trial."

"You're wrong. We have to keep an eye on the Blackhorse brothers, for their own sake. It's obvious to most of us that Joshua killed his father and then tried to kill the sheriff and his wife with a bomb. Left free to operate, he may succeed next time. We watch out for our own here, and you know it. What we're doing is paying our dues to Four Winds by making sure a killer is caught and punished."

"I'll come to one of your meetings, but don't expect me to turn what I hear into an indictment of Joshua Blackhorse."

"Listen, *then* make up your mind," Alex pressed. "And my offer still stands. I'll write the editorial, if you have problems bringing yourself to do it."

Joshua signaled Nydia, then they crept away from the alley until they reached the library garden, where no one was around. "You were right to zero in on Alex. Private meetings like the ones they were talking about, are meant to incite people. And the way Alex is talking, he's going to make sure the piece he wants to write runs in that paper, even if he has to sneak it past Ralph."

"It would be great to eavesdrop on one of those meetings, but it's way too risky for us. There's no telling what would happen if we were caught. We'll just have to rely on Ralph to let us know if things are getting out of hand. But let's not worry about that now. It's time to go see Sally and talk to her son. Peter may give us the edge we need to solve this case before things reach the boiling point in Four Winds."

Chapter Sixteen

The lunch crowd was mostly gone by the time they stepped through the diner's entrance. Sally stood at the counter, wiping it down with a wet washcloth.

Seeing them, she smiled. "You two hungry? We made some of my special pot pies today."

Joshua nodded. "That sounds great. Bring us two." As Sally left, he looked at Nydia. "We might as well have something to eat while we're here. It'll also help set the tone so she'll be more relaxed while we talk to her."

A short while later, Sally returned to the counter and set full plates before them. "I use fresh red and green chilies in my recipes. People seem to really notice the difference around here."

Nydia took a bite. "It's wonderful."

"You take your time, and if anyone comes in and hassles you, let me handle it. This is my property, and you're both welcome here."

"I appreciate that," Joshua answered. "Not many people feel the way you do right now."

Sally nodded, leaning heavily on the counter. "Yeah, I know. I've heard all the talk. It's pathetic, if you ask me. Most are saying that the sheriff's not doing enough, but then they blame you for trying to look into it yourself. Have you two come up with anything that will put an end to all this?''

Joshua shook his head, ''Nothing definite, but we have one lead, and there, you might be able to help us. I'd like to ask Peter a few questions about Ted Burns.''

Sally's expression changed dramatically. The sympathy and understanding etched there disappeared abruptly, replaced by fear. ''Please don't drag all that up again. That was a very difficult time for my son and for me. There's still a lot of pain buried back there.''

''I know,'' Joshua said gently, ''but it's your son's knowledge of Ted and his habits that could give us the lead we desperately need.''

Sally exhaled softly. ''All right. I owe your brother big time, so this is one way to pay him back. Come with me. Pete's doing the pots and pans.''

As they entered the kitchen carrying their plates, Peter looked up. His eyes grew wide, sensing trouble.

''Whatever it is, I didn't do it,'' he said.

''Relax, nephew,'' Joshua said. ''Nobody's accusing you of anything.''

Nydia's heart went out to the boy. He was young, but from the stories she'd heard, he'd had to do quite a bit of growing up in a very short time. She put her plate down on the counter and prepared to eat lunch, hoping that would normalize the mood.

''We need to know more about Ted Burns,'' Joshua said.

Peter threw up his hands. ''Nobody will ever really let me forget that. It doesn't matter how hard I try to prove myself.''

''Relax!'' Nydia's tone was sharp and held an unmistakable commanding air. It was a tactic that usually worked with her own son, and she was glad to see that it had worked on Peter, too. Startled, he'd lost some of his posturing. ''We trust you. All we want is to pick your brain for a while. It's your knowledge we need most," she said, appealing to his ego.

"My knowledge...you mean about Ted and what he was like?"

"Exactly," Nydia said. She made a show of turning her attention back to her meal.

"What do you want to know?"

Joshua met the boy's gaze. "Where do you think he got the explosives he used to bring down the library and barn?"

Peter shrugged. "I couldn't say. Ted never really confided in me. He told me things from time to time, but it wasn't a friendship, you know. He didn't feel close to anyone. All I was to him was someone to push around."

"Think back. When they were tearing down the old gym to build the new one, Ted was a student at the high school, wasn't he? Do you think he might have stolen some of the explosives the contractor was using?" Joshua pressed.

"We're not asking you to swear to it, Pete," Nydia said when he hesitated. "We just want your opinion, that's all. It would help to get your perspective on this."

Peter met her gaze and nodded. "Ted was always bragging and pushing his weight around. One time, he told me that he had a stash of explosives that he'd stolen from the construction crew's trailer, the one they'd parked at school. He threatened to use them to blow up this diner. But at the time, I thought it was mostly talk, him trying to scare me, you know? He was like that."

"After the mayor's son died, did you tell my brother what he'd said about the explosives?" Joshua asked.

"I meant to, I really did," Peter answered, staring at the floor with a frown. "But after getting shot, everything was crazy and I just forgot. I only thought about it again after the explosion at the sheriff's house. But I was too scared to bring it up. I figured people might think I had something to do with it. And it wasn't like I was sure it had anything to do with Ted anyway. Though it was possible someone had found Ted's stash, that bomb may have had nothing to do with him, either.''

"Okay, thanks," Joshua said.

As they came out of the kitchen, Gabriel was coming into the diner. He glanced at them, his eyes narrowing in speculation. "What's going on?"

As they finished their lunch, Joshua filled him in on what they'd learned. "According to the list I saw, there are still some materials to be accounted for."

"Good detective work, Tree. If you ever decide to go into another line of business, I can make a suggestion." He glanced at Joshua and Nydia. "Where are you two off to now?"

Nydia looked at Joshua and shrugged. At the moment, she had no ideas to offer.

"I think we'll go speak to Ralph. They're leaning on him pretty heavily," he said, telling his brother what they'd overheard at the feed store.

"There's also the matter of those anonymous phone calls that I think we should discuss with him...." Nydia added.

"You think he's covering for someone?" Gabriel asked.

"I don't know, but I'd like to sound him out a bit more."

As they walked to the newspaper office, Nydia noticed that the few people on the sidewalk stepped aside as they went by. Yet even in the face of their unfair judgments, it was hard for her to blame them. Though misguided, they were, in the final analysis, trying to avenge the murder of their former sheriff, Joshua's father.

She cast Joshua a sideways glance. He masked his thoughts well, but his expression was too controlled to pass as natural. Frustration slammed into her, biting and corrosive like acid. Nydia forced herself to meet some of the gazes, silently challenging, but people quickly looked away. Although she didn't feel hatred for them, she did feel contempt.

When they finally entered the newspaper office, they heard Alex and Ralph arguing. Hearing the door shut behind Nydia, the men stopped their discussion abruptly.

Ralph waved them to a chair. "What can I do for you?"

Joshua waited until Alex left the room. "Can we talk freely here, or would you prefer to do that elsewhere?"

Ralph stood, went down to the hall and closed the door leading to the back rooms. "He can't hear us now, not with the presses going," Ralph said. "What's on your mind?"

"We know about the meetings in Wilson's barn, and the pressure being placed on you."

"Then you must have also heard that I won't be a party to that type of journalism. There's a vigilante feel to this that makes my skin crawl."

"You might be able to help the Blackhorse family by playing along a bit more," Nydia said.

"How so?"

"It's possible you could find out who has been making the anonymous phone calls if you go to those meetings."

"If that's what you want, I'll try, but no promises."

"Alex probably knows far more than he's saying. Any chance he'll answer our questions?" Nydia asked.

Ralph shook his head. "What he wants is a confrontation."

"Then maybe it's time he got one," Nydia said. "Can you ask him to come in here?"

"I'll get him," Ralph said.

Ralph returned a moment later, Alex by his side. Alex gave them a suspicious look as he sat down. "You wanted to talk to me?"

"Yes," Nydia said. "We know that you've been very outspoken against Joshua. You've also been lobbying hard to get Ralph to let you do a write-up about this case. Why are you so determined to stir up trouble?"

"I'm not, but I do have a right to voice my opinion and have it heard."

"By phoning in news tips anonymously?" Nydia challenged.

"Don't look at me. A newspaper gets those kinds of phone calls all the time." He glared accusingly at Ralph. "But most editors-in-chief go after the story."

"Most go to even greater lengths to identify the source. That's what I did," Ralph said, his gaze resting on Alex unwaveringly.

Alex turned crimson. "If you don't need me anymore, I've got the next edition of the *Last Word* to run," he said, standing up.

Joshua stared at the closed door after Alex had left. "He definitely knows something about the source of the calls. My gut tells me he's the one phoning you with the tips, but I'm curious as to who is behind the information he's passing to you. He strikes me as the messenger, nothing more."

Ralph nodded slowly. "That's been my feeling, too. I haven't said anything because I can't prove one whit of this. To be honest, I think Alex is the one calling me, but I'm far more interested in his source."

"Is there any way for you to monitor his phone calls?" Nydia asked. "Maybe we can uncover his source that way."

"No. To listen in to his calls, I'd have to stand behind him all day. There's no way I can do that."

"Maybe my brother can help us with this," Joshua said. "He might be able to put a bug in the phone—that is, if you'll consent," he added, looking at Ralph.

"No problem. This is my business, and I intend to make sure this newspaper doesn't become someone's pawn," he said, placing the phone before Joshua. "You can call him right now, if you'd like."

Joshua picked up the receiver and dialed his brother. The arrangements didn't take long.

Joshua left with Nydia through the front door, knowing Alex was watching them. As they moved down the street, they ducked into the alley and hurried down to Gabriel's. "We'll be able to monitor his phone calls from my brother's office. He assured me he has the equipment. Let's go see."

Nydia felt his tension as sharply as she did her own. Soon they would have answers, but there was no guarantee that they'd be the ones they so desperately needed.

THEY SAT by a tape recorder and some sophisticated equipment that Joshua had never suspected would be available in Four Winds.

"Listen but don't touch anything," Gabriel said.

"How did you get all this stuff?" Joshua asked.

"It came out of a deal I cut with the sheriff in the next county a while back. All it takes is one phone call to our town's switchboard, and we're all set. Even the mayor doesn't know I have all this. It's good to keep a few secrets from the politicians."

"Why are you concerned about what the mayor knows or doesn't know?"

"The mayor is attending these supposedly secret meetings held in Darren Wilson's barn, but as of yet, he's never passed any useful information from them on to me. That worries me a bit, but there's another danger. I make confidential daily reports to him on the status of the case. If he confides in anyone there, he could undermine what I'm trying to do. The bottom line is that Burns is a politician, and his priorities are different from mine."

The first several calls Alex received and made were routine. Then the call they'd been hoping for came. They heard a man's cautious, whisper-soft voice, obviously disguised.

"It's me," he said.

Gabriel picked up another phone and started the trace.

"What have you got?" Alex asked.

"There was an attack launched against the singer and the woman with him. It failed, but the woman is now a target, too. There will be more attempts aimed at her."

"Anything else?"

"Not for now, but I'm not sure I should bother to call you anymore. You haven't been doing your part. I give you the news, but you don't print it."

"I don't determine what the paper prints. I just work here."

The phone rang in Gabriel's office. He picked it up. "Are you sure?" he asked.

Joshua looked at his brother. "Did you recognize the voice?"

He shook his head. "But that call is originating from Miss Alma's shop, though it has been locked up for months. I'm going over there. Will you two monitor the conversation? If the equipment fails, I'm going to need witnesses."

"You've got it," Nydia replied.

Hearing Joshua's name being mentioned, they quickly turned their attention back to the conversation taking place over the wires. Then they heard a knock, and someone came into the outer office.

Gabriel cursed. "I'll be right there," he said, then listened a moment longer.

"What if I could set up Joshua Blackhorse so that you catch him with his hands dirty?" the voice asked.

"I want no part of a frame. I work for an honest newspaper."

"*Now* you're getting self-righteous on me?" He laughed.

"I'm just telling you the way it is," Alex snapped.

Joshua glanced at his brother as Gabriel stepped out into the outer office and spoke to the woman who had just come in. He recognized Mrs. Stephens's voice, and she seemed very upset about something. His brother would lose precious time now, and neither of them could afford that.

Silently, Joshua slipped out of the office through the back door and made his way to Miss Alma's antique shop.

JOSHUA WALKED AROUND to the rear of the building, making sure no one at Rosa's grocery store next door spotted him. Seeing the side door to the antique shop open a crack, he moved forward. Suddenly, a figure emerged from the building, and Joshua ducked back to avoid being seen. The shadows in the alley obscured the caller's face.

Joshua hurried forward to follow, but as if sensing his presence, his quarry ducked into an adjoining side street that led back to Main.

Opting for a shortcut, Joshua went through the feed store's warehouse. He had almost reached the Main Street entrance when he heard an engine start outside, and a sudden, loud backfire.

Just ahead, a crowd was gathering in the middle of the street. Citizens huddled around something on the ground, but Joshua couldn't make out what. As he drew near, he felt an overwhelming sense of danger piercing him like a cold blade. His gut wrenched as he stepped around the shopkeepers and saw the woman he loved lying still on the ground.

Chapter Seventeen

Joshua pushed through the crowd to Nydia and crouched by her side. The wound at the tip of her shoulder oozed a little blood, but there seemed to be no other injuries.

She sat up. "Oh, cripes, my arm hurts!"

He hurried to tear open her sleeve and was relieved to see that a bullet had only grazed her flesh. "You'll be all right," he assured gently, wondering what had brought her out into the line of fire.

Taking some herbs from his medicine bundle, Joshua placed them carefully over the wound, then lifted her up into his arms.

"Should he be doing that?" he heard a woman whisper.

"They're two of a kind—let him," came a male voice in answer.

As Joshua carried her out of the street, people stepped aside, allowing him to pass. He'd just reached the sidewalk when Gabriel came running up.

"I couldn't get away fast enough. I had to make sure it was just one of Mrs. Stephens's crazy sightings and that she wasn't in danger. When I looked up, I realized both of you were gone."

Joshua glanced down at Nydia. "Why did you come?"

"The conversation we were taping ended abruptly. I

wasn't sure if the caller knew we were on to him or not, but I figured I should warn you."

"I ran after the person you were chasing, Tree," Gabriel said, "but he gave me the slip before I could get a look at him. Whoever it is knows this town like the back of his hand."

"Put me down," Nydia said, squirming. "I'm okay." As Joshua set her down, Nydia pressed the herb to her shoulder. "Let's not just stand here. Let's go turn over a few rocks and see what crawls out. Whoever that was shot me, and I have something to say about this!"

Joshua shook his head. "One step at a time. You need to have Shadow look at your shoulder, clean out the wound and bandage it."

"These herbs will do," she said, giving him a hesitant smile.

Gabriel's glance took in the crowd, still milling around in the street. "They're not dispersing. Take my suggestion. Go to Shadow's and wait for me there. I'll meet you as soon as I can."

As Gabriel strode off, Joshua walked to his truck with Nydia, staying protectively at her side.

They were halfway through a darkened alley when he stopped and gently turned her to face him. "Is it the old ways and my herbs you're now willing to trust, or is it me? If your trust is in my skills as a *hataalii*, then I should tell you that your faith is misplaced. When I saw you lying out on the street, all I felt was the need to pay back in kind what was done to you. Emotions like those make me useless as a singer. But that anger has its own satisfaction. I want to hang on to it, at least until I even the score."

She placed her hand on his chest, and with that simple gesture broke away the hardness that armored his heart. "Then I will help you find yourself again," she said softly.

"Do a sing for me, *hataalii*. Help us both find what we've lost."

He couldn't believe her words. He would have never refused her anything, but of all the things she might have asked, this was the most difficult. When he'd seen her hurt, all he'd felt was hatred, but now as he gazed at her, all he could feel was love. "We'll go to Shadow's, and there, I'll do what you've asked of me."

As they drove to Shadow's clinic, his senses stayed attuned to danger. He would not allow another assault on them.

"This latest attack means that we're getting close to catching the killer," she said, interrupting his thoughts. "It's good news for us."

"Nothing that harms you is good news."

Nydia reached out for him, placing her hand on his thigh. He almost groaned under the pressure building inside him. "I wonder if I'll ever have the ability to stay focused no matter what, like the legendary *hataalii*s of our tribe."

"You have that now, when you need it." She closed her eyes and rested her head against the back of the seat.

He looked at her, and saw her wince as she shifted in her seat. Seeing her pain brought his thoughts quickly into focus. "Maybe I do, *sawe*, but I need you by me to point it out to me," he whispered.

"What?" she asked drowsily.

"Nothing. Sleep for now. You've been through enough."

THEY WERE PARKED in front of Shadow's hogan, behind his clinic, twenty minutes later when Joshua wakened her. She opened her eyes as he lifted her into his arms to carry her inside.

"My brother isn't here now, so we'll wait in the hogan

instead of the clinic. There, I'll be able to do the sing as I promised you."

He carried her effortlessly, and despite the ache in her shoulder, she found herself shamelessly enjoying being held by him. Guided by the yearnings of her heart, she pressed a kiss to his chest.

He groaned. "No, don't do that, not if you want me to keep my word and do a sing over you."

"Do I distract you so much?"

"You don't realize half of what you do to me."

His words made her heart soar, but mingled with that was a sorrow that remained like a shadow over her heart. What separated them still remained, and the song he'd do for her was part of that chasm that kept them in different worlds. To her, it would simply be a connection to a past they both shared as part of the *dineh*. To him, it was the foundation of all he was and had worked to become—all that set him apart from her.

Joshua lowered her gently onto the sheepskin rug, but remained close to her. "For you, I'll do a *hozonji,* a song of blessing. It's a special one that can't be used too often because it loses its power, so only a few even know it. But it's one that I choose to share with you."

She listened as his song rose into the air, filling the small hogan. The chant was like a voice crying in denial of anything that created suffering. It was a statement of hope to a distant vision, and a quest for whose success anything was worth enduring.

It filled her with joy and with the expectation of promises to come. Peace settled over her. As his song ended, a stillness descended. It was as if the earth itself held its breath.

"Do you feel its power?" he asked, looking down at her. "That's the essence of the strength of the *dineh* and what gives our tribe the courage to face the future."

"And it is also a very dear part of you that you've chosen to reveal to me."

"That it is."

Love, stronger than any she had ever known, filled her. She allowed him to clean and tend her wound once more, aware of everything about him, the concentration he devoted to the simple task and his dedication to the powers he'd pledged his life to.

It was then that Nydia realized the simple truth that had somehow eluded her. Being a singer was what enabled Joshua to love with such depth of feeling. She would never be a poor number two in his life, as she'd once thought. His focus and commitment to whatever he gave his heart to meant that she'd be at the center of everything he was, not simply the woman who stood beside him.

That realization stunned her. The very thing she had thought would always keep them separated, his devotion to the knowledge of the old ways, was precisely what would bond them together.

"You're all right now." Hearing a truck approach and the squeal of shifting gears, Joshua moved to the entrance and looked outside. "That's Shadow's truck, but stay here until I make sure he's alone. There's no sense in both of us exposing ourselves to danger. One alone has a better chance of not getting caught."

"All right," she managed to say, still stunned by the magnitude of what she'd learned about him.

As Joshua left, she stood near the blanket-covered entrance of the hogan. How many Navajo women had seen their warriors go off like this? Her connection to the past felt stronger now than it had ever been.

A minute later, she saw Shadow and Joshua approach. As they spoke, she saw Joshua looking over at her frequently, as if assuring himself that she was all right.

Shadow unlocked the door to the office as she walked

out to join them. "Did something new happen?" she asked Joshua.

"No, but for what it's worth, I think we're close to finding the answers that will free me to go with you to the reservation. Then you can complete what you set out to do when you came to Four Winds."

His words filled her with an aching loneliness. She was suddenly excruciatingly aware that Joshua had never expressed a desire for a lasting relationship with her. Perhaps he wasn't ready to take that step. He was a *hataalii,* and as he'd told her many times, he needed harmony most of all in his life. Accepting an eleven-year-old boy and a modern woman in his life full-time was a lot to ask of him.

She thought of John, and her heart ached to see him. "I need to call home," she said as they entered the clinic. "May I use your phone?" she asked, looking at Lucas.

He led her to his office and waved her inside. "Help yourself. I'll see if I can find some food."

Eager to hear her son's voice, she dialed quickly. To her delight, her son answered instead of her mother-in-law.

"Mom, where are you?"

"I'm still here in Four Winds. How's your grandfather?"

"The same. I'm really worried about him. When will you bring back the *hataalii?*"

"It won't be much longer. Tell your grandfather. Ask him to hold on."

"You've never given me your word and not kept it," he said, as if reminding himself.

Tears stung her eyes. To him, everything was either black or white. Yet her situation here had myriad shades of gray. "Hang on and believe that I'm doing my best."

"I do, Mom," he said. "Make it happen, okay?"

She heard the worry in his voice. That seed of doubt spiraled its way around her, making it difficult to even breathe. She said goodbye, feeling a great weight settling over her. At that very moment, nothing mattered to her quite as much as not letting her son down.

She closed her eyes, tasting the possibility of defeat. What if her best efforts turned out to not be good enough? She brushed the thought aside. No, she wouldn't fail. She wouldn't even contemplate the possibility.

There was a knock at the door, and a moment later, Joshua peered inside. "Is everything okay? You look as if you've lost a battle."

"Maybe I have," she admitted. "My grandmother used to say that a Navajo never speaks for another Navajo. I wish I'd listened. In my overconfidence, I promised my family I'd bring you, but I had no right to make that vow."

"You shouldn't have—that's true," he said. "But what's done is done."

"John's never asked me for much, so when he made this request, I was so glad to have him coming to me for help that I agreed to it immediately. It never occurred to me for one moment that I'd fail."

"If you do, I share in that failure," he said wearily. "Your son is special, not only because you love him, but because he sees the value of our traditions. It's on boys like him that the fate of our Way depends. If I fail him, I'll injure the tribe. Believe me, I don't take that lightly."

Lucas joined them and said, "I hate to interrupt, but would you mind if I took a look at that wound?"

"It's scarcely a wound. It's just a really deep scratch, and your brother has already taken care of it."

"If it's deep, it wouldn't hurt to take a few bandages along with you. And before I dispense any supplies, I'd like to see what we're dealing with."

"All right."

Lucas undid the makeshift bandage that Joshua had placed over her wound. As he worked, he continued to talk, trying to keep her mind off any discomfort his touch might cause. "Have you two reached any decisions about where you'll be staying now?"

"Not yet," Joshua answered.

"Why don't you stay here?"

"This is the last place we want to endanger. Your clinic is needed," Joshua said.

"Exactly my point. If they attack here, they risk the only medical facility around for miles."

Joshua considered it. "I'm not so sure they'll stop to think things out."

"They also know I'm armed," Lucas said bluntly. "You wouldn't be sitting ducks here, and you'd have an extra pair of eyes to keep watch at night. I'm certain Gabriel would approve, too."

"I vote against it," Nydia said. "If they did attack here, many innocent people who depend on this clinic would suffer. I can't condone that risk. This town depends on you."

"Yeah, but I depend on my brothers, and this town's attacking one of them."

Joshua shook his head. "No, Shadow. I thank you for the thought and the offer, but it can't be."

"So where will you go?"

Joshua considered it. "The last place they expect us to go. We'll hide in the woods near the cabin."

"The canyon?"

"Yes."

"Well, at least nobody can sneak up on you there, and you do know that area."

"Precisely."

Lucas finished bandaging Nydia's shoulder. "You'll be fine in a day or two, but take some extra bandages anyway. I'd also like you to take whatever supplies I have in the kitchen and some lightweight sleeping bags," he said, reaching into the closet. "It will all come in handy."

Nydia and Joshua thanked him, packed up the truck and got under way. They were on the outskirts of town when Joshua spotted a slow-moving truck on the road ahead. The bed of the pickup was stacked high with everything from furniture to athletic equipment.

"Looks like someone's leaving town," Nydia commented.

Joshua pulled up in the next lane to pass, then recognized the driver. "It's Father Rogan. His parish is in the next town, just over the mountains, but a lot of our people here in Four Winds attend his church."

"Joshua!" The man waved, then signaled for them to pull over up ahead.

"You're not stopping, are you?" Nydia asked, realizing Joshua was slowing down. "You can't—"

"He's incapable of harming anyone. We're in no danger from him."

The priest was already walking toward them as Joshua parked on the shoulder and got out.

"I've been worried about you, son," Father Rogan said. "Our church has provided a sanctuary for many over the years. If you have need of it, you're welcome, though you're not of our faith."

"I appreciate that, Father, but right now, I need to stay here and work to clear my name."

"Terrible, terrible business," the priest said, shaking his head. "I know you had nothing to do with any of it, and I can't believe that there are people who believe otherwise." He waved at the things stacked on the back of his truck. "But that's the first step to healing the wounds left by the tragedy. Maybe by giving these away and letting the poor put them to good use, he will be granted some peace."

"Who, Father? To whom did those things belong?"

"Ted Burns, the mayor's deceased son. For the past few months, I've been counseling Bob Burns to let the past go, but he refused to accept what had happened. He kept that boy's room as a shrine, as if Ted would be coming back through the door any second.''

Joshua studied the possessions that had once belonged to Ted Burns. "What made the mayor let go of these things now? To him, these possessions represent memories and a last link to his son."

"It wasn't easy on him, the poor man, but he finally began the mourning process about a month ago. He asked me back then to come and take whatever I wanted from Ted's room, but when we started sorting through everything, it was just too much for him. He told me he'd take care of it himself and then call me. He finally did, as you can see from the back," he said, waving to the bed of the truck.

"Thanks for the information and your kindness, Father," Joshua said. "It was good to see you."

"You, too, son." The priest extended his hand toward Nydia. "I'm told you are a modernist, and may not mind this Anglo custom."

Nydia shook his hand. "Not at all, Father."

"I'll pray for both of you," he said, getting back into his truck.

Joshua's gaze remained on the truck as it slowly started down the road again. "This news about the mayor raises some interesting questions. It's possible that the mayor changed his mind about having the priest go through his son's things because he found something illegal there."

"Or suspected he would," she said. "One interesting note. Burns didn't give all this boy's possessions to the priest. The mayor was at the gas station when I first came into town. I remember him talking to the attendant wanting to sell a bicycle that had belonged to his son. There wasn't one in the back of the priest's truck."

Joshua looked at the fading sun. "This gets more interesting by the minute. Night will protect us if you're willing to go back to Four Winds. I'd like to talk to Charley about Mayor Burns.''

She exhaled softly. "That's risky. The gas station is right on Main." She knew that if she said no, he wouldn't insist, not after what they'd already been through. But she'd accepted the responsibility and danger when she'd insisted on staying with him. "Oh, well. Everything's risky at this point. Let's go.''

She felt the force of his gaze as it swept over her like a caress. Her body tingled with awareness.

"You have more courage than is good for you," Joshua said, "but I'm glad to have you by my side.''

Nydia suppressed the shiver that ran up her spine, knowing the futility of indulging these longings. Wishing things were different would never change the way things were.

When Joshua drove up to Charley's garage, everything was quiet, as it always was after dark. In the darkness, they could see Charley's garage light on, though the station was closed.

"He works late into the night, tinkering with his old cars," Joshua said. "It's his one love. He'll buy cars that barely run, then refurbish and sell them. I think that's how he really makes most of his money.''

As they approached, Joshua and Nydia kept a sharp eye out for a possible ambush. They'd almost reached the side door when they heard a rustling sound in the brush to their right. Without hesitation, Joshua pulled Nydia down, shielding her with his body.

Chapter Eighteen

Hearing the click of a revolver's action being pulled back, Joshua spun in a crouch, simultaneously kicking out.

"Whoa!" Gabriel jumped aside fast, evading the blow. "What the hell are you doing here, Tree? Don't you *ever* listen to anyone? What's it going to take to get through to you?"

Nydia exhaled loudly and stood up. "Sheriff, you practically gave us both a heart attack."

"Good. Maybe you'll finally realize that there's mortal danger here for both of you." He placed his service weapon back into its holster.

"We came back because we needed to talk to Charley," Joshua said. As he started to explain, the side door of the garage was thrown open.

Charley stood there, shotgun in hand, glaring at them. "What in the name of heaven is going on here?" His shotgun, though not pointed at any one of them, wasn't far from the ready position.

"Sorry we startled you," Joshua said. "It's my fault. I came to ask you some questions."

Charley glared at him. "I do have business hours, you know."

"This couldn't wait. My time's running out. You've seen the mood of this town."

"I've got to say, I'm not sure people aren't right about you," he snapped, but then stood aside and gestured for them to enter. "Okay, so what's so important it couldn't wait?"

Nydia took the lead. "When I first came into town, I stopped at your gas station to ask for directions. I remember Mayor Burns was there at the time asking if you were interested in buying some things that had belonged to his son."

"Yeah, so? His kid obviously had no use for them anymore."

"Can you tell us what items you bought from him?"

"An ATV. I tuned it up and sold it a few days ago to Bobby Pierce, the social-studies teacher. There was also a mountain bicycle I kept for myself. That's it. He had mentioned selling his son's fancy air rifle, too, but I guess he changed his mind about that because he never came back with it."

Joshua shot Gabriel a look. Nydia didn't miss it, and neither did Charley.

"Why are you asking about this?"

Gabriel shook his head. "I can't tell you just yet, and please don't discuss any of this with anyone."

Charley walked them to the door, muttering under his breath. "Don't worry. The last thing I need is to tell anyone I was discussing the mayor with the town's least popular citizens."

As Joshua and Nydia returned to Joshua's truck, Gabriel stuck with them. "I have some interesting news," Gabriel said. "I found the person who stole your hunting rifle, Tree, but he's not our father's killer."

Joshua stopped by the driver's-side door and faced his brother. "Are you certain?"

Gabriel nodded. "It was one of the high-school kids. He was told it was an initiation of some sort, a prank he was supposed to play if he wanted to join the Lettermen's Club. He's just a freshman, and he says he found a note in his locker telling him what to do. It was on a hall-pass form. The note told him where to leave the rifle. After he dropped it off, he went back to his locker and there was a school jacket there for him. The problem is he never figured out who was behind it, and he didn't keep the note."

"Are you sure he's telling the truth?" Joshua asked.

"Oh, yeah. The kid was genuinely embarrassed as he told me the entire story. He found out he'd been had when he wore the jacket to school and learned he's not supposed to wear a letterman's jacket until *after* he letters in a sport."

"I also tracked the slug that grazed your shoulder," Gabriel continued, looking at Nydia. "I recovered it from a tree by the curb. The bullet was misshapen, but I believe it came from a .44 caliber revolver that was missing from the antique shop. When we checked the inventory after the store became the town's property, that weapon was never found."

"We have another speculation to share with you," Joshua said, and told him about the blasting caps and the possible connection to Ted Burns.

"Now, that's real interesting, particularly because I've recently learned that Bob Burns reloads his own ammunition, and purchased a pound of gunpowder from a Santa Fe gun shop a week ago. That, and your lead to the blasting caps, gives us a tie-in to the pipe bomb and the bone ammunition, which was probably fired from an air gun."

"So now what?" Nydia asked. "It's all still circumstantial evidence, definitely no more solid than what the town is using to convict Tree. We can't lower ourselves to that level."

"No, but we can continue to pursue this, and see where it leads. Or more to the point, I can," Gabriel said. "I'm going to put a little heat on the mayor. I reached him on the cellular phone, but he's fishing out at Deer Lake, and the connection was lousy. I want to go talk to him eye to eye. In the meantime, I have a favor to ask of you."

"Name it," Joshua said without hesitation.

"It's dark now, and I'm worried about my wife. She hasn't been feeling well. I don't want her alone tonight. Will you go over there and stay with her until I get back?"

"We may bring her more danger," Nydia cautioned, avoiding the use of names as he'd done.

"Not if you go there without attracting attention. My brother knows the long way."

"Why didn't you tell us she'd been sick before? Is it serious?" Joshua asked.

"No, I don't think so. Fact is, she hasn't said anything about it, but I noticed that she's been sick to her stomach a lot in the morning. I think it's just stress."

Joshua glanced at Nydia, suppressing a smile. His brother, despite his skill as an investigator, could sometimes be as thick as a brick when it came to the simple things in life. "We'll stay with her."

"Tell her I'll call her in a little bit, okay?"

"No problem."

As they got under way, Joshua looked at Nydia. "I'd be willing to bet she's pregnant, and waiting for the right time to tell my brother. I can't wait to see his face when he finds out he's going to be a daddy."

She laughed. "He doesn't have a clue, does he?"

"I don't think it has occurred to him yet," Joshua said, then grew somber. "But then again, his mind has been on other things."

When they arrived at Lanie's, they saw her sitting outside in the porch swing. She stood up, concern clear on her features. "Is something wrong?" she asked quickly.

"No, not at all, little mother," Joshua said.

She smiled slowly. "You've always had a sixth sense

about people, haven't you? But I hope you haven't told Gabriel.''

"No, that's your news to give."

"Where is my husband? Will he be home soon?"

"In a few hours. He went to talk to the mayor, who's camped out at Deer Lake. He said he'd be calling you soon, but in the meantime, he asked us to stay here with you."

"Good," Lanie said, placing her hand over her belly. "I worry more than usual lately."

They went inside to the kitchen, where Lanie served lemonade. "Have there been any new developments?"

"A few, but nothing final," Joshua answered.

Lanie leaned back in her chair. "I'm really worried about you, Tree," she said quietly. "And you, too, Nydia. I can see the way you feel about each other."

Nydia shook her head. "This isn't like it was between you and Gabriel. When my business here is finished, I have a son to go back to."

"When I first arrived, I thought my leaving was inevitable, too. But love finds a way, not to mention Four Winds," Lanie added with a smile.

Although Nydia didn't agree, Joshua noted that this time she wasn't quite as willing to scoff. Perhaps she'd seen too much already, or perhaps the wish that things could be different colored her outlook.

He thought of how much he'd changed, too. Through this tragedy, he'd found a new source of strength. Nydia's unfailing support had given him courage and bolstered his confidence when he'd needed it most.

Yet he was too much in tune with everything around him to discount the reality of Nydia's situation. She had responsibilities on the reservation that couldn't be altered. Her wish to have a modernist husband be the parent of her son, rather than one who'd accentuate a way of life she didn't truly believe in, was something he could do nothing about. He could not change who and what he was, and he knew himself well enough to know he would not be able to stop himself from instructing her son if that was his wish. The boy's interest in the Navajo Way was too precious to waste. As his gaze drifted over Nydia, a heaviness of spirit encompassed him.

The loud ring of the phone interrupted his thoughts. Lanie leaped to her feet and picked up the receiver. "Hi, there," she greeted gently, obviously knowing who it was before she even heard his voice.

"Yes, they're both here and—Gabriel?" She shouted his name into the phone.

Her cry tore through Joshua. He felt her fear stab through him like a naked blade slicing his flesh. In a heartbeat, he and Nydia were by her side. Together, they reached out for her before she could fall.

"What happened?" Joshua tried to take the phone from her hands, but Lanie wouldn't relinquish it.

"Gabriel!" She screamed his name.

"Lanie, stop it!" Nydia's voice cracked through the air, and somehow managed to reach Lanie. "We need to know what happened!"

"There was this noise...an explosion, I think, then the phone went dead!"

"He may have had a blowout and dropped the phone to regain control of his Jeep," Nydia said, not at all convinced. A voice whispered one word in her mind over and over again like a chant. *Destiny, destiny.* She glanced at Joshua, and saw the fear shining in his eyes.

"We've got to find him!" Lanie rushed to the door.

"No, wait! He'll probably try to contact us here. Someone's got to stay at the house," Nydia said.

"I'm going over to his office and try to get him on the radio. That'll be the quickest."

"I'm going with you," Lanie said. "I'm the sheriff's

wife. Who better to let you into his office when he's not there? If you try to break in, someone might shoot and ask questions later.''

''It makes sense, but it'll be better if you just give us the keys. I know you're scared, but think this through. If the sheriff is under attack, then we're all in danger. Can you go stay with Marlee? You can take the cellular phone and have the calls routed to that in case the sheriff tries to contact you.''

''I'd rather go with you,'' Lanie said.

Nydia glanced down at Lanie's belly. ''It's your decision, but you've got another who needs you to stay safe.''

Lanie nodded slowly. ''All right. Here.'' She tossed Nydia the keys.

Joshua looked at Nydia. Every argument she'd used made perfect sense, but he was almost certain that she knew far more than she'd said. He couldn't ask her about it now, however, not with his sister-in-law present. His own sense of urgency assured him clearly enough that the web of danger was tightening around them all with each passing second.

NYDIA AND JOSHUA WENT down Main Street, alert for trouble. ''I keep hearing one word, 'destiny,' being repeated over and over again in my mind,'' she said.

He took a long, deep breath. ''I don't think my brother's dead. I...think...I would feel it...somehow, like I did with my father.'' Despite his hopeful words, despair as black as the darkest night slammed into him. His father was dead; now his brother's fate was in question.

Nydia placed her hand on his arm. ''We'll see this through together. Our enemy won't win.''

The warmth and gentleness of her touch wove a path to his heart, strengthening him. He would not lose hope. He would concede his enemy nothing except the one death he'd already caused. "You're right. We're still in the middle of this battle. If anything, we have to fight all the harder now."

They reached the sheriff's office and, using Lanie's key, quickly made their way inside to the dispatcher's room. As was routine office procedure at night, the dispatcher handled calls from a unit in her home.

Joshua clicked on the two-way radio, appraised the dispatcher, then tried to reach Gabriel. Only a burst of static came through. He tried changing frequencies, but to no avail.

"All this means is that his radio isn't working, either, or is turned off," Nydia said, more unconvinced than ever. Closing her eyes, she visualized the blanket, but nothing came except for the one-word litany. She shook free of its hold.

"I'm calling Shadow," he said.

Joshua switched frequencies, and this time the transition was smooth.

"Shadow, we've got trouble." Joshua gave his brother an encapsulated version of the events. "I know Gabriel's somewhere around the lake, but not the exact location. Where are you now? Can you stop by and check things out?"

"I'm on my way back to town, still about a half hour or so away. I was called out on an emergency, but it turned out to be a hoax. I'll contact the state police and ask for their help in locating Fuzz. But it sure looks like someone wanted us both out of town."

Lucas's words filled Nydia with dread. Someone had gone to a great deal of trouble to isolate Joshua and her. A fight was at hand, and this time, they'd either win or die. She felt it in her bones, though the inner voice was curiously silent now.

She looked at Joshua, who was staring pensively across

the room. Once before, she'd fallen in love, but Death had taken that man from her. *Destiny*. The word echoed in her mind. Perhaps destiny would once again demand she face the loss of the man she loved. The thought made her tremble. She shoved her hands in her pockets, afraid he'd sense her fear. She wouldn't undermine him that way. He needed all his strength now, and so did she.

Joshua's gaze was filled with love as it swept over her. "Don't be afraid, *sawe*. There's no reason to believe fate won't bring us exactly what we've searched for, my father's killer."

She nodded, not trusting her voice. Her most cherished dream, that which she'd kept hidden deep within her, and oftentimes even from herself, had little to do with finding a killer. It had everything to do with love.

Hearing a noise at the back door, he quickly turned off the lights. "Hide," he whispered.

Easy for her, she thought, but where did a man Joshua's size hide? She had her answer a moment later when she caught a glimpse of him ducking into the next room, and flattening his back against the wall.

A moment later, the door opened. In the light from the rear doorway, she saw Lanie and Marlee come inside.

Nydia felt her heart start beating again, and she came out from beneath the desk. "What on earth are you two doing here?" There was something in Lanie's eyes when she turned to look at her that made Nydia's blood turn to ice. "What's wrong?"

"I kept the cellular with me, in case Gabriel called back. Right after you left, it rang. Your mother-in-law tracked me down through the operator. She wanted you to know right away that your son is missing."

"Missing?" Nydia repeated, her voice sinking. "That's impossible. He wouldn't have left his grandfather's side."

"Your mother-in-law believes he took the bus, and is on his way here to find you."

Chapter Nineteen

Nydia felt as if the air had suddenly been taken out of the room. She clutched the back of a chair for support. "She must be mistaken. He'd never do that."

"What if he thought you'd asked him to?" Lanie said, her eyes filled with compassion. "Your mother-in-law found a note from you on his desk. She said that she discovered it by accident. She wouldn't have noticed his absence until school let out if she hadn't decided to clean his room."

"But I sent no note." Nydia struggled to clear her mind. This made no sense.

"Someone has lured him here," Joshua said softly, standing close beside her. "But if he's on the bus, we can make sure we're there to meet him. You can bet that he won't be getting off at an earlier stop. And the person who sent for your son will be there, too. He's embroiled in what's going on here, and won't be leaving town, not now, when everything's at a critical point."

"I guess," Nydia answered, unsure of everything. "I just can't think straight! All I know is that John's in danger!"

Joshua placed a hand on her shoulder. "Nothing will happen to your son," he said, then looked back at Lanie and Marlee. "When's the next bus due?"

"I'm not sure when exactly. I'll find out, but I'm sure

we have some time. It always comes into town late at night," Lanie answered as Marlee went to stand by the window to keep watch. "But there's more trouble brewing. I saw Mayor Burns as we drove in. He was with an angry group of people that included Darren Wilson. They didn't look too interested in upholding the law, and they were heading this way. I have a feeling that group with the mayor plans to take advantage of my husband's absence. You two need to get away from here." She took a deep breath and steadied herself. "Have you located Gabriel yet?"

"No," Joshua answered gently. "But we will. Shadow said he's calling in the state police to help."

"I have to meet that bus as soon as it comes into town and preempt whoever lured John here," Nydia said. "How can I find the bus schedule?"

"I'll take care of that for you." Lanie handed her the cellular. "Here. Take my phone. As long as you're not in the mountains, it'll work. While you search for Gabriel for me, I'll get the bus schedule and the information to you."

"My son is *my* priority," Nydia said. "I'll—"

Seeing the mayor's group approach, Marlee called out a warning. "They're coming. You better get going."

"I'll be there for John. Find Gabriel!" Lanie said. "I'll see what I can do about dispersing the crowd outside."

Joshua and Nydia hurried to the truck and got under way, but at the mouth of the alley, Joshua slowed to a stop.

"Why are you waiting?" Nydia asked impatiently.

He held a hand to his lips. "Listen. You can make out some of the conversation. Maybe one of them knows something about your son. I'm going in closer," he said, getting out. "Keep the motor running."

She rolled down the window and listened carefully. She could make out the mayor's voice. "The state police were on the sheriff's frequency when it happened. Apparently, the sheriff was trying to locate me, and asked for their help since they were in the area. I can tell you this, the tape recording of the radio transmission I heard leaves no room for doubt. Gabriel Blackhorse was ambushed by his brother, the medicine man. The sheriff tried to protect him, blinded by family loyalty, but this just proves how wrong he was to do that. We suspect the sheriff is dead, though we haven't located the body. In the meantime, the state police have issued a warrant for Joshua Blackhorse.''

Her heart sank. Someone had obviously faked a tape recording. Joshua's chance against this angry mob, particularly without the backing of his brothers, was slim. Fear shot through her. She wouldn't lose him, not this way. She placed the truck in gear, ready for a fast getaway.

"Let's go find Joshua ourselves,'' Darren Wilson said. "He can't hide from us. We know this town as well as he does.''

"We have to do this right,'' the mayor argued. "This tape is damning evidence, that's true, but it isn't conclusive.''

"Come on, Mayor,'' someone else she didn't recognize chimed in. "I heard that tape, too. The sheriff named his brother as the person attacking him. Then the static cleared, and there was only silence. Maybe Joshua planted another bomb, and this time it did its job.''

"I say we go after him,'' Darren pressed. "Justice, Four Winds style, is just what's needed.''

As voices were raised, she was relieved to see Joshua jogging back to the truck. Then, suddenly, a gunshot rang out, then another in rapid succession.

Nydia pressed down on the accelerator, and pulled up beside Joshua. In a heartbeat, they were on their way.

"They'll come after us,'' he said. "They've got some trumped-up evidence against me.''

A shot whizzed between them, putting a hole the windshield and spraying glass shards into the cab.

"Hang a right, fast."

They entered a narrow alley leading from Main to a residential street. "We can't outrace them in this truck, so let's leave it among the ones in that man's yard just ahead. I know a better way to lose the men after us."

As they drove down the alley toward the residential area, a truck screeched to a stop in front of them, blocking their exit.

Joshua reached into his medicine pouch, ready to use the only defense he had. Then he saw Ralph lean out the driver's-side window. "My truck looks like yours," he shouted. "I'll lead them away from you. Head for the library. Jake will help you there."

Leaving his truck in the alley, Joshua took Nydia's hand and raced toward the library. "We have to cut across this empty lot. It's open ground, so once we reach it, there's no slowing down. You ready?"

She nodded. There were few things that fostered speed as much as being shot at. "No problem."

They were halfway across when someone spotted them. Angry shouts rose in the air.

"They've seen us!" Joshua said, releasing her hand. "Keep going. I'll create a diversion."

There was no time for her to protest as Joshua ran around the large elm that stood in the center of the lot. His song rose strong, and out of nowhere, a cloud of smoke filled the air. As she raced for the library, smoke engulfed everything around her.

Even after the chant was finished, Nydia felt its power reverberating in the air. Through the haze, she could make out the library just ahead. There were shots being fired in the distance, but nothing seemed real except the anger in the voices around them.

"Don't slow down!" Joshua warned, suddenly right behind her. "They're closer than they seem!"

The smoke was clearing, and they had to reach the library before it dispersed and they were caught in the open. As she turned her head to glance back at Joshua, she caught a flicker of movement to her left.

"Look out!" Her warning came at the same instant that Joshua pushed her down. A shot rang out.

They tumbled to the ground together, but Joshua's arms were secure about her as he rolled with her out of the line of fire.

"Stay down!" he said, his voice strangely unsteady.

As he pulled away, she saw the blood that covered her sleeve. Aware of no pain, she suddenly realized that it wasn't she who was injured. With a gasp, she saw the hole on the side of Joshua's shirt and the blood that was quickly soaking downward from that hole.

The pain in his eyes tore through her like talons squeezing her heart. Nydia placed her arm around him. "The library's just ahead. Let's go."

"No. You go. Unless I distract them, you won't make it."

"We'll go together," she said stubbornly. "That's how we started this, and that's how we'll finish it."

Joshua didn't lean hard on her, but even taking some of his weight was difficult. Reaching inside herself, Nydia drew from a wellspring of courage and determination she hadn't known she possessed.

When they reached the library doors, a figure suddenly emerged from the shadows, shotgun in hand. Voiceless with fear, Nydia stopped in her tracks.

"It's me," Jake said quickly. "I heard what was happening, and grabbed my shotgun."

Jake saw the blood seeping down Joshua's side. "Can you make it?"

"Yes."

His voice was full of determination, and Nydia's heart filled with love and pride for everything he was and stood for. He had been willing to sacrifice his life for hers, but he was not through fighting yet.

As they staggered through the front doors of the library, Jake released his hold on Joshua. "I need to barricade the entrances and windows. Hang tight. I'll be right back."

"We're outgunned and outnumbered," Joshua said, looking at Nydia. "I won't let you or Jake come to any harm because of me."

"No. Jake made his choice to back you, like I did." The thought of selling Joshua out was as repugnant to her as the actions of the vigilantes outside.

"You have a son who needs you alive."

"I won't make a choice like that. I...can't."

A voice echoed one word in her mind, *Destiny*.

Blocking the voice, Nydia ran to help Jake move bookcases and tables against the doors and windows. "Can we hold out?" she asked him.

"It'll depend on how quickly we get help. Can you shoot?"

"Yes."

"What are you more familiar with, a rifle or a pistol?"

"Rifle."

"There's one in that closet and some ammunition, but don't shoot unless it's absolutely necessary."

"Do you think we'll get any help?" Nydia asked. "You know the people of this town better than I do."

"Joshua's brothers aren't going to sit idly by. We'll get help."

"We can't count on them," she said, then explained how Gabriel and Lucas had been lured away. As she did, Jake slowly nodded. "Had you known, would you still have helped us?" she added.

He grinned. "Of course. I served in the Rangers. We don't run from fights. Goes against the grain, you know?"

"Joshua is talking about giving himself up, if things get bad."

Jake turned another desk on its side, then wedged it beneath the knob on the front door. "It may turn out that he has no choice, but we're far from that point right now. Let's see what they throw at us, then we'll worry about what to do next."

"Fields, can you hear me?" A voice came through the gloom outside. "You're surrounded. Send Joshua Blackhorse out. We have no quarrel against you."

"So it starts," Jake said, motioning for her to get the rifle.

Joshua came up. "Do you have any other weapons?"

"My .45, in the file cabinet next to my desk, bottom drawer. The clips are in the drawer above it."

Joshua went to arm himself as Nydia stood by the window. "Did you recognize the voice?" she asked.

"It's Darren Wilson, I think," Jake answered.

"It's seven against three," the man insisted. "Give it up." As if to make his point, three shotgun blasts were fired at them. The door shook from the hits, and the massive door handle fell half out of the wood.

Fear surging through Nydia made her senses painfully sharp. Her hands began to tremble as she thought of her son arriving in Four Winds, greeted by enemies. Lanie was his only hope, unless they got out of this soon.

"Don't shoot back," Jake cautioned. "We can't afford to waste ammo unless they try to come inside."

Nydia glanced at Joshua, who held one arm close to his side as if movement was painful.

The voice that came out of the night shouted another warning. "Give it up, Jake. If we have to, we'll burn you out. If you stand with a killer, you'll share his fate."

"I won't let that happen," Joshua said quietly. "I'll turn myself over to them first."

"It's too soon to throw in the towel," Jake said. "We're far from finished here. First, they have to come up to the building, and that'll mean stepping into our sights. If one or two of them take a bullet, they may rethink their plan."

Suddenly, a woman's voice rang out clearly. "Stay inside, you three. You're not in this fight alone. Nobody's getting close to that building, not unless he's willing to risk his own life."

Nydia looked at Joshua in confusion. "That sounded like Lanie!" Just then the cellular phone that Lanie had given her rang.

"It's me," Lanie said. "The mayor's got John. He stopped the bus just out of town, claiming that the town was closed due to a police emergency, and got him out. He won't hurt him, Nydia. If he even touched that boy, the others would turn on him and he knows it."

Nydia stopped listening. All she knew was that John was in the hands of their enemies. She didn't struggle as Joshua took the phone and spoke to Lanie.

Darren's voice suddenly rang out. "Give it up, Mrs. Blackhorse. This isn't a scuffle on the school grounds. This matter is out of your hands."

"She's not alone, Wilson," another voice warned loudly.

"Ralph is with us," Joshua said, identifying the voice as he put the cellular aside.

"There are plenty of others here, too," Sally, the owner of the diner, added after a heartbeat.

"Nobody's taking Joshua Blackhorse anywhere." Ricky Miller's voice was firm as he added his vote to the others.

Joshua looked at Nydia, then at Jake. "It's as it was long ago."

"What is?" Jake asked.

"Flinthawk's story," Nydia said slowly. "The medicine

man who was almost lynched, but was saved by the townspeople.''

Jake gave them a startled look. ''You're right. History is
repeating itself. The teacher, the saloon owner and the others, each a new version of the old.''

''But what of my son?'' she managed to ask in a thin
whisper. ''In Flinthawk's story, the rancher's son was
nearly killed. That's part of the reason they wanted to lynch
the medicine man.''

''That part of the story will not repeat itself. My sister-
in-law is right. Your son won't be harmed. Hurting him
will only defeat their purpose,'' Joshua said firmly.

''If a fight is what you want, then that's what you'll get,''
Darren's voice rang out.

''Wait!'' The shout rang out like a whip. ''This is getting
out of hand. It's me, everyone, Mayor Burns. I'm coming
out into the open. Hold your fire, especially you in the
library. There's a young boy with me I think you all should
see.''

Fear screamed inside Nydia. She knew her son was out
there—with Mayor Burns.

''Mom?''

The sound of John's voice went straight to her heart. She
sprinted for the door, but Joshua's arms closed fast around
her.

''Let me go! My son is right in the middle of this. Don't
you see? Burns is the enemy who's been hunting us all
along. He killed your father!''

Joshua nodded, realizing the truth. Burns blamed the
Blackhorse family for the trouble that had claimed the life
of his son. It was the only thing that made sense. But the
revelation was anticlimactic, considering their situation.
''*Listen* to me,'' Joshua said, his voice soft but commanding. ''It isn't your son they want. Burns has convinced them
I'm a killer. It's me they want. I'll go.''

"You can't! They'll kill you. It's *my* son, *I'll* go."

"Stop thinking with your hearts!" Jake snapped. "They won't harm a child. The others in town would turn against them in a flash, and they know it. What they want to do is force both of you out in the open so Burns can have Joshua killed."

"You're right, my friend," Joshua said. "Our best chance lies in doing what they're not expecting. Right now, they're trying to manipulate you," he told Nydia, "because the ones Burns has duped see you as my accomplice. But I'm their real target. Let's use that knowledge and turn it to our advantage."

Chapter Twenty

Joshua stood beside Nydia as she called out to the mayor. "Don't hurt my son!"

"He's not hurt, ma'am," Bob Burns answered. "I want him away from this as badly as you do. The situation here is too volatile."

"Then let him go."

"Come out, and we'll negotiate."

"First, I want to make sure you haven't already hurt him. I want to talk to my son now, but not by having you stick him in the middle of a shooting gallery."

"What do you suggest?"

"Take him to a telephone, somewhere inside where he'll be safe, and have him call the library."

"All right. I'll see what I can do."

Making sure the small room he entered was completely dark, Joshua slid a bookcase away from the window with his good arm. His side throbbed painfully, but the herbs he had applied had stanched the flow of blood. As he peered out into the darkness, he saw Mayor Burns take the boy into Charley's garage.

Joshua joined the others and gave them the news just as the phone on Jake's desk rang. Nydia picked it up before it even finished the first ring. "I'm here."

"Mom?"

"Are you okay? Has anyone hurt you?"

"No, but don't come out. They'll shoot the singer, and then Grandfather—"

She heard a cry, then Burns got on the phone. "I would strongly suggest that you disregard his advice. No matter what else happens, I personally guarantee that the singer won't be walking away from this."

She glanced at Joshua, and he nodded. "If I convince him to come out, will you let me and my son go?" she whispered, biting off the words as if they left a foul taste in her mouth.

"I think that can be arranged."

"Give me ten minutes."

"You've got five before we take action."

Nydia hung up the phone. "That murderer has only given us five minutes."

"What's your plan?" Jake asked.

"It's dark now, so I should be able to slip out through the side window unseen. You'll go out the front," he said, looking at Jake. "Go slow and unarmed and tell them Nydia and I will follow. While they focus on you, I'll circle around until I'm across the street from the garage. Nydia will come out two minutes after you, slowly, like before. While all eyes are on her, I'll make my move and enter the garage."

"I'll make sure nobody hurts Nydia. Don't worry about that. Just do what you have to," Jake said.

"There's got to be another way!" Nydia whispered, her voice trembling. "You're still hurt. You're no match for anyone."

"Wounded, I'm still more than a match for Burns and Wilson. Just don't start having any second thoughts. There's no more time to waste."

Just then she heard the voice within her clearly. *The singer needs your faith. Destiny calls to all of us.*

Frustration tore through her. She wanted answers, not riddles. She saw Joshua looking at her and forced a smile. This was no time to sidetrack him. "I'm okay. Go and don't worry about us here."

Joshua went to the side window and slipped outside before Nydia noticed he had left the .45 on the floor.

"You forgot your pistol," she whispered harshly into the darkness, reaching for the weapon.

"I'm going to try and save a life, not take one. Leave the gun there."

His words sliced through her. She realized how easily that decision could make those words his last. Her heart ached with the knowledge that he was going out there, ready to sacrifice himself to save her son, a boy he'd never even met.

Destiny. Once again, the word came unbidden to her thoughts.

JOSHUA MOVED silently along the side of the post office, getting ready to cross Main Street. He wouldn't fail Nydia, no matter what the risks. Her son wouldn't be harmed. If he forfeited his life, yet accomplished that one thing, he would be satisfied.

He heard the shouts as Jake stepped out into the street. But then the voices were suddenly obscured by the rumbling of an approaching vehicle, blowing its horn.

Even before Joshua peered around the corner, he recognized Shadow's truck from the familiar screech of gears. As it passed by in the dim light, he saw two people inside. Lucas was driving. It was less than a second before he recognized Gabriel as the passenger.

Relief was sudden and welcome, and almost made him forget the fiery pain at his side as he raced across the street to Charley's garage. His two brothers were safe and nearby. Now the odds were more equal.

From his vantage point behind a gas pump, Joshua heard people cheering as Lucas screeched to a stop. Gabriel and Shadow jumped out, using the vehicle as cover between the crowd and the vigilantes. His eldest brother walked over to the armed men, his hand resting on the butt of his gun, and loudly ordered everyone to put down their weapons and go home.

As his brothers took charge of the situation outside the library, he made his move. Joshua slipped into the garage through the open repair bay. Up ahead, he could see a young boy standing between two armed men. One was the mayor, the other Darren Wilson.

The boy turned his head as if sensing Joshua's presence, and his eyes lit with recognition. Joshua gave the boy a nod of encouragement, then signaled him to remain quiet as he crept closer, hiding from view behind a car.

His side and left arm throbbed, making his movements clumsy. As he slipped past a counter covered with tools, he brushed against a screwdriver set that had been carelessly left on the very edge, and it rolled off onto the concrete floor with a clang.

As the men turned toward the sound, the boy acted. John clamped his teeth down on the hand of the man who held him, Darren Wilson. With a yowl of pain, Darren pushed the child away, right into the mayor. Burns cursed and slapped John hard, knocking him into a stack of tires.

Outrage twisted through Joshua, and he hurled himself at the two men, knocking them to the ground in a heap. Wilson stayed down, but Burns scrambled to his feet and tried to make a run for it. Joshua grabbed him by the collar and lifted him up into the air with his good hand. "Why?" he asked, fighting the urge to toss the man across the garage. "Why did you kill my father? You barely knew him."

"Revenge," he gasped. "It was the evil your family

brought into this town, that skinwalker bowl, that resulted in the death of my only son. I was going to finish you all off, father first, then sons.''

Hearing someone move behind him, Joshua tossed the mayor aside as if he weighed no more than a rag doll, and whirled around in a fighting crouch.

"Whoa!'' Gabriel said, jumping back. "I'm on your side. Wilson isn't going anywhere. You put him to sleep.''

Joshua sank down, aided by the wall at his back. "Finally,'' he whispered, pointing to Burns, "you have your killer.''

Noticing his brother's injuries for the first time, Gabriel shouted for Shadow, then pulled open his brother's shirt to check the wound. "Hang on, Tree.''

Taking advantage of the sheriff's distraction, the mayor tried to scramble to his feet, but Gabriel was on him in an instant, flooring Burns with an uppercut to the jaw. "You're going to prison, Mayor Burns,'' he said, handcuffing the man to Darren Wilson, who was just regaining consciousness.

Nydia raced through the open bay door, and saw her son at the same time that he saw her. The boy launched himself into her arms.

"Mom, you're okay! And the singer was *excellent!* You should have seen him. He pitched that creep aside with *one hand!*''

Joshua smiled at the reunion, but his gaze turned cold as he looked down at the mayor. "How did you do it? Nydia saw you at the gas station when she first came into town. How did you get to my father so quickly?''

"I already had your rifle, and knew where you'd be. When I saw my chance to have a witness to frame you with, I took Darren Wilson's pickup—after letting everyone see me leave town in my own car. If anyone had seen

Darren's vehicle racing up one of the back roads, they'd never think it was me behind the wheel.''

"And the tape?" Joshua asked. "How did you manage that?"

"I edited the department's own recordings, piecing together a phony conversation from some on file in the sheriff's office when no one was in. It wasn't hard. I have my own key, after all."

"Finally, justice can be done," Joshua whispered as Shadow reached him. Dark clouds began closing in on him. "I'm so tired."

Nydia knelt beside Joshua. "No way, my Tree," she said, pressing a kiss on his lips. "You're not fading on me now. Get used to the idea. You hear me?"

Her words seemed to come from far away, but as a blanket of darkness covered him, her voice reached out to him, showing him the way back from oblivion.

NYDIA STAYED outside the examining room at the clinic while Shadow tended to Joshua. Lucas had assured her his brother would be okay, that the bullet had passed cleanly through and he expected no irreversible damage from it.

It seemed an eternity later when she heard a commotion on the other side of the door.

"You can't go anywhere, Tree," she heard Lucas roar. "What the hell do you think you're doing?"

"To find Nydia. I have work to do."

"Get back in that bed, you big jackass."

Nydia heard a crash, then Joshua appeared at the door, Lucas trying to hold him back. She blocked the doorway immediately. "What on earth do you think you're doing?"

"That's what I want to know," Lucas added. "Get back in here!"

Gabriel came through the front door and, assessing the situation, joined Nydia in blocking his youngest brother's passage. "You're wounded, so I figure Shadow and I can take you. Don't turn this into a fight."

"No fight. But I have to go." He looked past Gabriel at Nydia. "Your father-in-law, how is he?"

"He's worse," she admitted. "That's why John came. The note that Burns used to lure him here said that I needed his help to get you to come to the rez. John knew his grandfather didn't have much time left, so he didn't hesitate."

"Then it's time for me to keep my word to you." He looked at Gabriel. "Am I free to go?"

He exhaled softly, then nodded. "There's no legal reason to keep you here. But if you insist on doing this, at least let me drive you. I can get a deputy from the next county to cover for me here for a short time. Besides, I owe you," he added with an easy grin. "If it wasn't for you getting Shadow to come back for me, I'd still be hiking into town."

"What did happen out there?" Joshua asked.

"Burns set me up. Seeing his chance to get me alone, he shot out a tire when I was rounding a curve, and my vehicle rolled over. By the time I got myself out and went looking for him, he was long gone."

"I'm glad we all made it," Joshua said, glancing at his brothers. "But now it's time for me to do what I trained for."

"Before we leave town," Nydia said, "I'd be grateful if we could make a stop by Tree's pickup."

"The peddler's gift?" Joshua asked.

"Yes. I'm going to take it back to the rez. I'll figure out what to do with it after we get there."

"Wait a minute. You never mentioned a gift from the peddler," Gabriel snarled at his brother.

Joshua grinned. "It didn't seem important at the time."

"We'll take that up later, when you're feeling better. And believe me, I won't forget it. For now, though, let's get going."

NYDIA SAT by the entrance of the hogan as Joshua did the life-enhancing sing her father-in-law had been waiting for, praying for success whatever the source. The effect on the elderly man was immediate and astonishing. Joshua led his patient in the final part of the chant, which had to be repeated word for word by her father-in-law. Lastly, he turned over the ritual basket, using it as a drum, as he invoked the aid of the gods.

Joshua continued, confident in Navajo beliefs that assured that if the chant was done precisely right, the gods would be impelled to grant the prayer.

At last, Joshua's voice rose in power, filled with the timelessness of the Navajo Way. "The trail is covered in beauty. Beauty surrounds us," he said, concluding the ceremony.

As silence descended over the hogan, a sense of expectation electrified the air.

Nydia's father-in-law stood up slowly and with halting steps went to his wife. Harmony had been restored. Energy and life burned in the elderly man's gaze as he looked at his family and nodded with a grateful smile.

Nydia looked down at her son, and saw the wonder in his eyes. At one time, she would have been horrified to think that her own flesh and blood would choose the old ways over the new. Yet now, she saw things in a new light. There was strength and power in the beliefs that had held the People together through time.

"That was just awesome," John said to Joshua, then hurried out to help his grandfather.

"Awesome?" Nydia chuckled, shaking her head over her son's choice of words.

Joshua smiled down at her. "He's everything our people have become, a blend of the old and the new. And that's a good thing. Our strength depends on kids like him who, seeing the new, still value the old."

Silence fell between them as they realized they were alone in the hogan. Nydia watched Joshua gather his ceremonial items, her heart heavy.

"There is one final favor I want to ask of you," she said, her voice whisper soft.

"Whatever it is, all you have to do is name it," he said gently.

"The rug. Take it and do whatever must be done with it. I've been thinking about this, and I've come to the conclusion that it's part of our destiny to right this wrong, too."

Joshua brushed her face with his palm, and the caress made her breath catch in her throat. "I agree. But are you sure this is what you want?"

She nodded. "I've come to accept that there are things that, because of their nature, won't fit within the framework of the Anglo world. But they still exist. Ignoring them isn't an answer."

He smiled. "Bring the rug to me."

When Nydia returned, she placed the cursed object before him. She watched as he carefully unraveled a thread leading from the middle to the edge, then began a sing. The words of the chant led them from the present world to the land where gods ruled. His song reverberated with the strength of a *hataalii* who had earned his rightful place among the legends of the *dineh* after a trial by fire.

At long last, he handed the rug back to her. "The line freeing the spirit of the weaver has been made, and Spider Woman has been appeased. All that remains here is its beauty."

As she took the rug from his hands, a great heaviness of spirit settled over her. They had reached the end of their journey, and as she'd known from the start, it was time for them to go their separate ways. Desolation wound itself around her heart in an endless, suffocating spiral.

She looked at Joshua, her throat burning. "And now you'll go back to Four Winds?"

"I'm needed there," he answered, just as her son came back into the hogan. "It's part of the legacy that was handed down to me."

John stood tall and proud before Joshua, his shoulders squared. "You are needed here, too, *hataalii*. By me, and the tribe. I want to be a singer like you. I need a teacher, and I want it to be you."

"When the time comes, I will be your teacher," Joshua agreed. "Until then, I have work elsewhere."

John looked at his mother, then back at Joshua, and smiled. Taking his mother's hand, he placed it in Joshua's. "I have to grow up more before I get what I want, but you guys don't have to wait for anything. You need each other. Anyone can see that! Teacher, you want her to be with you. So why don't you just ask her?"

"Hush!" Nydia said. "You don't understand." She looked at Joshua, tears welling in her eyes. "I've always known that this moment would come. I know how much you value the peace of your solitary life, and how much you need that as a *hataalii*. You're not bound by anything that's happened between us."

"It's my heart that binds me, *sawe*." He pressed her hand to his lips. "Come back to Four Winds with me. It's time we were a family."

"Mom, say yes!" John prodded in a harsh whisper, nudging her toward Joshua. "Sure, teacher, we'll all go with you. Right, Mom?"

Nydia laughed, then looked down at her son. "Don't you have something to do right now?"

"Oh—sure. I'll make myself scarce."

Joshua gently drew Nydia into his arms. "The old and

the new, you and me, side by side, throughout all the days and nights of our lives. How does that sound to you?''

As his lips covered hers, her answer became only a sigh that was lost in the desert breeze.

Epilogue

John assisted Joshua as he finished the blessingway for the town of Four Winds. "The people here saved my life, now I return the gift in the way I was taught," Joshua's voice rang out. "The legacy of good bestowed on Four Winds by my ancestor, Flinthawk, is now renewed."

A cheer rose from the gathered crowd as Jake Fields approached the singer. "As this town's acting mayor, I'd like to present you with this key to your new cabin. You are part of this town forever, Joshua Blackhorse. We need you here."

As Joshua accepted the gift, he glanced at his brothers. Gabriel smiled, his arm draped protectively around his pregnant wife. Lucas stood proud and alone. But as Lucas looked at Marlee, Joshua knew Shadow's life path was destined to change before long.

Joshua's gaze finally came to rest on the woman who would soon be his wife, and the boy who would become a son to him. "I do belong here, Mayor," he said. "And thanks to Four Winds, I now share in the greatest gift of all."

WELCOME TO *Love Inspired* ™

A brand-new series of contemporary inspirational love stories.

Join men and women as they learn valuable lessons about facing the challenges of today's world and about life, love and faith.

Look for:

Promises
by Roger Elwood

A Will and a Wedding
by Lois Richer

An Old-Fashioned Love
by Arlene James

Available in retail outlets
in October 1997.

LIFT YOUR SPIRITS AND GLADDEN YOUR HEART with *Love Inspired* ™*!*

Steeple
Hill™

LI1197

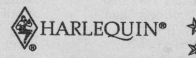

DEBBIE MACOMBER

invites you to the

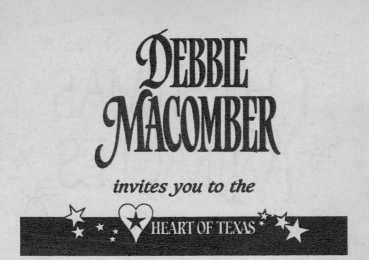

HEART OF TEXAS

Join Debbie Macomber as she brings you the lives
and loves of the folks in the ranching community
of Promise, Texas.

If you loved Midnight Sons—don't miss
Heart of Texas! A brand-new six-book series
from Debbie Macomber.

Available in February 1998
at your favorite retail store.

Heart of Texas by Debbie Macomber

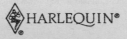

HARLEQUIN®

HPHRT1